# THE THIRD COINCIDENCE

# THE THIRD COINCIDENCE

A Novel

## David Bishop

OCEANVIEW PUBLISHING
SARASOTA, FLORIDA

ISBN: 978-1-60809-393-9

Published in the United States of America by Oceanview Publishing, Sarasota, Florida
www.oceanviewpub.com

2 4 6 8 10 9 7 5 3

PRINTED IN THE UNITED STATES OF AMERICA

To my sons:
Todd David Bishop and Dirk Bradley Bishop.

And my grandchildren:
Brandi Bishop, Kristopher Bishop, and Kaia Bishop
I love you all.

# THE THIRD COINCIDENCE

2. **Six Members of the Court constitute a quorum.**
   See <u>28 U.S.C. §1.</u> In the absence of a quorum on any
   day appointed for holding a session of the Court,
   the Justices attending—or if no Justice is present, the
   Clerk or a Deputy Clerk—may announce that the
   Court will not meet until there is a quorum.

# CHAPTER 1

The president is expected to announce his short list to replace deceased Supreme Court Justice Adam Monroe.

—*Sarah Little, NewsCentral 7, June 3*

"Hello, Jack. I'm just leaving the White House. The president would like you to join him tomorrow morning at eleven fifteen. It's about the death of Justice Monroe."

Jack McCall's monitor identified the caller as CIA Director Harriet Miller, his soft-spoken, efficient boss with the look of a librarian and the soul of a cobra.

"All I've heard is a heart attack," McCall said.

"Toxicology came in less than an hour ago," Miller said. "Poison. His ginseng had been laced with ground oleander. The president wants you on it."

"Oleander?" Jack asked. "Isn't that a flowering shrub?"

"That's it. I have one of the damn things in a pot in my sunroom. The lab people tell me the stuff's high on the poison scale, particularly for Justice Monroe; the guy was way over eighty and had a bad heart."

"But we're not a domestic agency."

"Debate that with the president if you wish," Director Miller replied. "It'll just be the two of you. Use the West Executive Avenue checkpoint." Then she hung up.

It would not be the kind of meeting Jack wanted right now in his life.

As a special assistant for strategy and planning to the Director of Central Intelligence, Jack had spent the afternoon at his desk reading the latest high-level releases on America's covert activities—updates put out internally at intervals based on the sensitivity of each operation and global time differences.

After Director Miller's call, Jack left the agency and walked to his car, a newspaper held above his head sopping up the light rain. Thirty minutes later he walked out of a three-chair barbershop after having a half inch taken off his brown hair that had started curling over his ears.

At rush hour, the road home was nose-to-butt cars, their drivers all in a hurry to get somewhere, with the result that no one was getting much of anywhere. As Jack approached the Virginia entrance to the Key Bridge, traffic slowed even more.

Gravel-sized raindrops began hitting the windshield like kamikaze beetles. He moved the wipers from intermittent to constant, turned on his headlights, and in a few minutes fell under the spell of the rhythm of tires squishing water.

Jack had never questioned that intelligence work would be his career, never until two years ago when his younger brother, Nick, lost his life in a covert Middle East operation on which Jack had been the on-the-ground leader. Dr. Christopher Andujar, a psychiatrist and friend, had explained that Jack experienced "survivors guilt," born from the momentary relief that it had been his brother and not himself.

Men died in battle. Nick had understood that, but Nick had died because of someone's greed and traitorous behavior. The mission plan had included a refueling stop where a Kuwaiti base worker had tipped off the terrorist training camp. The National Security Agency had intercepted that call, but not deciphered its meaning until after Jack's special forces team had been ambushed. Jack had taken revenge, but it hadn't rid him of his black mood.

Ten months ago, on his forty-sixth birthday, Jack had been promoted to his current agency desk job. After twenty years of Foreign

Service, he was finally stationed in the U.S. and had bought his first home, an older house with a detached garage. More important, the desk job meant men directly under his command would stop dying.

When he got home, he left his car in the driveway, turned off the wipers, loosened his tie, and went in through the side door to the kitchen.

He poured three fingers of Maker's Mark over ice, walked into the living room, and stared out the window while sipping his drink. The rain hadn't stopped, but it had softened into the kind that didn't bounce when it landed and made no noise of its own, while quieting other sounds that had largely gone unnoticed until muted. At this moment, the world seemed at ease and he longed to feel the same. But all he could think of was how the meeting tomorrow morning with the president might pull him back toward his past.

# CHAPTER 2

The new nominee for the Supreme Court will face the
traditional questions about abortion and the many faces
of civil rights. And, perhaps, a controversial new one—
a gay person's right to marry and adopt.

—*Washington Post, June 4*

At seven the next morning, U.S. Supreme Court Justice Herbert
Clarkson Montgomery's driver stopped at the curb on Pennsylvania
near Seventh Avenue. After more than thirty years on the nation's
highest bench, the justice still loved Washington, D.C., loved to
walk the last few blocks, feel his heart quicken as the courthouse
came into view. The rain had stopped a half an hour earlier so he got
out and walked down Seventh turning into the National Mall.

Monty looked back toward the city's towering buildings pocked
with windows, then up at the charcoal clouds that had stubbornly
hung around for days, intermittently dispersing sprinkles, down-
pours, and pauses. The crisp air along with an accompanying light
breeze had just enough zing to make him feel alive.

From the Mall his routine path took him around the Capitol,
across First Street NE, and up the white stairs to the courthouse.
Despite having to pause frequently to catch his breath, he liked the
exercise of climbing the steps. The exhilaration of looking up at the
marble neoclassical building that housed America's premier Court.
He also preferred entering through security at the main door so he
could walk the Great Hall filled with creamy Alabama marble. From

there, a short elevator ride delivered him to the upper floors that held the justices' private chambers.

The Mall's grounds crew ignored a very old niblick golf club Monty kept hidden behind a dense bush. He could no longer play golf but, in the early mornings, he often lingered to chip for a while, most shots flying less than ten yards, his niblick barely trimming a few blades of grass.

For Monty, an important fringe benefit of being a Supreme Court associate justice was that few people recognized him without his black robe. Anyway, at this hour, he rarely saw anyone.

The sun broke through the gray pallor that roofed the city, the brightness bleaching the deeper hues of the grass. Monty took a golf ball from his pocket, turned it in his hand, and let it roll off his fingers to drop onto the wet grass. Then he reached for his niblick. It wasn't there.

He shuffled closer to the bush and leaned in farther.

A strong hand grasped his arm.

# CHAPTER 3

Nominees for the Supreme Court are being vetted.

—*Philadelphia Inquirer, June 4*

Later that morning, Jack McCall walked into the National Mall with the trees slapping back at the summer wind. Deeper into the Mall, near a rest area called the Summer House, he found a uniformed officer and two detectives standing around the body of an elderly white male, a mere skeleton wrapped in skin as frail as wet tissue paper. The victim's sparse hair, the color of dust. His jaw loose. Black flies dotting the gaping wound across his neck that had leaked onto dirt to form a soupy scarlet puddle. Age had shrunken the man, but not each part equally. His head looked oddly large in proportion to the rest of his body.

Jack's gaze swept the area with the ease of someone familiar with making a quick assessment of his surroundings: a golf ball on the grass a few feet from the body, an old golf club under a bush with a broken branch, but no footprints in the planted area.

Thanks to an earlier call from his office, Jack knew this was Supreme Court Justice Herbert Clarkson Montgomery. He also knew that events were conspiring to push him into the middle of this—whatever this was—even before his meeting with the president. He need not take the assignment the president would soon ask of him. The wealth his grandfather had left him assured a comfortable living. The man, born in Canada, his paternal ancestors trappers, had made his modest fortune using his knowledge of the Great

Lakes to slip Canadian whiskey into the States. Jack's father moved to the Chesapeake Bay area as a young man and legitimized the family through a long career in the U.S. Navy.

In any event, Jack didn't need to decide his answer to the president now, but the question hung.

Jack approached the two plainclothes detectives, flashed his credentials, and got their names: Lieutenant Frank Wade and Sergeant Nora Burke.

"While I'm here, I'll be in charge," he told Lieutenant Wade, a formidable black man with the indefinable aura of a film-noir cop. The kind that skipped his prayers and kissed the butt of his gun, a detective whose appearance said he had been there and back.

Wade twisted his mouth, then mumbled something. Jack waited a beat, the two of them looking uncomfortable enough to be wearing each other's shoes.

"The FBI's sending over an ERT," Jack said. After noticing a quizzical look on Sergeant Burke's face he added, "evidence response team." Then he instructed the two local detectives to tell him what they knew.

"We got zip." Wade said, raking his thick fingers down his stubbled cheek. "The cut severed the old guy's jugular, but not the carotid artery. That would have sprayed like a fountain. The medical examiner will tell us whether he bled to death or drowned after his blood back-flushed down his severed trachea. Either way, he hasn't been waiting long to be found."

"We've only been here a few minutes," Sergeant Burke added. "You got here fast from Langley."

"I was in town." Jack said. "Who was first on the scene?"

"Carlyle," Wade bellowed. "Come over here and tell this man what you told me."

"Some tourist flagged me and my partner when we stopped on Pennsylvania," the uniformed officer said. "The tourist hadn't recognized the old man. I did only because Montgomery always waved whenever we saw him walking. One day he introduced himself."

"Did he walk often?" Jack asked.

"Every morning, 'cept in shitty weather."

"Where's the tourist?"

Carlyle pointed. "My partner's with him."

"Any other witnesses?"

"Not a soul," Carlyle said. "The next six or eight people who had arrived at the scene, I had stick around. Sergeant Burke had them wait over there." Another point.

"Anything else?" Lieutenant Wade asked.

Carlyle shook his head and started to leave. "Oh, Lieutenant," he said, turning back. "I called Mall maintenance. They're bringing over some stuff to close off this part of the Mall."

"Good work, Officer Carlyle," Wade said. "Protect the scene until the techs arrive."

Jack turned to the lieutenant. "The small group of folks who came later, any of them know anything?"

"Little chance, Agent McCall—is that what we should call you?"

"That's fine. You were saying?"

"That's it."

"Okay. Take those people's names and find out how to contact them. Then, assuming they don't know anything, let them leave. While you're doing that, I'll take Sergeant Burke and we'll talk with the man who found the body. Then your sergeant can fill you in."

Wade nodded. His lips tightly clamped.

"Sergeant Burke, you go on over and take the lead," Jack said. "I'll come along in a minute or two. Don't introduce me. I'll fly low. And send Carlyle's partner back to help lock down the scene."

A rumble came from the dark clouds. Jack looked up and shook his head. He needed the weather to hold until the FBI's evidence response team had done their thing. He started up the incline behind Burke, who was wearing a black pair of those stretchy pants that held her butt close. The wind at his back brought a noise. He looked over his shoulder. The Bureau's ERT had arrived and was setting up for a grid search.

"I think there's eight, no nine," Jack heard one of the technicians say. "I'm pretty sure now that I think about it. The ninth is the chief justice. I don't know their names, let alone their faces."

"The chief justice is Thomas Evans," another said. "I've heard of this Montgomery guy, but I couldn't pick him out of a lineup. We all really need to pay more attention to these guys."

Burke pushed back a strand of strawberry-blond hair and started questioning the man who had found the body. After he repeatedly claimed not to have seen anything but the body where it lay, she jotted down how to contact him and let him go.

"I heard a rumor this morning," Burke said, turning toward Jack, "that Justice Monroe didn't die last week of a heart attack."

Jack nodded. "Poison."

"Montgomery makes two justices murdered. We'll have more."

"What makes you say that, Sergeant Burke?"

"Because people die. Hatred doesn't."

# CHAPTER 4

Capitol killings and terrorism: Are they connected?

—*Detroit Free Press, Editorial, June 4*

The watcher observed tonight's prey, Federal Reserve Governor J. T. Santee, back out of his driveway as the sun slid behind a high ridge in the Pocono Mountains. The red taillights on Santee's new Jaguar glistened off Winding Trail Road, wet from the drizzle falling along the fringe of the huge storm system pelting Washington, D.C.

He had considered capturing Santee to learn why he and the others like him would sell out their country, but he already knew the answer. They lusted for the intoxication that came with being able to largely ignore the Congress and the president of the United States.

The watcher had spent his life on the lower limbs being shit on by the big birds sitting on the higher branches, but he had dedicated himself to change that. He'd take no unnecessary chances. In and out. Quick hits. Disappear.

The taste of damp eucalyptus flavored his lips as he held rough-textured binoculars to his eyes to see Santee lower his driver's side window, then a red dot brightened as the man drew on the cigarette in his mouth.

*Smoking will kill you, old man.*

Three minutes to go.

The families of the five houses clustered near the peak were all home. The Santee estate held the kingly spot at the very top with a view to die for. The killer smirked at his unintentional pun.

A previous reconnaissance had disclosed this road to be a favorite of the local area's sex-charged youths, the wild card in the hand he would play tonight.

Two minutes.

He rolled his pant legs up above his knees, tossed his red baseball cap onto the front seat, slipped an old housedress over his head, and pulled on a woman's gray wig. Last, he lifted a baby carriage from the back of his Explorer.

At that moment, a shooting star streaked the night sky, cutting a widening swath as the clasp on a lowering zipper spreads material. The time had come for his next step in restoring America to a government of the people, by the people, and for the people.

One minute.

The baby carriage bumped oddly as he pushed it across the blacktopped road to the spot where he would stand just out of sight. Santee's speed alone would carry the Jag nearer the right side of the outer lane. Centrifugal force would protect the watcher standing on the white line just beyond the sharp turn. He eased the baby carriage into Santee's lane and waited. It would not be long.

Forty seconds.

Santee felt the pulse of his sleek machine through the leather-wrapped steering wheel. The Jag's premium speakers, blaring a classical CD, blotted out the squeal from the tires as momentum carried the Jag to the outer edge of the narrow two-lane road. The cool night gave him goose bumps. His breathing deepened. His heart raced.

At the three-mile post he lifted his foot from the accelerator and kept it off the brake. More than once he had promised his wife he'd stop, but she didn't understand. Some older men in power cavorted with younger women, but he had seen such behavior revealed to ruin professional lives. Instead, when he got behind the wheel, he was seduced by the challenge of his road game.

Tonight he would bust his record. Then, by God, he'd keep his promise.

Santee slammed the accelerator to the floor. The eucalyptus-scented air poured through the moonroof to rustle his thinning hair. He felt young.

His Jag entered the turn.

*Oh, my God.*

Fear grabbed his throat.

Right in front of his speeding car stood an old woman pushing a baby carriage. For an instant his mind asked why she would be there, but there was no time for reasoning. He hit his high beams.

Her eyes brightened. Her mouth opened. Her hands shot up shielding her eyes from the glare.

He screamed for her to move the carriage, but the tightly built Jaguar suffocated his voice. He jerked hard to the right, strangling the steering wheel as his Jag smashed through the feeble guardrail. The left front tire clawed at the graveled edge, then spun freely in the air.

He watched with horror as the rocks below appeared to be reaching up to embrace him.

His last awareness, the humiliation of surrendering control of his bowels.

The rain spotted the watcher's face as he rushed to the broken guardrail. The full moon, ducking in and out among the rushing black clouds, revealed a mangled mass more resembling an accordion than a car. A moment later the Jaguar exploded, the crash having apparently ruptured the gas tank, its contents somehow reaching the old man's cigarette. He had not anticipated a glorious explosion.

*The red glare, the bombs bursting in air.*

His lower jaw quivered. He wanted to stay, to watch, to feel the warmth wafting up from below. But he could not risk it. The local teens could start arriving at any moment. They would see the broken guardrail, look below, and report the accident.

The night clouds veiled the moon while he concealed the carriage, dress, and wig in the back of his Explorer. He had left the vehicle parked just around a bend, on a gravel-covered shoulder. The bushes on the downhill side absorbing the headlights of any cars coming up the hill. After making sure there was no traffic approaching from either direction, he moved his SUV onto the road and went back to be sure there were no foot or tire tracks.

The rain had stopped. The crickets were again reporting their positions to other crickets. There was little ambient light, but some bright dots from the nearest town could be seen far below. He drove the first mile down the mountain slowly with his headlights off, passing no one.

His plan was well along the way; he could not be stopped. America would be saved.

# CHAPTER 5

President Schroeder: "There is no evidence of a conspiracy."
James Bernard: "Still, Monroe, Montgomery, and Santee are dead."

—*Fox News, last night*

The morning sun and clear air made the White House appear a symbol of all that was good. From closer, the symbol was now surrounded by so many barricades that the bastion of the free world appeared a fortress imprisoning itself.

At the security gate, Jack was cleared by an attractive brunette with white polished fingernails holding a clipboard. She was small in the way a driver's license describes a woman, but big in the way a man does.

After parking, Jack buttoned his double-breasted, dark blue suit and reached for the door to the White House just as it swung open in the hand of an older woman.

"Mr. McCall, I'm Gruber." A single hair grew through a mole spotting her thin neck. In contrast, her smile said she had a good dentist and, working for the White House, a generous dental plan.

"You may not remember me," she said.

"Yes, ma'am, you were with President Schroeder, then our Ambassador in Kuwait."

"In your line of work I suppose remembering people is routine," said Gruber. "The president is looking forward to seeing you again. Please follow me."

As they moved through the hallways, everyone seemed to be talking at once. Phones were ringing constantly, with people rushing about while talking back over their shoulders as they moved.

Then Gruber opened the door to the Oval Office.

President Samuel Schroeder looked as Jack had remembered. His hair was a little grayer, his forehead a little higher, and his paunch a little larger. But his clear blue eyes and casual manner were the same. A presidential face.

"Hello, Jack. How do we get so busy that we lose contact with people we never meant to?" Schroeder came to him, extending both hands.

"Hello, Mr. President. You've certainly kept yourself busy."

They sat facing each other on two gold brocade couches near the fireplace. Almost immediately Crockett, the president's collie, came over and rested his chin on the knee of his master's black slacks.

"I often think about those nights we spent in embassy kitchens eating your homemade ice cream," the president said, reaching down and scratching Crockett behind the ears. "Some of our best ideas were hatched that way. Do you still make those Grand Marnier bonbons?"

"I thought about bringing some today." Jack grinned. "But they'd've become a puddle getting through security."

"One of the more damnable aspects of this job. Which reminds me, drinks are on the side table. Help yourself. Lunch will be brought in soon. I've told Gruber that if we're interrupted, she'd better have a first-class reason." Then the president lowered his voice. "I was sorry to hear of the loss of your brother."

"Thank you, Mr. President."

"You've had no action since that fiasco?"

"Nothing official, sir."

"Yes. I heard about that unofficial thing. Perhaps I've got just what you need. A direct, hands-on assignment."

"Sir, before you begin, may I say something?" The president nodded. Jack edged forward on the couch. "I've been considering, well, leaving the CIA."

The president held his gaze on Jack. "I don't want to lose you. Why don't I find you something outside the agency?"

"No. Thank you, sir. I should have said, retire from government service."

Jack was surprised when, instead of reacting to what he had just heard, the president changed the subject and asked if he still played chess. But he had long ago recognized the wiliness of his commander and chief.

"Yes, sir. When you're single and working the globe, chess fills the spots of personal time."

"You were always too good for me. Whom are you playing with now?"

"I play correspondence chess," Jack said. "To not disclose my identity, I use the name Carl with my sister's address in Phoenix."

"How does that work?"

"Different groups or games are handled differently. For some time now I've been involved in a tournament. Moves are posted on a bulletin board on the Internet."

"I may look into that." The president's brow wrinkled as his eyes narrowed. "Have you made your decision about retirement?"

Jack grinned. Schroeder remained a grand master at conversational countermoves. "No, sir, I just felt you should know."

The president moved Crockett's head, got up, and began pacing the room, just as Jack had often seen him do while an ambassador.

"I'd like your thinking even if you decide to go ahead and retire," he said. "Did you catch the morning news?"

"Only a quick read about Santee's auto accident."

"Such a sad ending," the president said. "But, I was referring to a smaller story, further back, that said I was going to appoint you to look into these deaths."

"I didn't see that. How did the paper get it? Who knew?"

The president squeezed the back of the couch he stood behind. "Your boss over at the CIA, the directors of the FBI, the Defense Intelligence Agency, and the National Security Agency, also my chief of staff."

"No one else?"

"No one else."

"Then one of them leaked the story."

Jack's guess would be National Security Advisor Robert Quartz based on nothing more than his low regard for the man. The intelligence community had shaken its collective head when Quartz got the job. His family's money and contacts built during prior generations had brought this fop to the highest level of government. Shit floats.

The president stopped on the gold seal woven into the Oval Office's blue carpet. "Yes. One of them," he said. "Trying to keep something quiet in this town is like saving water in a sieve, but we can't solve that now. Three men are dead."

Dead. There it was again, a word as crisp and final as the act. Jack had always hated the word, even when he had delivered it to a deserving person.

The president pressed a button on his desk, took off his jacket, and turned up the cuffs on his white shirt. "Lunch is on the way. We're having one you might remember from the old days: beefsteak tomatoes and mayonnaise on toasted dill rye bread with chips and a bottle of root beer. The kitchen called Gruber to confirm." He laughed. "It's a long way from the typical lunch around here. I can tell you that."

As always, Sam Schroeder had a knack for disarming those with whom he met. "Have the other agencies been able to connect these deaths?" Jack asked.

Schroeder shook his head. "Do you think this is coming from across the pond? What's your gut telling you?"

"If Islamic terrorists are involved," Jack said, "it's a major tactical shift. Targeted assassinations of Americans have not been their thing. They like to kill us in bunches. That and the absence of electronic chatter tell me this is homegrown."

"The first time we met, I believe it was in Egypt, you said that two unexpected events with a common thread may be coincidental, but when confronted by a third, a connection must be assumed until proven to the contrary."

Jack inclined his head. "That remains my view, sir."

"We're going to proceed under that assumption," the president said, frowning. "You'll have whatever you need and I've got your back, so don't worry about the political crap that flies around this town. Will you take this assignment?"

Jack pinched his bottom lip between his teeth. Politics soured things. Rotted people. He'd often seen the gangrenous result of the whole mess while posted through the State Department, not to mention his own agency. Hell, particularly in the CIA. He didn't want to get into all that any deeper than his present desk job had put him. In particular, he hated the thought of again being in a position where people under his command could die. Still, these killings were happening on our home court, with the potential of disrupting both the government and the economy. On a more personal level, there was Sam, the man, his friend; a good first-term president with no chance at a second term without this killer being stopped soon.

"Well, Mr. President, we can't just go around making liars out of the morning news, now can we?"

They grinned while shaking hands. The purpose for the meeting had been resolved.

"What are the Israelis saying, sir?"

"Spoke to their prime minister this morning. The Mossad has nothing. Like I said, we'll play it domestically and keep an open mind."

"What about the task force itself?" Jack asked. "Who? How many? Whom do I report to?"

"You pick the size, subject to future events, the staffing I'll leave in your hands. You know the best people better than I, and whenever this office gets involved in staffing, politics end up dirtying the water."

"There's a civilian I'll want on the team."

"You will be responsible for him."

"I accept that, sir."

"I'm going to run this through the White House, so there's some political realities. It'll need to be a multiagency task force. You'll need to include at least one person from the FBI and Defense. You're the CIA's only involvement. FBI Director Hampton has requested someone specific, an Agent Rachel Johnstone—her file suggests you may have met her."

Jack pictured Rachel's face, her jet black hair and eyes the shade of washed blue denim. He had forgotten a lot of women he had known since, but would never forget Rachel. She had been a bit aggressive in letting him know she was available, but then he had been a bit stuffy in those days about protocol.

"We met some years ago, sir. Ms. Johnstone was with naval intelligence. She helped on an assignment I did for the Defense Department. She's tireless and a solid thinker. If Director Hampton suggested she be put in charge, she must have developed into a fine agent. That doesn't surprise me. I'll take a look at her file and consider making her second in command. That'll strengthen the CIA-FBI coordination. From Defense, I'll want Colin Stewart."

The president furrowed his brow. "I know that name."

"The Kuwaiti Embassy. Colin sat with us while we structured the contingency plan for the possible evacuation."

"Oh, yes, I remember. When my wife saw him, she said that he had cheekbones sharp enough to cut cold butter. It was an odd thing for her to say."

"The ladies say he's ruggedly handsome." Jack shrugged. "Go figure."

"You asked about authority. You take orders only from me. But, please, do your level best to avoid ruffling the feathers on my big birds. I'll want periodic reports on my request or when you feel it's warranted. Here's the jacket on Ms. Johnstone. Take a look after we're done. Give it to Gruber on your way out. If you need anything, call Gruber or my chief of staff, Clarence Stafford. He prefers Clancy. Should you think it necessary, call me directly. You will be given the same access as my cabinet members. Any questions?"

*Here I go again,* Jack thought, *one more for the Gipper.* "Not now," he said, "but I'll likely have some later."

On the way to the lunch table, the president picked up a book from the credenza near his desk. "Have you read this?" he asked, angling the book. *"The Politics of Oil and Terrorism."*

"Finished it last weekend, sir." They sat down and unfolded their linen napkins.

"I finished it last night," the president said. "How did it strike you?"

"A solid book, sir. The extremists want our influence out of their part of the world. They could likely get it done by destroying the oil industry in the Middle East. But they're pragmatic enough not to have done so because, indirectly, a chunk of their funding for terrorism comes from our oil purchases."

The president held up his sandwich. "God, I've missed these." He took a big bite and used his tongue to erase the mayonnaise comma punctuating the corner of his mouth.

"I don't think I've had tomato on rye since we were together in Kuwait," Jack said, feeling a bit odd. Here he was having an ordinary lunch with the president of the United States, talking about shared books and world issues the way they had so many times, so long ago when the man was just Sam."

The president put down his sandwich. "After air, water, and food, oil is the most vital commodity to our way of life. And the production and distribution of much of the food and water are dependent on oil, not to mention getting the American consumer to the food. Our reliance on the most volatile region of the world for a huge portion of our oil borders on insanity. And that doesn't even take in the fact that OPEC is a monopolistic cabal that couldn't exist under our laws. So, where else should we go for our oil?"

Jack knew that in America every major issue came down to the two main political parties striving to make the other look bad by always opposing whatever the other party wanted. Still, with political resolve, solving our oil dependency was doable.

"Untie our oil industry's hands so they can develop our own fields," Jack said, answering the president, "and there's Mexico. If we diverted a third of our OPEC buys into increased purchases of oil from Mexico, we could, through bringing that quantity of our buys into our region of the world, further stabilize our sources of oil while enhancing the Mexican economy. The good-paying jobs created in the process would reduce the motivation for illegals to cross our border. As part of the oil deal, we could likely barter for real cooperation on their side to slow down human and drug smuggling. I hope I haven't been too candid, sir."

"Nonsense. I asked, but we need to leave that discussion for another day and get back to why you're here."

Twenty minutes later, Jack drove out through the same White House security checkpoint. With his focus on assembling his team, he failed to notice the dark Ford Explorer that turned from F Street onto Seventeenth to fall in two cars behind.

# CHAPTER 6

Security is tight at the Supreme Court. There's talk of an early summer recess, and whispers now and then about resignations.

—*Sarah Little, NewsCentral 7, June 5*

Rachel Johnstone left the FBI building in a snit. She had just finished meeting with the FBI's beefy director, Fred Hampton, where he'd assigned her the murders of two Supreme Court justices and the suspicious death of a Federal Reserve governor. Then came the almighty *but*. But, she would be working on a task force under Jack McCall.

She knew her desire to lead the investigation exceeded her résumé. But the lead had not just been taken from her, it had been taken from the bureau and given to a spook, and not just any spook, Jack McCall.

*Why me, Lord?*

Thirty minutes later, Rachel walked into her one-bedroom apartment, dropped her keys in the basket on the mahogany sofa table just inside the door, ruffled the head of her cat, Jingles, standing next to the basket, filled the cat's bowl with dry crunchies, and started shedding her pantsuit. She hung her blouse over the back of a chair and reached back to pop her brassiere. Then, using the remote she turned on some bluesy piano player that fit her sultry mood, the overhead fan cooling her sweaty skin.

She doubted Jack McCall would remember her. Not unless he

remembered all the women who had come on to him, women he had shunted aside with one excuse or another. With her he had used the unimaginative "regulations do not permit personal involvement among intelligence personnel." It had been a putdown and she had not forgotten.

It wasn't her appearance, heaven knows. She didn't think of herself as vain, but certainly there was no shame in being conscious, even proud of one's appearance. More frequent high reps with low weights would tone a few spots and keep her breasts firm and high, but all in all the curves were still in the right places.

*Not bad for forty-three.*

Ten minutes later she stepped out of the shower. After toweling the loose water out of her hair and patting the moisture off her face, she responded to the chimes of her cell phone.

*Speak of the devil, Jack McCall.*

"I believe you know why I'm calling," he said.

She knew that for him, becoming an intelligence operative had not been a random choice made during some overwhelming campus career day. The job possessed him. He lived it. She wondered if the years had worn the edge off that intensity, and how his well-muscled six-two frame and boyish face had changed. She also remembered that he believed in the chain of command, so she opened with the needle.

"Hi, Spook. Do you remember me?"

"Of course," he told her. "Seven years ago. The Persian Gulf. We worked together for two weeks."

Cradling the phone with her shoulder, she sat on the bed, drew her knees up against her still wet, bare breasts and wrapped her arms around her legs. Jingles jumped up and began dragging his body across her damp calves.

"Is spook okay?" she persisted, determined to get under his skin, "or do you prefer Agent McCall?"

"Listen," he said patiently, "I know you wanted to head this task force, but you're not. When no one else is around you can call me whatever you wish. My concern is whether or not I can count on you to follow orders and be a team player."

She used the side of her foot to push Jingles off her bed.

"I've been given my assignment. I'll do my job."

"How do I know you mean that?"

"Trust me. I work for the FBI."

"Now that's the funniest thing I've heard today."

"I *do* work for the FBI."

"You know about Monroe?"

She scooted back and leaned against the headboard. "Poison. His death was assigned to me the day he died. We all saw it as waiting for the autopsy to confirm heart attack. So the toxicology report brought us up short. Today, the director also put me in charge of the murder of Justice Montgomery and the death of Santee. You figure he was murdered too?"

"Probably. It could be an oddly timed accidental death, but I doubt it."

"That's how Monroe looked at the beginning," Rachel said, "like an accident, well, like a heart attack. I'm not sure what we're going to be chasing here, but we're holding the loose end of a big ball of something."

"Listen. I'd like us to talk in person," he said. "Tonight. In the morning we need to hit the ground running. Shall I come to you or do you prefer to come here?"

"You didn't ask if I already had plans."

"If you do, cancel them."

"And which charm school did you attend, Spook?"

She heard him take a deep breath. "I'm sorry if you had other plans."

"Give me directions."

She jotted down what she needed and said, "I'll be there in twenty to thirty minutes."

"Have you eaten yet?" he asked.

"No."

"I'll throw a couple of burgers on the grill. They'll be ready when you get here."

She knew that McCall had made a gesture with his offer of a casual meal and she appreciated it. And she knew the two of them meeting before his entire team met was a good idea.

After trying on several outfits, she hooked a pushup bra, slipped on a scoop-necked blue jersey and white shorts. Her outfit, didn't say FBI professional, but she didn't wish to convey FBI professional.

*Eat your heart out, Spook,* she thought. *Next time I'm turning you down.*

"Except for those very busy two weeks seven years ago," Jack said to Rachel, "I know nothing about you. Tell me about yourself."

"What do you want to know?" Rachel asked.

"Oh, just start somewhere and end somewhere else."

As he listened, he noticed she was wearing her dark hair a little longer than he remembered. Shoulder length with a softer look along her forehead. A thin nose above a mouth a little wide, and at times a little too smarty, an intelligent face with a gentleness that avoided the hard cynical look that all too often leeched in from their work.

While eating, his glances caught her studying his face. Line by line like Sherlock Holmes with a microscope. Jack considered his face to be ordinary, but found himself hoping she thought it was a good face.

After dinner they discussed the case over a bowl of Jack's homemade vanilla ice cream studded with Maraschino cherries. Their only clear decision: they should, at least at the start, include the two D.C. homicide detectives Jack had been with at the Justice Montgomery murder scene. Lieutenant Wade and Sergeant Burke would provide a local element to further the president's desire for a multi-agency face.

She ran her tongue across the end of her ice cream spoon before clanking it into the melted white pond at the bottom of the bowl.

"So, Spook—I'm sorry, I need to stop calling you that."

Strangely enough, Jack found that he didn't care whether she did or didn't. He had come to terms with the quirks in their relationship, if he could yet think of it as a relationship.

"What were you going to say?" he asked.

"How do you think you'll like working out in the open in the real world?"

"The real world?" Jack said, his eyebrows raised. "Just what do you think I've been working in all these years?"

"Some parallel universe where madmen and patriots engage in large and small evils justified by some definition of the greater good."

"That sounds like something you read on the editorial page of the *New York Times*," he told her. "I expected better from you."

"I probably expressed that view more profoundly than I hold it." She shrugged. "Let's change the subject. You've got a nice place here. You needn't have straightened up on my account."

"I pick up after myself as I go along and have a housekeeper in once a week. Next time I can make a mess here and there, if it'll make you feel more at home."

"I can handle neat." She stood, turned, and bent down to lift her purse off the couch.

He watched the white material tighten across her butt, then the trim muscular curves of her calves as she moved toward the door. Rachel was obviously a strong woman, yet very shapely and feminine. He got up and followed.

"We made some progress tonight. Thanks for coming over."

At the door, she stood close. Jack felt the warmth in her breath.

"Maybe we can work together." She looked up at him without tilting her head back. "But don't underestimate me."

He grinned lopsidedly, willing his eyes to avoid her cleavage. "I will never do that."

"Yes, you will," she told him. "To quote V. I. Warshawski, 'Never underestimate a man's ability to underestimate a woman.'"

"V.I. who?"

"You don't know V. I. Warshawski? She's only the world's greatest fictional female private detective."

Rachel's lips turned up at the corners, her teeth filling the crescent of her smile. She opened the door, spilling a corridor of light into the night, and stepped out onto the porch. He held the screen door open, half hoping she would boldly change her mind and stay. But she turned her back and walked down the hall of light that widened as it reached for the curb.

After she had shut her car door, the headlights sent two piercing beams into the night, spreading until they illuminated the leaves of the trees along the edge of the Potomac river.

Jack stood there looking into the darkness, wondering what waited out there in the abyss.

Rachel drove home knowing more about Jack McCall than she had known before, and wondering if perhaps that had been his purpose for the invitation. He liked sea kayaking, Zinfandel wine, stage plays, and in films, mostly film noir, but his favorite movie was *True Lies*, particularly the scene in which Jamie Lee Curtis did a sexy dance for a man in a hotel room without knowing that man was her husband.

She had told him her favorite movie was *The Sting*, but they had both liked Dustin Hoffman in *Tootsie*. She dug light jazz while he favored traditional pop and show tunes. They had challenged each other to a game of golf, after the case of course. He carried a nine handicap, she carried a ten.

Rachel parked behind her condo building in the Kalorama Heights area of D.C., north of Sheridan Circle, and sat in her car to take a personal call before going inside.

For the first time she could remember, Jingles was not on the entry table meowing when she slid the key into the lock, thrusting his nose into the crack when it opened. Tonight, her furry friend sat quietly on the entryway floor, his tail wrapped neatly around its own legs.

"What's wrong, Jingles?" she said, bending down to stroke the cat's ears. "Yes, I know. Every time I come home I need to fill your crunchies."

Jingles ignored his freshly filled bowl. Instead, following her into her bedroom, hopping up on the bed and caterwauling while she disrobed.

"My gosh, you're certainly a chatterbox tonight." She sat on the edge of the bed and rubbed the cat's head between her cupped hands. "Let me shower and put in a load of clothes. Then we'll play. Okay? Now settle down."

As the shower spray worked its way through her hair, cascading down over her breasts, she relaxed and imagined the water washing away the stress of her day—the stress of again seeing the mysterious Jack McCall.

She had never forgotten the afternoon the two of them stood together on the forward part of the weather deck on a naval vessel off the coast of Egypt. When he had paid her a compliment, she took it as a comment from a man on the make. But he hadn't been because he later turned away her advances. In a strange way that had made the compliment seem even more special.

Fifteen minutes later, wearing a cotton nightie, she dumped the hamper on her bed and began sorting out her underwear for the washer only to discover that her bra, the one she had just taken off and dropped onto the bed, had disappeared.

*Maybe I put it in the hamper.*

Suddenly she had a sense that someone had been there. Which was absurd, of course, and yet that would explain Jingles's unusual behavior when she first came home. Had he been there while she sat naked on the edge of the bed petting Jingles? While she showered? Was he still here? Her heart slammed back and forth inside her chest like a clapper pounding a bell.

After tearing the room apart looking for the bra, without finding it, she got her 9-mm Beretta, checked the closet, and the locks on the front door and the windows. Then she slid the gun under her pillow, turned out the light, and went to bed.

CIA Special Assistant McCall will handpick his own
squad and report directly to the president, without
interference from the other intelligence agencies.

—CNN *Headline News*, 6:30 *a.m., June 6*

The skin on his cheeks and neck had been chewed by teen acne in
the way aphids disfigured a young rose leaf. He had purchased a
ticket to San Francisco using the name John Kimble and dressed as
an ordinary traveler with a carry-on bag, just another passenger reading a newspaper while awaiting his flight.

He recalled his father repeatedly fulminating at the breakfast
table about the Supreme Court justices and Federal Reserve governors constituting the unelected government that was really *the man,*
strangling the representative government put in place by our forefathers.

His father would have gone ballistic if he had lived long enough
to see the Supreme Court set aside the people's election and anoint
their own choice for president of the United States.

The nobility of his cause excited him. Once aroused he could
find calm only through sex. Because he felt more alert afterward, he
believed these dalliances should be work-related, tax-deductible ex-
penses.

His mother had left enough money to fund both the completion
of his father's work and the satisfaction of his cravings.

During the flight he reflected on the last few days. Events were escalating just as he had expected. Years ago, as a young member of the FBI's electronic surveillance unit, he had been a face in the crowd at a large joint CIA-FBI meeting headed by Jack McCall. When he had heard on CNN that the president would meet with McCall, he had watched the White House entrance often used for quiet meetings. He had recognized McCall when he pulled up to the security gate, and waited to follow him home. That night he had staked out McCall's residence and saw a woman arrive. With his laptop and her license plate, he learned her identity and address. While she had been with McCall, he went to her apartment and had not gotten out by the time she returned home.

He had fought down his desire to take her when he had seen her body in the bathroom mirror, but he could not resist the playful act of stealing her underwear. Had he killed her and McCall, the government would have been more careful about protecting the identities of their replacements. They didn't know him, but he knew them and where they lived.

After landing in San Francisco, he took a cab to the downtown Marriott Hotel, paid cash and checked in as John Powell, a different alias than he had used to buy his plane ticket. In the unlikely event McCall somehow picked up his trail, the ticket name could not be tracked to the hotel where they might find his fingerprints or DNA.

From his room, he called an escort service and spoke with the manager, telling her he wanted a woman with medium-length black hair and large breasts, but not the streetwalker look.

*Momma had never looked cheap.*

After the manager's assurance that she would send one of her best girls, the man flopped into the overstuffed chair that accepted him as a catcher's mitt accepted a fastball. After plopping his feet onto the cushy ottoman, he took out his laptop that held more than two years of information on the habits and movements of all the current U.S. Supreme Court justices and Fed governors, and their families. He had also started putting together data on some of the leading candidates being floated in the press to replace the now departed justices. Also files on the rumored nominees to fill the vacancy he had created on the Federal Reserve Board.

*And there will be more. I promise.*

He had bestowed the honor of being the next sacrifice for America upon Supreme Court Justice Donald Quincy Breen. At first, bachelor Justice Breen had ranked poorly because his movements had been too unpredictable. All that had changed when Justice Breen and a Baltimore attorney, Ms. Judith Ashcroft, unexpectedly announced their wedding plans.

It had not been difficult to get information on Judith Ashcroft, a thirty-six-year-old ex-beauty queen, who had grown up spoiled by her old-money family. She believed in the government's responsibility to care for those not capable or willing to provide for themselves. Another family of rich pigs longing to practice largess using money taken from hardworking Americans. If she really felt that way, she'd use her own money. The media colored it a solid marital merger with the more liberal wife expected to take the edge off Breen's reputation for being right of the political center.

The killing of a U.S. Supreme Court justice and his bride on their honeymoon would guarantee coast-to-coast headlines. After using his toes to leverage off his loafers, letting them drop silently to the plushly carpeted floor, he hacked into the e-mail of Mrs. Cordelia Ashcroft, Breen's new mother-in-law. Several days ago, in her inbox, had been an e-mail wherein Judith told her mother that she and her new husband would not, as reported by the media, honeymoon in Maui. Instead they would quietly slip away to spend June seventh, eighth, and ninth in the honeymoon cottage of a resort near Depoe Bay on the coast of Oregon.

He glanced at his watch and saw that it was six, an hour before his escort companion would arrive. In the classified section of the local paper he found a private party trying to sell a used Chrysler van. He agreed to the seller's asking price, subject to his seeing it the next morning. After that he dropped to the floor and did fifty pushups and fifty situps. Then he went into the bathroom and washed his armpits and crotch.

At seven sharp he heard a soft knock, and opened the door to see a naked leg slide out through a slit in the woman's floor-length coat. "Hello," she said, before smiling. "I'm Kitt."

Her voice made him think of a hot fudge sundae. A perfect opening act before tomorrow's main event.

# CHAPTER 8

Highly placed sources report that NSA Director Quartz told President Schroeder: We don't need McCall.

— *Washington Times, Editorial Page, June 6*

He left the downtown San Francisco Marriott feeling contempt for the beautiful people living in their high-priced, ocean-view mansions, while the disadvantaged lived in vacant buildings and drove grocery carts stuffed with their possessions through back alleys. His father believed America could no longer remain a country of opportunity. That America must become a country of obligation. The government had to care for its citizens and assure equality for all. Once he had restored representative government, America would enter an expanded age of social engineering.

The cab he had hired outside the hotel took him to the home of the man from whom he had agreed to buy the used van. After checking to be sure the brake and taillights worked, he paid the full price in cash, telling the seller he was in a hurry and would return tomorrow to complete the transfer of the title.

*Yeah, right.*

Despite a cool ocean chill, while crossing the Bay Bridge he lowered the driver's window to taste the salty air. From there, he moved onto Interstate 80 north toward Sacramento.

Near Sacramento he again veered north, taking I-5 toward Portland, Oregon. When the interstate angled eastward, the sunlight collided with his windshield. He slammed down the visor while, at the same time, cursing a woman driver who had sped down an on-ramp and cut in front of him. He honked his horn. Her arm snaked out her window to give him the finger. He stuck his head out, and with the wind rippling his cheeks, yelled, "Fuck You!"

When he calmed down, he smiled. His life was right where he wanted it. No job. No identity. As loose a life as a yacht freed from its anchor. He had done his research, and he now had the time to do what he had long known was his reason for being.

He parked facing east in a rest stop south of Grants Pass, Oregon, and slept behind the wheel. When the rising sun woke him, he got back on the road. Later, he turned off the interstate and pulled into the first gas station where he was told that, under Oregon law, drivers could not pump their own gas. A stupid law, but his mother would have loved it. She always hated to pump gas. Said it made her hands smell.

While driving, he pictured the resort where he would meet up with Justice Breen and his new bride. He had not been there, but the resort's Internet site was chock-full of pictures, including a map of the grounds. Even pictures taken inside the honeymoon cottage where he would join the newlywed's celebration.

Two hours later he stopped for lunch, then continued north until exiting to make a toll-free call from a pay phone at a rest stop near Salem, Oregon's capital. The crunch of the gravel near the phone booth reminded him of the sound of Santee's Jaguar skidding off the shoulder of the road just before smashing through the guardrail.

"Resort at Depoe Bay, how may I direct your call?"

"I'm interested in reserving your honeymoon cottage." The receptionist put him on hold and his ears were instantly filled with the sounds of "Come Fly with Me," sung by Steve Tyrell.

The song stopped. "Reservations. This is Peggy. How may I help you?"

Her voice had a smiley tone like the voice of his mother's favorite singer, Doris Day. He moved close to the booth to shield out some of the road noise.

"Peggy, my name is John Kimble. My fiance and I are considering your resort for our honeymoon."

"I'm sure your bride will love it here. Our honeymoon cottage is beautifully appointed and secluded near the rear of the property."

He imagined Peggy to be a woman who, through sitting all day, had a bottom three sizes bigger than her top.

"It does sound special," he said.

"Thank you. What dates would you like?"

"It's a bit last minute, but June seventh, eighth, and ninth."

"Oh, I'm so sorry. As you said, it is short notice. Those nights have been booked. May I offer any other dates?"

"I doubt any other dates would work, but if they will, I'll call again after talking with my fiance."

Before leaving the Salem area he stopped at a chain discount store where he purchased a white long-sleeve shirt, a bow tie, a red baseball cap, and a roll of duct tape. At the checkout counter he threw in a Lou Rawls CD, paying cash for everything. A few minutes later he began drumming his fingers on the steering wheel and singing a duet with Rawls of "Fine Brown Frame."

In Portland he took the Burnside Street exit to a part of town where research indicated he could purchase a gun on the black market. For the buy he wore boots with higher heels, a hat, and thick-rimmed fake glasses that would not distort his contact lenses. A 9-mm Colt 2000 with a fifteen-round magazine and a noise suppressor, came high. The seller took him to a location where he could test fire the weapon.

After completing the purchase, he returned to the interstate and went back the way he had come. At the junction for Highway 20 he turned west. This route would take him through lightly populated areas, bringing him out in the coastal town of Newport, Oregon, about ten miles south of Depoe Bay.

# CHAPTER 9

"Apparently, Jack McCall was the choice of
only one person: President Schroeder."

—*Fox News, June 7*

After Colin Stewart left Defense Intelligence for the day, he stopped at the Best Way Supermarket. A raven landed on a grocery cart left in front of his parking space. The bird looked right at him, chirped, and flew directly over his head, rising fast until catching a supporting thermal that allowed the black bird to soar effortlessly. This act by the raven was an ancient Gaelic sign indicating that his life would soon turn in a new direction.

The supermarket's double doors whooshed open automatically, revealing an attractive woman of about thirty-five tugging a grocery cart free from its row. She wore tight black shorts and had her strawberry-blonde hair back in a ponytail. She glanced at him and smiled before turning her cart up the first aisle. He saw her again in the produce section and again they exchanged smiles. Later, in the vitamin section, he went up to her.

"Will you please stop following me?"

She placed the palm of her open hand on the chest of her yellow jersey and blinked innocently. "If anyone is being followed, sir, it is I." Her laughter gently moved her.

When Colin introduced himself, she extended her hand. "Nora Burke. It's nice to meet you, Colin Stewart."

"After we check out, will you join me for a cup of coffee?"

"I'd planned to go home to eat and watch the rest of the Dodgers and Diamondbacks game." She grinned.

"We do need time to figure out just who's following whom," Colin explained. "Join me across the street at the sports bar. I'll have them put your game on one of their televisions. They also serve food."

She leaned on the side of his grocery cart and looked at its contents. "It appears you eat most of your meals out, Mr. Stewart."

"The six boxes of cereal gave me away, eh?" They laughed. "Are you ready?"

She released her hair from its ponytail and shook her head. "I still need a few things. I'll meet you across the street."

Maybe there was some truth to the old story of the raven.

The sun had climbed just above the horizon when Colin returned to his apartment to shower and change before reporting to the base. Still holding last night's groceries, the cell phone on his belt rang. He dropped the two bags on the counter, and opened his phone to hear Jack McCall's voice.

"I need to see you in two hours at the CIA," Jack said.

Colin flipped a box of cereal in the air, caught it, and put it in the cabinet. "I'll need to clear it with DOD."

"Taken care of. The president spoke with General Crook."

"The president?" Colin set two more boxes of cereal on the shelf.

"Yep. This time we're working directly for our commander in chief. Keep it under your hat. No one else in military intel knows about this yet."

"What's up?"

"Let's plow that ground later. I need to call Millet. We'll go see him together."

"Jack?"

"What?"

"I'm glad we'll be working together again," Colin said.

After their adventures in Kuwait, and being along with Jack on the operation in which Jack's brother, Nick, had been killed, Colin knew that working with Jack meant cliffhanging excitement and plenty of it.

# CHAPTER 10

"One minute the story is that McCall will have a small, quick
force, then talk circulates about a new heavily staffed
department being assembled within the CIA."

—MSNBC, June 7

"What the hell does he want?" Harry Mandrake demanded after his
secretary told him that FBI Director Fred Hampton was on the
phone.

"It is true I've achieved the high office of secretary to Washington, D.C.'s chief of police," she replied, "but you don't figure the
FBI director explained his purpose to me, do you, Chief?"

Mandrake admired his secretary's competence, but she was a
wiseacre. "Put him through," he said before straightening his computer keyboard and picking up the phone.

"Chief Mandrake."

"Good morning, Chief, Fred Hampton here. Can you meet me
for coffee? It's urgent."

"It always is with you feds. I feel like a cheap date. You only call
when you're already excited. Where?"

"The Bakery Café. Sixth and Indiana. I'm half way there, talking
to you on my cell."

Chief Mandrake removed his coat from a hanger suspended on
the coat tree along the side wall, used his off hand to take the swing
out of the now unoccupied hanger, and headed out the door of his
fifth floor office in the Henry J. Daly building.

At the café, he found Hampton sitting at a corner table.

"Hello, Chief," Hampton said, his perfunctory smile containing no joy. "It's good of you to come on such short notice."

"Good morning, Fred. I delayed another meeting, so let's get to it." Mandrake sat across from Hampton, then took a moment to straighten the plastic spoon on the paper napkin in front of him.

The waiter brought two coffees. The thin Mandrake sipped his black and watched the lumpy Hampton ruin a perfectly good cup of coffee with three packets of make-believe sugar and a generous measure of cream. After a small sip, he added one more packet and another splash of cream.

"Chief, I need you to authorize Frank Wade and Nora Burke to work with a multiagency federal task force being headed by Jack Mc-Call."

Mandrake stopped his cup before it got to his lips. "So CNN had it right about McCall?"

"We're not happy that got out."

A young couple came in and sat two tables from them. Director Hampton lowered his voice. "The president asked me to contact you. Officially, Wade and Burke will still be your homicide detectives. Unofficially, they'll be part of McCall's team. Any paperwork you feel is needed should be held at your desk, for now. The task force will eventually be acknowledged, but for now we don't want this perp to think we're saddled up."

Mandrake hated it when the feds came waltzing in to tell him what and how, even the director of the FBI. But Mandrake had learned it came with the job; Washington, D.C. had its own protocols.

A bakery employee headed toward them with a tray of donuts. Mandrake waved him off while asking Director Hampton, "When?"

"Have them meet McCall for lunch at noon at LaBamba's. The backroom's ours. Ask for the Harkness table."

"By noon?" Mandrake exclaimed. "Without any official records? That's pretty fast."

Hampton grinned. "Hey, they don't call you Mandrake the Magician for nothing."

"Yeah, right, you owe me, Fred."

"You know my door's always open to the D.C. chief of police."

"Yeah, right, you owe me, Fred."

"You're repeating yourself, Chief, and you've got another meeting, remember?"

Mandrake grunted, gulped the last of his coffee, and used his napkin to wipe the lip of the cup. After refolding the napkin and replacing the spoon at its center, he dropped a five dollar bill on the table and walked out, cast in the late-morning shadow of the rotund FBI Director.

It was just like the feds, Mandrake thought. Director Hampton had asked for the meeting, taken his two best detectives, and stuck him with paying for the coffee.

Jack and Colin pulled up in front of the home of Millet Yorke, a modest one-story house east of Marion Park, shoehorned into a mixed cluster of painted and natural brick homes. Both sides of the porch cover sagged, giving the entry the look of a pouting mouth.

"Holy Shit!" Millet's voice reached out to them at the curb. "You never know what the dogs will leave on your stoop. How the hell are you two?" Before they stepped onto the porch, Yorke, who was wearing a striped shirt and plaid Bermudas, asked, "Is this visit about the deaths of the two Supremes and the big-money guy?"

Jack grinned.

The heels on Millet's untied brown chukka boots slapped the floor as he led his visitors inside.

Millet's place looked as if everything had been left where Millet had last finished with it, including a pair of his Jockeys balled up on the cushion next to Jack. Millet himself looked unshaven and disheveled, with wisps of unruly hair that caught the light at odd angles.

"Whoever's doing these killings," Colin said, "must be a madman. He's literally attacking the United States government."

"In the dark ages," Millet interjected, "the mad ones were considered the special children of God."

Colin rolled his eyes. "When do we start, Jack?"

"We'll meet at four this afternoon at the CIA. Millet, you'll get all the computer goodies you'll need and—"

"No fucking way, Jack. I ain't going into that den of death."

So nothing had changed, Jack told himself. As usual Millet preferred working at home where he could get loud and vulgar whenever he wished, and dress however he wanted. Hell, he did that anyway or so it seemed.

"I know you prefer to work here at your own place," Jack said, "and I usually go along with that. But this time I need more than your computer. I need your mind in the entire process."

"Jackman, you know I love ya, but my privacy's important. It's gonna cost you—big time. Double the usual?"

"It's great working with you two again," Jack said.

"Back at ya, boss," Colin replied.

Millet just shook his head. "We still got more negotiating to do. I'll come to the meeting at four to hear more, but for now, I'm in just today."

Jack knew that Millet loved his country, just perhaps not as much as his privacy.

"Anything I can do until four?" Colin asked.

"Reach your best military intel sources here and abroad," Jack told him. "Operatives at the grass roots, find out what they've heard. What they suspect. Keep it under the radar."

"What about me?" Millet pleaded. "Don't leave me out."

Jack knew then that Millet was just playing hard to get. "Start your computer digging."

Millet grinned. "I'm on it."

"Millet. The president has authorized top-secret clearance for you."

"Well, super dickie do." Millet dug his finger into his ear. "Don't that beat all? Me with a secret clearance."

Jack frowned. "The president hesitated because you're not a government employee and have never had clearance at any level. I assured him you were essential and no risk."

"I feel like a kid with the key to the candy store," Millet said.

If you embarrass me on this," Jack said, "I'll parachute your sorry ass onto *The Island of Dr. Moreau*." After Millet smiled, Jack said, "This is not a challenge for you to prove the president wrong."

"Maybe just a little," Millet said with his eyebrows raised. "It's good for them politicos to get brought down a notch or two from time to time.

Jack fixed Millet with a stare and spoke firmly. "I'm not fooling here. I had to speak up to get you that clearance."

"Jesus Christ. . . . Okay! . . . scouts' honor."

A little of Millet's eccentricities went a long way. He was a royal pain, but the man had delivered the goods in the past. Jack was hoping he could do it again.

# CHAPTER 11

He stood ankle deep in the ocean, the legs of his pants rolled up above his knees. The sea speaking loudly enough to be the voices of all who had died within her. He looked down as the ebb tore the wet sand from around his heels, dragging it across his bare feet. He hated the look of his second toe being longer than his big toe.

A hundred yards out into the surf, boulders, some as tall as three-story buildings, defied the violence of each crashing wave. He pictured himself as one of those boulders standing strong against the forces of evil.

Before leaving his house, Jack opened the chess forum on the Internet. Two days ago he'd received his opponent Harry's latest move: a castling of his white king to the king side, posted as 0–0. His opponent would not likely move his king again in the next few moves as the piece was under no immediate threat. So, Jack used his move to position his black knight and posted that move: Nba6, in the English algebraic notation system used in the U.S. Chess Federation tournament.

• • •

Thirty minutes later, Jack walked into the room at the CIA head-quarters that would become their ops center. Millet had arrived, sitting alone, slouched at the only piece of furniture, a large confer-ence table with five matching swivel chairs and five unmatched straight backs. The room looked to be about three thousand square feet but with just the table, the space had the feel that comes with empty.

Millet had dressed for the meeting by putting on long pants with horizontal stripes and tying his chukka boots, but he still wore the same striped shirt he had worn at his house.

"This is why I like working at home," he barked, before getting up and standing near the window. "Its five minutes to four and some of your folks aren't here yet. If we don't start on time, I'm gone."

"You're being paid, Millet, and rather well at that," Jack re-minded him.

Rachel came in, her dark-green blouse shifting under her tan blazer, her arms crossed. She sat in one of the swivel chairs. Her arms remained crossed. Next, Colin came in, introduced himself to Rachel, took Millet by the arm and the two of them joined Rachel at the table.

Jack had given the front desk a list of his squad with instructions to bring them back as they arrived. When the expected knock came, he ushered the two D.C. Metro homicide detectives in and made the necessary introductions. Jack noticed the change in Nora Burke's expression when she saw Colin. They knew each other.

"I could give you the long speech," Jack said when they were all seated at the table, "but there's more than enough long speeches given in this town. The short one goes like this: The nation is won-dering. The world is watching. And this is happening right under the noses of our agencies, so let's move right into doing the job.

"Right now, each of us knows some of the data on one or more of these deaths. Before we leave tonight, I want us all to know every-thing. We'll go around the table. When your turn comes, tell us what you know and what you think and answer questions from the others."

Everyone was looking at Jack except for Millet who sat gazing at Nora like a smitten-eighth-grader. "Millet," Jack said, bringing the eccentric's attention back to the group. "Let's start with you. Did your computer digging come up with anything?"

"Way too early, Jackman."

Jack pointed to Colin. "Did you learn anything from your international calls?"

"Nothing yet. Maybe later."

Jack wasn't surprised. He would keep the international angle alive, but as he had told the president, none of the trapping of these assassinations pointed outside America.

"Rachel?"

She opened a folder. "The CTC, in case any of you may not know, that's the counterterrorism center, gave me the long list of terrorist and militant groups."

Jack got up and moved behind her chair. She leaned forward toward the document, uncrossing her legs. He heard the whisper of nylon. The soft fragrance of her perfume entered him when he inhaled.

She ran her finger down the list. "CTC had nothing that points to any specific group, still, we can safely conclude that all these people are pleased this is happening."

Jack wanted to hear the specifics about the autopsy and evidence workup on the poisoning of Justice Monroe. Rachel had brought the reports from the FBI, but Jack knew Lieutenant Frank Wade had received copies, and Jack wanted to find out if Wade had kept himself current. "Frank, have you gone over the report on Monroe's death?"

"Sure."

"Sum it up for us."

Frank stood, draped his jacket over the back of his chair, and opened the collar on his button-down blue shirt.

"The medical examiner estimated that Supreme Court Justice Adam Monroe died about ten thirty the morning of May eighteenth.

Monroe had a congestive heart condition and diabetes—the type that does not require insulin injections. At first Monroe's death appeared to be a heart attack, but the toxicology report changed all that. Cause of death: he died of ingesting ground oleander that had been mixed with the contents of his ginseng capsules. Monroe kept the ginseng in his chambers and took some each day about mid-morning. Many ginseng users believe it should be taken between meals."

Millet blurted, "Oleander?"

Frank laughed, a laugh that seemed high for a thick man with a chest like a wine cask.

"That's the plant. It has a toxicity rating of six. Arsenic is five. In Europe, ground Oleander is sold to poison rats. The stuff grows like a weed in warmer climates. My ex-wife has a potted dwarf oleander in her sun room. She's been barking at me to come by and move it outdoors for the summer."

Wade reset his glasses and glanced at his notes. "Monroe's law clerk found him dead in his chambers at the Supreme Court. The FBI checked out the clerk, nothing suspicious there. They checked into the vitamin company. Nothing. The remaining ginseng capsules in the bottle were also compromised."

"Rachel. Anything you wish to add?"

"Good summary, Frank," she said in reply to Jack's question.

Jack sat down, clasped his hands under his chin, and put his elbows on the armrests of his chair, the sleeves of his white shirt forming the sides of a triangle. "Okay then. We've got copies here of all the reports from all the agencies, including the ones Frank and Nora brought over from Metro PD. Everybody reads all of it before tomorrow."

Jack noticed Rachel slipping out of her shoes. The skin on the backs of her heels looked smooth. He found it strange that he was so physically aware of her.

"If this were a routine murder," Colin asked, "what would the local cops do next?"

"Everyone associated with the justice had both means and opportunity," Nora said, "so we'd look for motive."

"I wonder if Monroe's doctor had anything to do with the justice taking ginseng?" Rachel asked. "Maybe the doc gave it to him?"

"At the Montgomery scene Jack told Nora and me that this was still officially a Metro case, so, we followed up on that angle when we didn't see anything in the FBI reports." Frank crossed his Popeye-sized forearms. "And, incidentally, the doc's a she. Doctor Joanne Hayworth had been Monroe's doctor for twenty years. Bottom line: Doctor Hayworth didn't even know Monroe took ginseng."

"Good work," Jack said. "Anything else?"

"I interviewed the justice's wife," Nora said. "Mrs. Monroe told me they had no visitors that morning or the prior night. And Dr. Hayworth never made a house call."

"At least that part of the case makes sense," Rachel interjected. "Doctors quit making house calls the year Norman Rockwell quit painting."

Millet slouched in his chair like a bored kid in church. "We're wasting time looking at families and coworkers."

Jack held up his hand for quiet, turning toward Millet. "Update those background checks for all the employees and staff who worked closely with any of the three victims. Credit records, arrests, financial records, bank accounts, travel in the past year, relatives who live outside the U.S., and so on."

"Wilco, Jackman."

"We checked out all forty-some law clerks and secretaries who work for the justices," Rachel added. "We threw in the security and cleaning personnel and the people who work in the gift shop in the area open to tourists. The Supreme Court Police had extensive background checks on those people so it went pretty quickly. We just updated them. I agree with Frank and Nora. We've got lots of folks with means and opportunity, but no one even remotely suspicious as to motive."

For the next few hours they shared what they knew about the

murder of Herbert Montgomery, the justice nearly decapitated in the National Mall.

Jack liked the way his team was coming together. The local cops weren't slackers, and Rachel looked as capable as he had hoped she would be. Colin and Millet were knowns, but the others hadn't gotten past getting acquainted. The real work had not yet begun.

# CHAPTER 12

National Security Advisor Robert Quartz
refers to McCall's squad as lightweights.

—*CNN, June 8*

Soon after dusk he pulled into the Resort at Depoe Bay, parking near
the back of the lot. After twisting the rearview mirror to be sure his
bow tie was straight, he tugged down his red baseball cap, popped an
antacid, and stepped out, holding the vase of flowers he had bought
on the outskirts of Newport Beach, Oregon.

A series of precise circles of light were thrown to the ground by
the dome-covered landscape lighting lining the path to the honeymoon cottage. As he moved, his warm breaths turned into small
clouds, defeated by the chilly air. At the end of the path he stepped
through the bushes and slowly worked his way around the cottage
until he found a window with a narrow sag in a carelessly closed
drape.

Justice Breen sat near the sliding glass door to the cottage's private garden, a fluted champagne glass in his hand. His bride stood
near the center of the room. She wore a white thong, thigh-high
black sheer stockings, red high heels, and a low-cut white halter top
with tiny red bow ties around her neck and wrists. She ran her hand
suggestively up the neck of the champagne bottle, then playfully
eased her index finger around its head.

The groom reached for her.

She backed away teasingly.

A fist of tension balled in the watcher's belly. His nerve endings tingled. When she bent down to refill the flutes, her butt protruded toward the window. Perspiration dotted his forehead like pimples on a teen. He reached inside his pants, taking himself in his hand.

He picked up a fallen pine branch, using it to rub out his tracks as he circled back to the path near the door. After rechecking the duct tape he had applied to seal the legs of his pants to his white athletic socks and his sleeve cuffs to his latex gloves, he reached out and knocked.

Breen's voice boomed. "Who is it?"

*Oh. Pudgy Judgy. Did I interrupt something?*

"I have a delivery of flowers, sir."

"Who from?"

Confident Justice Breen would not refuse flowers from his new in-laws, he said, "The card reads, 'from Mom and Dad Ashcroft.' Do you want them, sir?" The watcher, anticipating that the judge would look out through the peephole, stepped back and held up the vase of flowers.

The door opened.

Breen's eyes circled when the Colt 2000 appeared from behind the vase. His lips moved, but his first word drowned in the spit from the noise suppressor.

Breen's black boxers twisted as he coiled unevenly against the carpet.

The shooter stepped closer and fired again, this time striking Breen in the forehead. After kicking the groom's foot out of the way, he shut the door and looked for the bride. She was not in sight. As he started toward the glass slider, he heard a low vibrating sound, then saw light slicing out from under a side door.

*Of course, she stepped into the bathroom when Judgy came to answer the door.*

The narrow strip of light went dark and the fan died with a tinny whimper. The door opened. Judith came out, her halter top dangling from her fingers. The candlelight cast its shadowy hands across her bare breasts. When she saw her husband on the floor, she opened her mouth to scream.

The silencer made no more sound than the amplification of a woman's leg sliding into a nylon stocking.

Judith collapsed against the wall. Her knees buckled. She went down. Dead.

He pulled the drape over to close the gap he had watched through, then held the candle closer and watched as the flickering light changed the look of her body.

Some sicko might have sex with her, but he would not. Time was of the essence. He needed to get back across the state line, and he couldn't chance leaving his DNA behind. Instead he carried her to the bed, where he gently spread her soft hair on the pillow, creating a loving yellow nimbus around her head. Then he rammed a long serrated knife up into her and felt his satisfaction gush.

He went through the judge's wallet and the bride's purse, removing anything identifying. The local cops would have only their names from hotel registration, which he felt confident the Breens had disguised in some manner to keep their honeymoon site secret from the media.

After blowing out the candles, he eased open the door, smelled the wet pines, and heard only silence. He picked up the vase of flowers, hung the do-not-disturb sign on the outside knob, and quietly reentered the world he was changing.

In today's world, political power, sex, and gore guaranteed headlines. This elimination, having all three, would quickly become his most publicized elimination. The FBI's evidence response team would find hairs and fibers and secretions from countless honeymooners, but no trace of him. He had been too careful. He had been too smart.

At the bottom of the hill he turned south onto Highway 101, back toward Newport. Along the way he stopped in the parking lot of one of Oregon's spectacular beaches, the moon reflecting the ocean's natural phosphorus, creating a silvery shimmer. He changed clothes next to the back of the van and put his delivery outfit, including his shoes, into a black metal drum along with the lovebirds' identification and the flowers, squeezed a full can of lighter fluid into the jumbled mess and dropped a lit match. The gun, he'd left at the scene. The knife, well, the knife, he had left in the scene.

Newlyweds dream their honeymoon will last forever. For the Breens he had made that a reality.

And then there were twelve.

# CHAPTER 13

The Middle East remains conspicuously
quiet on the American assassinations.

— *FOX News, June 8*

At nine that night, Jack turned his straight-back chair around, strad-
dled it and plopped his arms across the backrest. "Fill us in on Santee, Nora."

"The local police in the Poconos concluded Santee accidentally
drove off the cliff," she began. "Their local M.E. confirmed the time
of death matched Mrs. Santee's statement. She said her husband
played a game in which he raced his Jaguar down the mountain
road." After a smirk of sorts, Nora added, "One thing we can be sure
of, men never grow up."

Rachel and Nora smiled at each other while the men protested.

Fostering camaraderie was a part of Jack's reasoning for tonight's
meeting, along with getting everyone up to speed. He knew they
needed to bond to have a good chance to complete their mission,
particularly in this town where the common denominator was: everything becomes a political football.

So far he had heard no media leaks since the one he discussed
with the president, and that one had come from the president's inner
circle. Rachel had a history of working FBI cases without leaking to
the press, and he had shared lots of classified stuff with Colin and
some with Millet. He trusted them. If there was anyone to worry
about it would be Frank Wade or Nora Burke, but they hadn't leaked

anything after he pushed them to the sidelines at the Montgomery murder scene, so he doubted they would now that they were back on the inside.

"You should all be aware that CIA Director Miller is a close, life-long friend of June Santee," Jack told the others. "She's also the god-mother of one of Santee's children. We need to be sensitive to that whenever she's around. Director Miller told me Mrs. Santee had spoken with her on more than one occasion about her husband speeding down that mountain road."

"Whoever is behind these killings has done their homework," Rachel said. "The killer knew about Monroe's ginseng, Montgomery's penchant for morning walks through the National Mall, and Santee's regression behind the wheel of his Jaguar. This guy has a spot picked out for each target."

"Frank, you and Nora, tomorrow morning, go to the Federal Reserve here in D.C.," Jack said. "Talk to the head of security. After that, stop to see Chief Oscar Wiggins at the Supreme Court Police. I talked with him after I left you guys at the Montgomery scene. He'll give you a CD detailing the security breaches, crank stuff, and threats over the past few years. Other than that, carry on the same as you would have if you had never heard from me."

Rachel slipped her shoes back on before asking Jack, "What's your take on all this?"

"As you just laid out, each victim died doing something that was part of his normal routine. Whoever is behind these killings has done reconnaissance and carefully planned when, where, and how. With that in mind, tomorrow, take Colin and make contact with the rest of the Fed governors and the justices. Encourage them to change their habitual routines as much as possible."

"When do you want us back here?" Frank asked.

"I expect to have this place outfitted tomorrow, by three. Millet, this is the last late meeting we'll pull without some food."

Millet winked at Nora. The corner of his mouth moved more than his eye, morphing the effort into a startling expression.

After the others had drifted out, Rachel walked over to Jack, her blue eyes intense.

"You've assembled quite a team," she said, hands on her hips, "two local cops, a strange computer geek, and the mysterious Colin Stewart. And that's without mentioning you and me. I figure Colin for a military sniper, right?"

"Colin is one of the best long-range shooters in the wor—"

"Like I said, a sniper. That's okay. The FBI has snipers in their SWAT teams."

"That's true," Jack said. "But FBI snipers usually arrive in a comfortable truck, accept the risk and take the shot, then go back to the truck and back to their homes and families. A military sniper crawls through the muck, and often waits in the same position for hours, even days, then takes the shot and crawls out hoping to escape with his life. Colin's been with me on four or five covert operations. He has a sixth sense that's uncanny. Trust it. I do. As for Millet, he's different. I grant you that, but I've used him many times. He fights me. He's even antisocial. But he's never failed to find what I need and without being slowed down by rules or authorizations."

"He's a hacker," Rachel said with a cutting edge to her voice, "like the hackers arrested by the bureau's White Collar Crime Division."

Jack shook his head. "I grant you Millet wouldn't fit in over at J. Edgar University. In the end, no one on this team will be more important than Millet. Not me. Not you."

He had to get Rachel out of her FBI button-down mind-set. He didn't want to lose her, and he was coming to realize he meant that on more than one level.

Like the unfolding wings of a bat waking from a long day of sleep, the assassin could feel his expanding thirst for blood as he continued to reassure himself that his eliminations were justified by both his love of country and loyalty to his father.

After driving south late into the night, he pulled off the interstate at Redding, California, to get something to eat, use a prepaid phone card for a long-distance call, and send a FedEx package.

The time had come to abandon the pretense of coincidence and turn the law dogs loose to chase his phantom militia.

At midnight, Jack stood on the second floor deck on the front of his house with his nightly three fingers of Marker's Mark. Between drinks he rolled his shoulders up and back, then stretched his head from side to side until each ear touched each shoulder. He then swirled his glass and sent the last swallow to exercise his insides.

This case alone would define his career. Twenty years of successful overt and covert operations wouldn't count. This time the battleground was America. Success would allow him to leave the government with the best wishes of his president and a grateful nation. Failure would be, well, failure.

He went inside, back down to the kitchen and poured two more fingers, not quite covering the cubes in his glass. He was back in the death business. Seeing it. Trying to prevent it. Perhaps dispensing it. At the kitchen table his mind replayed that night in the sand in Iraq, his last night with his younger brother.

"Oh, Jack. It hurts. Jack."

"Hang in there, bro. The chopper's had it. We'll have to get out on foot."

"I can't, Jack. Oh, God it hurts. You go. Get out of here."

"Stuff that talk, soldier. We'll make it. Together. Like we always have."

"No, Jack. No. You go. I love you, bro. Live for us both."

Jack had sat in the sand with Nick's torn head on his lap. Nick's eyes on Jack's face, scared eyes trying to be brave. But neither of them had said another word.

Jack had gotten out. And Jack had taken revenge. But Nick was still gone.

Why had he taken Nick on his mission? To impress him? To train him? To show off for him? Always the same questions. Always no answers. The memory always ending with the same words, "No, Jack. No. You go. I love you, bro. Live for us both."

He walked into the living room and put the glass on the piano without bothering with a coaster. Then sat down to play, determined to shake off his funk. He started to play Fats Waller's "Rumpsteak Serenade," a song that made him think of his sexy neighbor, Janet Parker. Before he reached the end, the phone rang. He hit the talk button. "Jack McCall."

"Why haven't you fucked Rachel Johnstone?" the voice said. "You must know she wants you to."

Jack clenched his teeth. "Who the hell is this?"

The caller sucked in a breath. "Your new friend. And you have no idea just how friendly we're going to be."

# CHAPTER 14

The president's opponents scream: "Schroeder's using McCall's squad as a forerunner to forming a Presidential Secret Police."

—*Cleveland Plain Dealer, June 8*

He left the van in an empty lot in a high-crime area of Oakland, California, tossed the keys next to the plastic explosive, and set the timer for ten minutes.

Four blocks away with his hand on the door of a taxi, the blast brought him up short. Fighting the desire to laugh, he parroted the cab driver's expressions of concern.

During his flight back to Baltimore, he went over what he had compiled about the next aristocrat who would die for his country: Charles (Chip) Taylor, the Federal Reserve Bank governor from the Cleveland District.

Taylor lived in Pepper Pike, an affluent Cleveland residential neighborhood about twenty-five miles from the airport. The kind of neighborhood that had strategically placed garden club bag stations so the residents who walked their dogs on cold mornings could bag their steamers.

He had periodically surveilled Chip Taylor for more than a year, and, for the past few weeks, bugged his home telephone. Taylor lived with his wife, Susan, a woman obsessed with trying to stay young, and his invalid mother who, suffering with advanced Alzheimer's, spent afternoons twice a week in therapy. Killing all three, after the eliminations of Justice Breen and his bride would shock the nation's financial markets and legal system.

After deplaning in Baltimore, he took a taxi downtown where he purchased a pair of running shoes, an expensive jogging suit, a new red baseball cap, and a backpack.

A different cab brought him back to the Baltimore-Washington International Airport where, as Robert Campbell, he purchased a ticket for the next flight to Cleveland.

Outside Hopkins International Airport he hailed a cab into downtown Cleveland. After walking three blocks, he entered a public parking garage where he recovered a detonator he had hidden there on an earlier trip, after having picked the lock on Taylor's kitchen door and rigged a bomb in their basement.

From there he went to the corner of Green and Mayfield Roads and entered a bicycle shop where he paid cash for an assembled red Jamis Ventura road bike and two cans of black aerosol bicycle paint. He pedaled five miles on Green Road and then Lander Road before turning into the heart of the Pepper Pike neighborhood. Street after street of pristine homes lived in by upper-class Americans who had stood aside while their elected leaders sold out their generation's stewardship of the country. Two turns later, he stopped across from a dark brick home, reached down for the water bottle suspended on the bike's frame and, while taking a drink, casually glancing at the light edging around the drape in Taylor's second-floor rear-bedroom window.

Constance Harding spent her days watching soap operas and her nights watching old movies, particularly musicals. Last summer she had tried to become friends with the older woman in the house behind her, the widow Lucille Taylor, who lived with her son and his wife, but it hadn't worked. Lucille, addled to the point where she had trouble recalling her own daughter-in-law's name, never remembered Constance from one visit to the next.

Constance's son, who lived in Pittsburgh, drove over with his family on the first Sunday of every other month to take her out to dinner. Other than those visits she had been alone since her husband died eighteen years ago. Except for the news hours between ten and eleven at night, the television was her best friend. She could not stand the steady recitation of gloom and doom that filled the news, never speaking to the good in people, the God quality that Constance believed could be found in every person. For a while she had watched *I Love Lucy* reruns during the late news hour, but eventually she started to simply turn off her television in silent protest.

Tonight, as she did every night, weather permitting, she sat in a chair on the screened-in porch at the front of her house, feeling the pulse of the neighborhood she had lived in for forty years, the first twenty-two with her dear departed husband. At that hour, the neighborhood was quiet. She rarely saw anyone except for an old man who walked his dog between ten and ten thirty—perhaps his own silent protest against the news. She had often thought about walking out and introducing herself, but she never did.

Right then, Constance saw a biker pull to the curb. She thought she knew everyone in the neighborhood, at least by sight, but not this man. Pepper Pike had become so transient. In her forty years she had lost all her neighbors several times until now no one remained who had known her Roland. The biker took a drink of something and moved on.

A hard push on the right pedal got him going again. Two quick left turns and he would soon pass the home of Charles Chip Taylor. The biker sat back on the seat, reached into the pocket of his zippered lightweight jacket and pressed the remote on the three-minute timer for the blast that would launch a thousand Chips.

*Okay, that was corny,* he thought, *but even a revolutionary patriot should have a sense of humor.*

He stopped where Lander Road at Country Lane crossed over a creek. After wiping the remote clean he tossed it into the water under the bridge. A block later his watch pulsed, and he turned to see pieces of the Taylor house, maybe chips of Charles himself, twist and turn against the night sky. In less than a minute, he heard the sirens.

*The authorities always give fast service in the ritzy neighborhoods.*

Two minutes later he coasted his bike into a vacant lot near I-271. After putting the bike down on its side in the weeds, he cut the seat and splatter sprayed the bike with the black aerosol paint. Then he walked to a nearby hotel where he put the cans in their Dumpster. At the street entrance, he hailed a cab pulling out of the hotel after dropping a fare. Feigning a cough he held a handkerchief against his mouth and used it to shield his hand when he touched the taxi.

He changed into jeans and a Cleveland Indians' baseball cap in a downtown gas station bathroom. In the next block he walked behind a bar, stuffed his backpack and the clothes he'd worn on the bike into the Dumpster and dropped in several lit matches.

Eight blocks later he hailed a second cab to take him back to the Cleveland Airport where, as Robert Campbell, he cleared security and boarded his flight.

On his way home from the Baltimore airport he stopped at his father's grave to consecrate the identities he had used in Oregon and Ohio.

*We're inside a dozen, now. You were so right, Father. They didn't hear your warnings. Your noble attempt cost you your life. My way is costing them their lives. Tomorrow will be stimulating.*

# CHAPTER 15

Some say it's foreign terrorists. Others say American
extremists. To vote your opinion, visit the Internet
site shown on the bottom of your screen.

—*All News Network, June 8*

Jack left home early enough to catch a glimpse through the trees of
the sunrise glistening off the Potomac River, the sheet of moving
water broken here and there by small whitecaps.

Last night he had endured another attack of insomnia. When
he was on assignment, sleeping was like being trapped in a fighter jet
doing an endless roll. Last night he had watched one of his favorite
movies from his collection of film noir: Humphrey Bogart's great
characterization of Dashiell Hammett's Sam Spade in *The Maltese
Falcon*. Throughout the movie his mind had wrestled with the unan-
swerable: could the man who had called about Rachel be the man
they were hunting? Nothing factual connected them. His instinct
did. If the caller was the killer, it meant that assassinations weren't
enough. The killer wanted to play. This was a new piece of the profile, and Jack needed to tell his squad and warn Rachel.

The sun was filtering through the surrounding trees when Jack
pulled into the CIA lot. When he arrived this early, he rarely saw
anyone other than Lana and Zaro Kindar. The Kindars provided coffee service in the CIA's New Headquarters Building that comprised
1.1 million of the CIA's total 2.5 million square feet secreted within
the trees in the Langley neighborhood of McLean, Virginia.

In the late 1980s, after Saddam Hussein's forces killed their three sons, Lana and Zaro took jobs working as housekeepers to high officials in Iraq's Republican Guard. In that job the Kindars secretly passed on information and documents they could copy to an American agent, Jack McCall. The afternoon before McCall and his squad were to be extracted from Iraq, the Kindars were arrested and taken to a small military camp near Tikrit, north of Baghdad. Jack had taken a few men, including Colin Stewart and with the support of the Kurdish Underground, fought their way in to free the Kindars. After their return, General Crook helped Jack walk Lana and Zaro through immigration. And Harriet Miller, the CIA director, had them employed as independent contractors to provide the coffee service in the nonhighly classified sectors.

The CIA's facilities staff met Jack at the door to his squad room. He explained the layout he wanted, the conference table at the far end, with a six-foot marking board on the wall next to the table's long side, covering the rest of that wall with pin board. He would ask Rachel to set up half the pin board as a bulletin section with pictures and particulars on the sitting justices and Fed governors. With the other half developed as a graveyard section holding the pictures and information on each of the victims, and the details of the deaths.

Desks were to be put at the end near the door, and in the space between a couch, some occasional chairs, and the food and beverage area that becomes essential once an investigation takes on a 24/7 life of its own.

About the time the facilities people left, the Kindars arrived to set them up with fresh coffee, snacks, and fill the refrigerator with sodas and bottled water. They even put a bowl of red apples and green seedless grapes on the conference table.

By early afternoon the furnishings were in place, and the installers had assured Jack that the computers and other high-tech goodies were ready for use.

At four the members of Jack's squad started coming in. Millet arrived, still grumbling about not being able to work at home. Jack had talked him into working at the CIA, in part, by going along with Millet's request to name their squad room the Bullpen. Jack immediately took to the name, feeling the connotation of the word captured the independence and solidarity he wanted his team to feel.

Millet headed right for his computer area, and spun on his heels when he saw an autographed picture of Tommy Lasorda, longtime manager of his favorite team, the L.A. Dodgers, hanging above his monitor. A card, wedged into the edge of the frame read: "From a fellow Dodgers fan, Nora Burke." The already smitten Millet ran his hands through his undisciplined hair.

After everyone got something to drink, they settled in around the conference table.

"Tell us about the meetings you and Frank had with security at the Fed and the Court," Jack said to Nora.

"Security at the Fed had nothing out of the ordinary. Chief Wiggins at the Court gave us this." She held up a CD and scooted it down the table toward Millet. "Crank calls and threatening letters during the past five years."

"Set that up so we can cross-reference names," Jack told Millet, "also misspelled words, colloquialisms, whatever with anything we may get later."

"Wilco, Jackman, I'll also rig these computers so we'll know if anyone tries to hack in. And, while I've got the floor, I went through the financial records and newspaper morgues for all the folks working at the Court or the Federal Reserve here in D.C. I included the other property owners on Santee's Winding Trail Road. In one word, nothing, zip, well, I guess that was two words."

"Anything more from the Poconos on Santee?" Colin asked.

"The case officer's just waiting for his chief's okay to officially book Santee as an accident," Nora said. "To quote him, 'It'd already be rung up thata way if Santee weren't no big shot.' "

Jack told them about his mysterious caller and what he had said about Rachel, wondering as he did so, if he should have said something first to Rachel. If she was upset by what Jack had said, she did not show it, although he had seen the glint of something in her eyes.

"If my caller's the killer," he continued, "it likely eliminates Islamic extremists. Fanatical Islamists would not make such references to a woman."

"Did we ever really suspect al-Qaeda or Hezbollah?" Millet asked.

"Not really, but we can't fully discount it. . . . Colin, anything on your remaining phone calls? Or yours, Rachel?" When they both shook their heads, he asked, "Frank, Nora, you have anything to add to what you've already reported?"

"Nope," Frank replied.

"Rachel," Jack said, "what's the latest on alerting the possible targets to alter their habits?"

"We're beating our heads against the wall on that one. Oh, they're frightened. No doubt of that, but they're also vain and used to feeling private and secure."

Jack's insides told him that would soon change.

# CHAPTER 16

Almost a week has passed without another government official being assassinated: is it luck or is the beefed up security working?

*—Portland Oregonian, June 8*

Mabel, the senior maid, stuck her head inside the housekeeping office at the Resort at Depoe Bay. "It's after two, girl, and them honeymooners still ain't gone."

Joyce Griffith, the director of housekeeping, knew guests often left without stopping at the front desk, leaving the hotel to charge the credit card imprinted at check-in. After calling the cottage and receiving no answer, she followed Mabel to the cottage, moving slowly because Mabel's bunions had been giving her a fit this week.

"It smells ugly." Mabel said, after she opened the door.

"Ugly's not a smell, Mabel," Joyce said, covering her nose with one hand. "Makes me think of week-old ribs and molasses sauce."

When they pushed through the door and saw what was inside, Mabel was the first to scream. A moment later Joyce made it a duet. They held each other and, too frightened to stand still, began to bounce.

In the parking lot, Jack suggested they all go for some dinner. Nora recommended Bisby's, a local eatery where patrons barbequed their own steaks over an indoor mesquite fire pit and helped themselves to beans, salad, fries, and corn on the cob.

By eight all the others had left except for Rachel and Nora, who sat toying with the remains of their dinners.

"What's the story on the old couple who bring the coffee?" Nora asked. "They treat Jack like he's their son."

Rachel told Nora what she had scrounged up through a friend in classified records. "Their names are Lana and Zaro Kindar. You probably noticed Lana has no pinkie finger on her right hand. The Iraqi Republican Guard had been torturing her while interrogating her husband. The Kindars had been spying for our side. Jack had been their control. He and Ringo and some of the Kurdish freedom fighters fought their way in and saved their bacon. Jack got them brought here and helped get them the coffee work."

"Wow. That's movie material."

"You got that right, but it's one of the stories that'll never see light." Rachel refilled Nora's beer mug. "Now, tell me, what do you think of our team?"

"I can't say I'm up to speed on what constitutes a federal task force," Nora told her, "but if Jack had followed the book, a couple of local cops like Frank and me wouldn't be on it."

"Jack says Millet's our secret weapon."

Nora laughed and pushed back a runaway strand of hair. "That man reminds me of the mad scientist in the movie *Back to the Future*."

Rachel grinned. "It's obvious Madman Millet is attracted to you." She remembered challenging Jack about the unorthodox members of his squad, and in particular Millet. Maybe she had been a little too rigid.

"I want to be Millet's friend," Nora said, "so that's how I'll play it. But if he hits on me, I'll have to shut him down."

Rachel stacked her empty dinner plate on top of Nora's and pushed them to the side. "When did you decide to be a cop?"

"I was around ten," Nora told her. "My mother had died and my dad and I went to live with his father, a retired beat cop. Grandpa loved that old black-and-white TV series *Superman* and I'd sit and watch them with him. I don't know if you remember, but Superman would open the show standing with his fists on his hips while some badass's bullets bounced off his chest. Then the baddie would throw the empty gun and Superman would duck." She grinned. "I asked Grandpa why Superman needed to duck the gun when the bullets just bounced off him, my Grandpa laughed, turned to my dad and said, 'We got ourselves a third generation cop and dontchuknow, this one'll be a detective.'" Nora grinned at the memory.

"And with that a career was born," Rachel said. They both grinned.

A waiter came to the table, held up their empty pitcher and raised his eyebrows. Nora shook her head and made the universal gesture for their check.

"You can tell me it's none of my business if you want, but from the way you look at Jack McCall when he's not looking at you, I figure you two have some history."

"Well, Ms. Burke, looks like your grandpa was right. You are a detective."

"Hey, you said you liked having another woman on the team. So answer the question, Ms. Johnstone."

"No. Yes. I don't know. I admit I once had the hots for him, but, well, he didn't feel the same way. I guess."

"The man must be gay."

"He's not gay, definitely not gay. I've got a friend in the diplomatic corps and she told me that Jack, what should I say, has had flings with a lot of women in this town. Plus the man's—a damn neat freak."

"He does keep his desk orderly."

"Orderly! You should see his house."

Nora nibbled on her last french fry. "Rachel, the man's organized at work so of course he is at home. If you're trying to put him out of your mind, you'll need something more than, he's neat."

Rachel ran the tip of her finger around the ridge at the top of her glass. "So, anyway, that's my story on America's super spook. Now enough about me." She raised her glass and drained it. "What about you? Who's in your love life?"

"I just ended a long thing with an assistant D.A.," Nora told her. "So, I'm between lovers, for lack of a better phrase."

"No prospects?"

"I did meet someone just the other night," Nora said. "In the supermarket of all places, but who knows when we'll hook up again. I'm going to be busy working with all of you, and I got the impression his work would be keeping him busy for a while too."

# CHAPTER 17

The president's press secretary confirms Schroeder
gets regular briefings from McCall, but beyond
that it's, "No further comment at this time."

—*Mel Carsten, D.C. Talk, June 9*

Sergeant Hector Mendoza from the Lincoln County, Oregon, Sheriff's office stood in the doorway of the Depoe Bay's honeymoon cottage alongside one of his deputies. Mr. Pritcher, the general manager of the resort stood behind them.

The sergeant instructed his deputy to tape off the cottage and the walkway leading to it from the parking lot, including the cottage's small private patio and the grounds around the patio. Pritcher, a frail man in his late sixties, leaned against a post near the door. "Nothing like this has ever happened," he said his voice quivering. "No one has ever been killed—murdered in our resort."

"Don't touch anything, Mr. Pritcher," the sergeant said after the manager stepped through the door. "Please wait outside."

The manager went out and put a cigarette in his mouth, lit it, and took a long puff. He spoke with smoke leaking around his words. "We have guests arriving to stay in this honeymoon cottage. They'll be here in about two hours. We don't have another cottage for newlyweds." He coughed, then lit another cigarette from the embers of the one he had lit only moments before.

Mendoza turned to Pritcher. "Who were the guests?"

"I checked before you arrived, Sergeant. A Ms. Ashcroft reserved the cottage using her credit card. We imprinted it when they checked-in. They registered as Ms. Ashcroft and friend. No first names. That's unusual for the honeymoon cottage, but it happens. Not everyone who reserves it is married. You should speak with Peggy Fallow in reservations. She and Ms. Conners, the concierge, handle the newlyweds."

Sergeant Mendoza left the resort three hours after arriving. He had spoken with the maids, Peggy Fallow, Ms. Conners, the bell-man who took the Breens to their rooms, and the restaurant staff. The Breens had arrived in a cab, eaten no meals in the restaurant or from room service, and had not been seen by anyone since the bell-man took them to the honeymoon cottage.

The Lincoln County Sheriff's Office would retain the lead on the investigation because the crime had first been reported to the sheriff's office. Standard procedure for that area of Oregon called for such crimes to be handled by a cooperative task force made up of the sheriff's office, the Lincoln County District Attorney, the Oregon State Police, and the police departments of several small area cities in what they called their coordinated Major Crime Team.

By seven that evening, Sergeant Mendoza completed his police report:

> Ms. Ashcroft and her friend were killed some time between the late afternoon of June 7, the day of their arrival, and 2:00 p.m., June 9, the time when the maids found their bodies. I estimate the approximate time of death, subject to the coroner's findings, as between 5:00 p.m. and midnight, June 7 based on their not being seen by the resort staff, their ordering no meals, and on the conditions of their bodies: The deep-purple blood settled to the lowest parts of their bodies did not shift when I changed their positions. No blanching occurred when I pressed my finger against the discolored skin. Both bodies were cool to the touch and flaccid except for the largest muscle groups.

The only other homicide Sergeant Mendoza worked had not included much time between the death and the discovery of the body. His estimate had come more from the textbook than from field experience.

He signed his report, turned it in, and went off duty.

The newlyweds' desire for anonymity was still holding.

# CHAPTER 18

No word of progress from Jack McCall.
The nation holds its breath.

—*The Evening News Hour, June 10*

Jack ended his day standing in the shower, the hot water pounding a hard scar on his hip, a souvenir from a firefight during a pre-Gulf War incursion, when his cell phone rang. He stepped out and picked up.

"It's Rachel, Jack."

"Oh, hi. What's happened?"

"Nothing. Just wanted to tell you I thought the group dinner was a good idea. The squad seems to be coming together."

"Are you feeling any better about the members?"

"Yeah. I'm sorry for being a jerk about all that. It's just, well—"

"No sweat. I had expected you to be critical. If you hadn't come around, I would've taken another look at who we had. You have any new ideas? Any time you do, I wanna know it."

"Okay, but I don't now. Just wanted to say goodnight."

"I'm glad everyone enjoyed tonight. I don't know how many more quiet evenings we'll be getting."

"As soon as we hang up, I'm going to pour a glass of wine, take a hot shower and shave my legs. What about you?"

"I've had the drink and the shower. As for the legs, I'll keep 'em hairy."

By ten thirty Jack was in bed, his head filled with thoughts and images of Rachel. Today she had taken the edge off her attitude. He was pleased because she was a capable agent and maybe more.

Four hours later his phone rang again. It was his boss, CIA Director Harriet Miller, telling him she had been awakened ten minutes ago by Fred Hampton. The Cleveland Police had called the FBI.

"Whomever you're hunting just blew up the home of Cleveland Federal Reserve Governor Charles Taylor," she said. "His wife and mother died with him."

"Set up to look like another accident?" Jack rubbed his eyes.

"Not this time. Plastic explosive. They knew we weren't about to buy a fourth coincidence."

Jack squeezed his eyes shut and shook his head in an attempt to dislodge the cobwebs sleep had spun in his mind.

"Director Hampton has dispatched his closest ERT," she went on. "We should have some kind of report by ten. I told Fred you would meet with his squad leader when he returns from Cleveland. That's all we know now. Pleasant dreams."

Jack yawned. "I'll see ya in a few hours."

He had set his alarm for six and drifted off again only to be awakened by another call from Harriet. "There's been another killing," she said.

"You've already called me."

"No. They struck again."

Jack rolled out of bed. "Who? Where?"

"Supreme Court Justice Breen and his bride were found shot to death in a honeymoon cottage in Oregon. The locals just identified the victims. Fred has dispatched his ERT from Portland. We should have their report sometime mid-afternoon."

Jack strode into the bathroom and while holding the phone, used his other hand to splash cold water on his face. "Tell Director Hampton I want the leader he sent to Cleveland to meet with my entire team in our ops center. I want them to hear what he has to say. I'm going to try to see the president around four. Ask Hampton to have the Oregon report sent over one of your secure lines and have your people bring us seven copies."

After showering and shaving Jack called the others. He asked Rachel, Millet, and Colin to be at the Bullpen no later than eight thirty. But he told Frank and Nora, not before nine.

Colin and Millet had already taken seats when Jack arrived and grabbed a cup of coffee and a carrot muffin. Rachel stood at their pin board removing the pictures of Justice Breen and Fed Governor Taylor from the bulletin section and repositioning them in the graveyard section.

Jack started talking while Rachel finished. "Our first order of business: do we keep Frank and Nora or send them back to Metro PD?"

"Keep them," Rachel said without hesitation. "They don't have the locals versus the feds chip on their shoulder. They think well and they fit in."

"Anybody disagree?"

"I like Nora," Millet said from the beverage area where he had just emptied a little packet of chocolate powder into a cup of hot water. "Frank's okay, too."

"Colin?"

"They should stay."

"I agree," said Jack. "They'll be here in a few minutes. Rex Smith, the agent in charge at the scene in Cleveland will be here after a bit."

Rachel turned toward Jack. "I know Rex. He's a good agent. Who'd the FBI send to the Oregon coast?"

"Lillian Beecher from their Portland field office; she went over with their ERT. We should have those reports later today. Every American will now know none of these deaths were accidents. The stock market will get skittish or worse. Sam Schroeder's opponents will turn up the heat. And we'll begin earning our pay. Let's break until Nora and Frank arrive. I've got to set an appointment to see the president."

"So our perps are out in the open," Nora said as she came through the door wearing taupe slacks, a white blouse with a cowl neckline, and two bangle bracelets. Her lipstick looked like she had put it on in the car. She took a chair next to Rachel who had just finished updating their bulletin boards.

"Looks that way." Jack leaned back in one of their new swivel-and-tilt leather chairs and clasped his hands behind his head. "All these cases are now officially federal." He turned to Frank who had come in right after Nora. "You and Nora can stop faking working for Metro. You're on this squad, unless you want off. All I'll promise is long hours and lots of stress. And, I would guess, a loss of the overtime pay you've been getting from Metro."

"Wow, Jack," Nora said, "you certainly know how to charm a lady."

"Can we have a minute?" Frank asked. "We'd like to give you one answer."

"Go out into the hall," Jack said, knowing that he would release them back to their local police work if they showed any signs of struggling with the decision to stay. The journey they were all starting would be tough enough even with total commitment.

Almost as soon as the door closed, it reopened. "We're in," Frank said. "Thanks for asking. We don't like stopping short of the goal line."

Three hours later, Jack met FBI Special Agent Rex Smith at the Bullpen door. Rex was an average-sized man on the shy side of forty-five. Freckles dotted the bridge of his nose and his cheeks. His chestnut hair hinted it would have curls if allowed to live longer between cuts. His body announced that he ran and pumped iron.

Jack pointed. "Coffee's on the side table along with some snacks."

"Thanks. I haven't eaten since," Rex looked at his watch, "dinner last night." Rex put an ice cube in the bottom of a cup and filled it with steaming coffee, then piled some fruit on a plastic plate and added a large croissant. Millet had used the pause to pour himself a glass of cranberry juice as a chaser to his hot chocolate.

Rex walked around the table dropping a file in front of each of them. When he paused next to Rachel, leaned in, and handed her a copy, she glanced up. Their eyes met and they shared an easy smile. Jack felt a little annoyed, which he knew was absurd. She was only being polite. Friendly. And besides, he had no claim on her.

"These folders," Rex began, "contain my report, the ERT's prelim, and a copy of the report from the local Cleveland detective first on the scene. The neighbors were all reading, watching television, or sleeping. The Taylor house is dust. So are the three inhabitants: Fed Governor Charles Taylor, his wife, Susan Taylor, and his mother, Lucille Taylor. The killer used plastic explosive."

"Anyone else hurt?" Jack asked.

"The houses there are well spaced," Rex replied. "The neighbors got a little collateral damage but no injuries. The explosion occurred under Taylor's house. The FBI will try to trace the explosives unless you want your squad to handle that."

"We'd appreciate the bureau doing that," Jack replied, before glancing around the table. "Any questions for Rex?"

Frank leaned forward so he could look past Millet to see Rex. "What's not in your report? Your instincts?"

"It felt like a killing by someone from out of town. I can summarize all this paperwork in a few short sentences: Plastic explosive. House gone. Inhabitants dead. No leads. The end."

Jack had been in harm's way more times than he could count, and here he sat listening to a report on the death of a governor in the Federal Reserve Bank who lived an important but relatively safe life, only to be murdered in his own bed in a comfortable American neighborhood. On some level, that alone seemed a bit screwy.

Millet gestured with enough animation to slosh some of his cranberry juice on the table. "Do the rest of you agree we can now quit chasing the families and coworkers?" He swiped at the spill and wiped his wet, red hand on his shirt.

"Millet," Nora said in a deliberate voice, "we all agreed with you from the start. But until something more happened we had only what we had."

Rachel raised her hands and then let them drop onto the table in a gesture of helplessness. "Our killers could be anybody in the frigging world."

"So we'll start with what we've got," Jack said with his hands spread. "Millet, cross-check the hate and threat letters received by the Fed and the Court. See if any of those names match any names on the list of terrorists Rachel got from the agencies."

"Done it early this mornin'. If you're going to keep up, Jackman, you gotta think faster than that."

"And?"

"No matches."

Jack heard a sharp noise from near the door. He looked up, his hand instinctively going toward the butt of his Sig Sauer, as Director Miller stormed in. Harriet's brown hair was pulled back so tightly that, from a distance, it appeared no more than a smear on her scalp. She was waving a piece of paper.

"This is a hard copy of a communiqué just broadcast by the ABC-TV affiliate in Phoenix, Arizona," she announced loudly. "It arrived in a FedEx package posted in Redding, California. The package contained a CD-ROM from a group calling itself the American Militia to Restore Representative Government. They're claiming responsibility for all the killings. The communiqué is signed by a Commander LW."

Jack dropped his croissant. "Get somebody out to that station—"

"Already done," Director Miller said, punctuating her words with the eyeglasses she held in her other hand. "The FBI's Phoenix office is fingerprinting and taking DNA samples from everyone at the station who has handled the package or CD. A military jet from

Luke Air Force Base, just outside Phoenix, will get the CD to our lab ASAP. No doubt the package got contaminated before anyone knew its contents. Our linguists are already working it over and the FBI's Behavioral Analysis Unit will take a shot at profiling the person who wrote it."

"Excellent." Jack wiped his hand across his mouth. "Ask General Crook to also have his geniuses at defense intel take a run at it. His people are really good at detecting which country a writer is from or what other languages the writer might speak. Have the NSA do it, too. This is supposed to be a multi agency effort, so let's act like it."

When Director Miller left, Jack and his team circled the communiqué as if it were an enemy encampment.

### A Communiqué from the Headquarters of the American Militia to Restore Representative Government:

It is time to return to a government of the people, by the people, and for the people. America's financial system is run by the Federal Reserve Bank. The unelected Fed governors regulate investment margins, the rate of interest Americans must pay, and, by extension, decide which Americans can afford to buy a home, or keep the one they already have. This must stop. We named our militia for this cause. The only thing that can stop this second American revolution is for the government to take the action demanded in this communiqué.

Our forefathers intended America to have three equal branches of government: the executive, the legislative, and the judicial. The job of the executive and legislative branches is to propose and pass laws. They are the people's elected representative government. The courts are supposed to penalize those who violate those laws. The Supreme Court has arrogantly evolved into seeing itself as the final government. If they disagree with a law, they rule it unconstitutional. They have even decided one of our presidential elections. This tilting of the balance of power must end. The Court must acknowledge that its job is to judge those who violate our laws, not the laws themselves.

To evidence our good faith, we will stop eliminating these aristocrats under the following conditions: The Supreme Court justices are to stand down. They must hear no more cases and make no further rulings until they reaffirm their proper limited role. Legislation banishing a Federal Reserve System, by any name, must be passed. That legislation must make it a crime punishable by death for any American to again promote or encourage a privately owned centralized banking system.

You have thirty-six hours to take the first step.

*Commander LW*


Jack whistled long and low. "Initial observations? Anyone?"

"I see two," Rachel said, her blue eyes darting back and forth between the communiqué and Jack. "Repressed anger not sated by the killings is all over this message. Secondly, their demands will not be met."

Jack stood and walked around the bench to Rachel's seat. "Is this militia or Commander LW on any of the lists of terrorists or militants you got from the CTC?"

"I don't think so." She pulled the lists from a folder. "Nothing even close."

"Keep everybody talking, Rachel," Jack said. "We need a plan to put us on the offense. I'll be home for the next hour preparing for my meeting with the president—I'll be back around six."

The media wolves would soon be circling the White House. And Jack would soon find out if the president meant what he'd said about having his back.

# CHAPTER 19

With two assassinations and a news release in the past twenty-four hours, the rogue Commander LW is picking up the pace. Can McCall catch up? What's really going on?

—Mel Carsten, D.C. Talk, June 10

"Happy anniversary, Jack. I was just reading some of your old press clippings. Today is two years from the night your brother lost his life during your failed desert mission. What makes you think you can protect these officials when you couldn't even keep your brother alive? "

"You bastard." Jack took a deep slow breath. "It's my job to stop you however I can, now I'll enjoy taking you down."

The caller hung up.

After the first call from this person, Jack had the FBI set up his phone so they could trace all incoming calls, but the caller had hung up in under a minute. Not long enough.

Jack half watched and half listened to the news networks he had running on his two home televisions. Conjecture about the American Militia flourished on one television talk show after another. He turned up the volume when Mel Carsten, the host of D.C. Talk, walked on stage. Carsten's narrow nose and high cheekbones gave him a strong face; his open-collar blue shirt, black slacks, and tan loafers adding a casual look. Carsten took a seat in his red chair between two blue couches angled on a vee toward the cameras.

"Today," Carsten began, "we have with us Charles Nesbit, a former member of the CIA's Counterterrorism Section."

Jack had known Charlie Nesbit for over a decade. The man could eat everything in sight and remain racehorse thin. He had always admired Nessy's ability to project a casual relaxed air even when deadly serious, his appearance indicated that nothing had changed.

After the usual pleasantries Carsten asked, "Mr. Nesbit, does our government know who these people are?"

"I wish I could say yes. But to my knowledge the U.S. intelligence community has no information on Commander LW or his militia."

"Off the record, those officials, who will tell us anything, say this LW is homegrown."

"Looks that way. At this point there's nothing that suggests an out-of-town team."

"What could make this Commander LW do these horrible things? It's not as if America fosters revolution by oppressing its citizens."

"This kind of killer comes up with an excuse so that he can feel he's more than what he is, a murderer. He sees injustice not seen by the rest of us. In his demented mind he assigns himself a mission to right the wrongs he perceives. A classic example would be John Wilkes Booth the man who assassinated Abraham Lincoln."

"When you say 'he,' how sure are you that this LW is a man?"

"The histories of these things suggest a man, but it could be a woman."

"Either man or woman, you see this person as mentally deranged?"

"Often militias consist of one psychotic, charismatic leader and a group of weak-minded followers," Nesbit told him with an uneasy grin. "But the leader is always a nutcase. The Reverend Jim Jones, whose followers joined him in a mass suicide in Guyana some years ago is the sort of twisted leader I'm talking about."

• • •

President Schroeder slammed his hand onto the arm of his couch. "This son of a bitch isn't going to shut down anything."

Jack could not remember seeing Sam Schroeder snap like that. The pressure on the president had to be enormous. Jack poured himself a glass of water and added a lemon wedge, giving the president a moment to calm himself.

"What do we know about this militia and Commander LW?" Schroeder asked.

"Not very much," Jack admitted. "Nothing, is more like it. Until we got this communiqué, we didn't even have the name. Your agencies' preliminary findings should reach us in about an hour. We're hoping they were able to connect them up."

"I've spoken to the agencies," the president said. "No one has anything. Have you been able to narrow the field at all?"

Jack swirled his water and looked inside the glass as if it were some magical potion that might reveal better answers.

"Other than ruling out you and me, sir, I'm afraid not much."

"Any clues from the crime scenes?"

"No, sir. I can tell you nothing encouraging, except that we do know more today than we did yesterday."

"And just what would that be?"

"LW has a passion he's dying to talk about. I'm expecting there'll be more communiqués. If we listen carefully, the odds are decent he'll eventually put his foot in his mouth."

Schroeder leaned forward in his chair, his eyes narrowing. "I can see your wheels turning. Come on. Give."

"The first three killings were only the officials. The most recent two included family members. This escalation could be intentional to ratchet up the level of terror or an indication that this guy is losing it."

The president rubbed his chin thoughtfully. "How can I help?"

"The likely future targets seem to be the eleven remaining governors and justices. We need to cover those officials and their families twenty-four hours a day. Electronic surveillance should be installed to see and hear anyone approaching their homes, offices, and cars. I'd like you to have the agencies handle that. Expanding my team to include protection would slow and distract us from catching this bastard. Excuse my language, sir."

The president grinned. "I would've said worse. The Supreme Court Police is charged with protecting those justices. However, the demands here may exceed their manpower. The U.S. Marshal's Office is responsible for protecting all our other federal judges. I'll ask them to assist and have them both coordinate with the FBI."

"I'll need an agent from each protective detail with whom we can interact, Mr. President, in the event we develop any information that suggests the next target."

"Done. Anything else?"

"Yes, sir. Before electronic surveillance is installed, we need to go over their homes, cars, offices, and any other places they predictably visit to look for listening and explosive devices."

Schroeder rose and closed the drapes over the west windows to shut out the late afternoon sun. "I'll call the chief justice. You said, 'seem.' The eleven 'seem' to be the targets. What did you mean by that? Or did I misread your inference?"

"No, sir, you did not. We know the identities of those killed, but that doesn't mean LW won't branch out beyond those target groups."

"Who else?"

Crockett, the president's collie, trotted over to lie next to his master.

"Wild guesses are all we could have at this point, sir." Jack spread his hands wide.

"Let's have them." The president said, reaching down to pet the top of his dog's head.

Jack lowered his eyelids, his brows moving closer together. "I think the Federal Reserve Act originally provided seats for the Secretary of the Treasury and the Comptroller of the Currency. My recollection is as ex-officio members. However, you should have my recall checked for accuracy before relying on it. If I'm right, those two are possibilities. LW could blame congressional leaders. In addition, the Federal Reserve has district banks, each of which has a president. They could be targets. He could come after you, sir. People have a way of blaming the top guy."

"Sack the quarterback, eh?"

"Something like that." Jack grinned, joylessly.

Even though the president's body language telegraphed that the meeting had come to an end, Jack decided that there was one other matter he needed to discuss.

"There is one more thing, sir. I'd like a letter over your signature authorizing and instructing all federal, state, and local personnel, including the military, to give my squad immediate cooperation. Please include a phone number they can call if they wish to verify or complain. Otherwise, they're to fully comply with whatever we say. I don't want us losing time over turf issues or foot dragging."

"I'll have the letter brought to your office," Schroeder assured him. "What did Harriet Miller tell me you call it?"

Jack felt his cheeks redden, "The Bullpen, sir. The name promotes a bit of esprit de corps. Millet Yorke came up with it. I'm not too sure he didn't have that purpose in mind before I realized it."

The president chuckled. "Before you go, any advice on this for my press conference in the morning?"

"Don't bait him, Mr. President. I know you'll need to say his demands will not be met. Say it plain. If and when it becomes necessary to call out this LW, that'll be my job, sir. And I don't know enough yet to play that card."

"I'd still like to tell him to go take a flying—but I see your point." The president patted Jack on the shoulder as he escorted him to the door. "Didn't LW's communiqué use the term 'stand down'?"

"Yes, sir."

"That's a military term. Could his background include military service?"

"That term along with his knowledge of explosives, could point in that direction," Jack admitted. "That's very observant, sir. I wish you had the time to be a full-time member of our squad."

"Now, your sounding like a politician," the president said, scoffingly. "Leave that unpleasant task to me and get on your way. I want this LW and his militia put out of business, and as soon as possible. We don't need to lose any more loyal Americans."

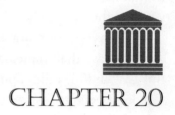

# CHAPTER 20

Rumors continue that the president is meeting
regularly with his secret McCall squad.

—*Atlanta Constitution, June 10*

"Welcome back, Jackman. What's the word from Numero Uno?"
Millet asked as the squad gathered at their oblong conference table.

"The president has authorized a check for bugs and bombs in
the haunts of the remaining big money guys and the Supremes—as
you call them, Millet. He's assigned the protection and surveillance
primarily to the FBI. We have only one job: stop LW."

Rachel gave Jack a thin smile.

"What did you guys come up with?" he asked.

"In his communiqué," Colin said, "LW used eliminate, not kill,
murder, or assassinate. We saw this as consistent with his delusion of
a higher purpose. His use of several terms suggested that the militia
has at least a few members. This may be further supported by the ge-
ographic spread of the two most recent killings, the honeymooning
Breens in Oregon and the Taylor family in Cleveland. Maybe the
agencies will have more."

"The president had their reports," Jack said. "They have nothing."

Rachel kicked off her shoes. "We had one more idea."

"Give."

"We develop a timeline for the Breen murder in Oregon and

work up a list of all passengers who flew into the major West Coast airports in Seattle, Portland, and San Francisco, also the smaller airports, that match up with that timeline. We do the same for the other killings, screening passengers out of the airports in Cleveland, Pittsburgh, Philadelphia, Cincinnati, D.C., and Baltimore. It'll be a big job but it puts us on the offense. Millet says he can write programs to cull out the passengers and flights that could fit at least one of the assassinations. We gather background information on as many of those passengers as possible in order to pare down the list. We can also build a database of the passengers' descriptions to have on hand for when we find someone who has seen this guy or one of his militiamen."

"Once we have those names," Millet added, "we can check car rental agencies to see which of them rented cars with mileage adequate for a round trip to the murder scenes. And match up the car rental names with the air passengers."

"How about the military and law enforcement angle?" asked Rachel.

Jack turned to Colin. "Get us a list of current and former agents and military personnel with a history of violence. And get confirmed locations on the dates of the killings for current personnel that fit that criteria.

"Frank," Jack continued, "you and Nora visit the Oregon and Cleveland crime scenes. Rachel, arrange a military jet to meet them at six in the morning. Take a copy of the president's letter. There should be experienced homicide cops in Cleveland who'll likely open up to you more than they might to the feds. Depoe Bay, Oregon, is much smaller so the locals won't likely have much experience. And find us some witnesses who saw something. Anything."

The night wind crossing the CIA's parking lot tossed Nora's hair.

"Colin Stewart," she said, putting her hand on his arm. "Is that Scottish or Irish?"

"Colin's Scottish, probably ancient Gaelic."

"Is Stewart Scottish too?"

"Stewart's just a name I took."

"What do you mean a name you took?" Nora asked, looking at him askance. "What's your family name?"

"My parents left me on the doorstep of a Catholic orphanage. I grew up there and when I got old enough I claimed Stewart as my last name."

"Why Stewart?"

"An old man who worked at the orphanage died the night before my tenth birthday, well, my anniversary of coming to the orphanage. I use that as my birthday. He told me he had no family. He was kind. A good man. I took his name."

"So you have no known family?"

"The old man. We had each other. Now the U.S. Army is my family."

Nora had lost her mother, but still had her father and grandpa. She couldn't imagine growing up without the roots of a family.

"I'm so sorry," she said.

"For what? The orphanage was swell. I got no complaints."

The faces of some of the punks Nora had arrested who had used their disadvantaged upbringing as an excuse, flashed through her mind. She looked at Colin and thought, *You're a good man, Charlie Brown.*

She unlocked her car door using her remote, then looked back at him, the wind pushing her hair back from her face. "Try to get some sleep," she said. "I'll see you tomorrow."

"I'll fall asleep thinking about you," he told her.

"I'll be thinking about you too."

"Then take me home. Doing is better than thinking."

"Oh, Colin, I'd like to. Really I would. I mean, our first night—but maybe we ought to cool it for now. That first time we didn't know we'd be working together. You know?"

"Meet me for breakfast."

"Frank and I are flying to Oregon and Cleveland in the morning, remember?"

He looked at her then in a way she had never seen him look at her before, and knew that she had disappointed him.

# CHAPTER 21

Jealousy infects the intelligence community. No one
likes McCall answering only to the president.

—*Headline News, June 10*

Rachel got out of her car outside her apartment building a few minutes before midnight. She dropped her purse, and swore as the contents spilled out over the pavement. After gathering up her lipstick and wallet and other odds and ends, she went upstairs and got blinded at the top of the landing by the streetlight that shined just over the roof of her building. It had happened before. She groped for the keyhole in her door, then felt the key stagger into the lock.

"Jingles. I'm home," she called out. Then suddenly felt wary. With her vision still impaired, she couldn't see her cat, but she should have heard his familiar squeaky meows.

*Jingles is always right at the door.*

She shut her eyes tight and saw the dancing dots of lights. She considered turning on the lights, but her instincts told her not too. She pressed her back against the wall, extended her foot over and pushed the door until she heard it latch. Her breathing went shallow. And she waited, wishing she were invisible while her eyes hunted for enough light to let her see.

*I always leave the drape over the side window open so Jingles can lie on the sill to catch the morning sun. But it's closed. Someone has been in here. Maybe still is?*

Fear wet her armpits. She slipped off her shoes, braced herself by spreading her legs and leaning hard against the wall and drew her Sig Sauer. She reached over with her hand to confirm the door to the front coat closet was closed. It was; that door always creaked, so she could move past it and trust her ears. She eased down into a squat with her back still against the wall. Her eyes found enough light for her to see the outlines of her living room furniture, the kitchen, and the hall reaching back toward her bedroom and bath. She focused down the center and relied on her peripheral vision.

Someone was here. She was sure of it. If not, Jingles would be weaving back and forth between her feet.

As her vision improved, the white refrigerator took inexact shape, then she saw the handle on the fridge.

She swallowed, licked her lips, tossed her purse onto the far living room chair, and quickly moved to the back of the couch. Nothing had moved but her.

There were no shadows that shouldn't be there. Then one leaped toward her, and collapsed. Rose again. Rushed her, and then disappeared, all without an accompanying sound.

She crouched next to the end of the couch, and cradled her gun in the palm of her other hand. If he had wanted her dead, he would have attacked as soon as she came in, before her eyes began to adjust. From her position she could drop the invader with a shot to his legs. But there weren't any legs, only a fast shadow. She held her aim, fighting to even out the ebb and flow of her breathing. Then the shadow rose again. Moved again. She had tightened the slack in the trigger when she realized the source of the shadows. The wind was blowing the small curtain over the bathroom window she left open to help dry the shower. Still, someone had to be here. If not, her cat would be with her.

She rose to a crouch and moved into the space between the two bar stools on the living room side of the kitchen island. In a sudden move she pushed the covered pan from her morning oatmeal over the edge of the island.

Clang. Bang. The pan noisily settled onto the floor.

Then nothing.

Her safe zone now included the kitchen. She could call the bureau for backup and hunker down to keep the bastard from getting to the front door—the only way in or out. While keeping her eyes on the hallway, she stepped to the chair in the living room area and reached inside her purse for her cell phone. It wasn't there. The slot just below the top flap was empty. She reached deeper. It wasn't there. She raked her hand hard across the bottom of her bag. It wasn't there. She moved to the counter and dumped the contents and glanced down. Her phone wasn't there.

*It must have fallen out when I spilled my purse,* she thought. *Christ, I should've installed a land phone.*

She couldn't go out and look for her phone without giving the intruder the time to get out, and she wasn't about to let the bastard escape. He had to be in either the bedroom or the bathroom.

She stood still. Alone in the dark lifeless kitchen. Listening. One minute. A breath. Another minute. Another breath.

*Screw this. I'll finish it right now. Alone.*

The apartment's one bathroom had two doors, a pocket door into the one and only bedroom, and a hinged door to the hallway. She couldn't go down the hall to her bedroom without exposing her back to the bathroom's hallway door. She needed a plan to clear the bathroom without leaving herself vulnerable to an attack up the hallway from the bedroom.

From near the refrigerator she saw a faint reflection of the bathtub in the mirror over the sink. The clear shower slider stood half open.

*I always pull it closed. With the window open, it dries faster.*

She could enter the bathroom quickly and close the door to the hall. No. That would allow the son of a bitch to recapture the space between her and the front door. She could stop in the hall and pull the bathroom door shut, then proceed to the bedroom. But that would momentarily leave her vulnerable from the dark bedroom.

She eased open a kitchen drawer, removed a flashlight, held it against her stomach and turned it on. It worked. She flicked it off and slipped it inside her waistband. From an upper cabinet she took two large water glasses, shoving the fingers on her left hand deep inside. Then, holding her gun in her right hand above her shoulder, she rushed the bathroom, smacking the door with her right shoulder. The door slammed against the wall, the knob gouging out its shape in the drywall.

She watched the open pocket door into the bedroom while listening for movement in the hallway. Hearing nothing, she slid one foot toward the door she had come through and quickly glanced down the hall toward the bedroom. Nothing.

The silence ended when she shattered the first glass against the hallway floor, while keeping her focus on the pocket door. Then she smashed the second water glass the same way. Now, if the intruder entered the hall from the bedroom, she would hear him.

The bedroom was as black as her hair. The uninvited guest had closed the blackout drape over the small window on the far side of the bed, the one she opened each morning so Jingles could catch the afternoon sun.

She eased her bathroom handheld mirror through the pocket door. The closet sliders on the far wall were shut.

*Men get in my bedroom by invitation only, you son of a bitch. Ready or not, here I come.*

She squared her shoulders to the opening in the pocket door and tossed a round plastic bottle of hand lotion so it would roll across the bed until it dropped off the far side. She trained her gun on the darkness along the wall, but got no reaction when the lotion bottle hit the floor. Nothing. She stepped through the door, stooping beside the bed, and listened.

Quiet.

Dark.

*The bastard's still here, he must still be here. If he got out, my cat would have met me at the door meowing his head off. Oh, my God. That's what Jingles did the night my bra disappeared.*

She moved to the wall beside the closet, reached over, and used her fingers to find the recessed cup handle in the slider. When she had it, in one violent motion she thrust the slider as hard as she could. The door bounced off the far jamb.

"Toss out your weapon. Crawl out here on your knees. Slow. Hands empty or you're dead. Now!"

Nothing.

Quiet.

Dark.

Rachel crouched and squinted. Then flipped on the flashlight, the stark light blunting against the clothes. She moved the beam lower. She had not before realized just how many pairs of shoes she owned, but none of them had feet in them.

*He has to be in the front coat closet.*

She pushed the bedroom door to the hallway closed, circled around through the bathroom pocket door and into the hall beyond the broken glass, closing the bathroom door behind herself. At the panel of switches near the front door, she raised her gun, flipped on the closet's inside light, dropped to one knee, and flung the door open.

Coats and umbrellas. Only coats and umbrellas.

A sense of relief struggled with her anger. Someone had been here. But now he was gone. And so was Jingles. Her nerve endings began tingling as her adrenal gland shut down.

After a futile hour of looking for Jingles outside, during which she found her cell phone under her car, she stood at the top of the landing softly calling for Jingles. She wrapped her arms around herself and shivered as if a seam in time had allowed December to visit June.

Back inside, she put her gun on the kitchen counter, and cleaned up the broken glass.

She put on an oversized T-shirt and went into the bathroom,

turned on the light, and looked at herself in the mirror. Her skin looked wet and felt hot. She splashed her face with cold water, ran a rung-out washcloth over her neck and down her arms. As she turned, her field of vision included the toilet bowl where she saw a dark shadow against the stark white porcelain.

Jingles.

His eyes had been gouged out.

# CHAPTER 22

The Supreme Court is effectively standing down.

—*Eric Dunn, freelance columnist, June 11*

The way McCall had watched Rachel Johnstone leave his home that first night had convinced LW that Rachel would be the perfect messenger. She would tell Jack about her stupid cat, and he would understand: stop interfering.

LW screwed the cap off a bottle of red wine and sat down to watch MSNBC's rebroadcast of its earlier edition of *D.C. Talk*.

But what he heard was not what he had been expecting. He flailed his arms, sloshing wine onto the floor. "Fuck you, Nesbit," he shouted at the TV screen. "Don't you get it? This is not about me! It's about stopping the unelected officials who really run America." You Goddamn fool! It's blasphemous to compare me to John Wilkes Booth and the Reverend Jim Jones.

"Charles Nesbit. I sentence you to death."

Chief Justice Evans paused outside the conference room and took a deep breath before walking in to face his five surviving associate justices. At six four the chief justice towered above the others. At a signal from him, his fellow justices took their seats in accordance with the Court's long tradition: Justice James Dunlin, the senior associate justice, sat to the right of the chief justice. Michael Roberts, the second senior associate justice, sat to the chief's left. Justices Penelope Budson and Harold Sanders, the third and fourth senior, sat second to his right and left respectively. The fifth surviving and newest Associate Justice Jonathan Phineas Huckaby faced him across the table. The seats where those killed would have sat, remained empty.

"The president has asked that we move our families away from our homes," the chief justice told his associate justices, choosing his words with care. "Today. The FBI and our Court police will accompany us during these relocations and each of us and our families will thereafter remain under surveillance."

When several of them started to speak, he held up his hands. "I know," Evans said. "I know. This is a sad day. The FBI is checking our automobiles for bugs and explosives. I took the liberty of giving them permission. I trust no one objects. We're to leave unannounced as soon as we finish this meeting. When the FBI tells us our homes are clear, we can return our families to them. While we're gone, the FBI and our Court police will electronically sweep our chambers here and the private and common areas of the courthouse before installing cameras and listening devices."

Justice Penelope Anne Budson, an elderly woman who's gray hair had bluish highlights, spoke first. "Mr. Chief Justice. How are we to proceed with our duties? Our deliberations must be confidential."

"There will be no listening devices or cameras inside this conference room. We'll post security outside this door twenty-four hours a day, seven days a week. This room will be used for all our discussions about the cases we have under deliberation. In our respective chambers we will need to watch what we say and make more use of e-mails and memos."

"But still—" Justice Budson insisted.

"Penny," the chief justice interrupted, "how can we proceed with our duties when one of us per week is being murdered? We cannot expect to go forward without some inconvenience. Let us hope inconvenience is the worst we suffer."

"Excuse me, but this appears to transcend mere inconvenience," Justice Michael Roberts said, his voice sharp with annoyance.

"You're quite correct, Mike. But then, calling it whatever you prefer, the situation remains."

Senior Associate Justice Dunlin dropped his pincer glasses onto the notepad before him. "Perhaps," he said in his Maine accent, "we should, for now, suspend our work as this Commander LW has demanded. Our summer recess is fast approaching. We could claim an inability to proceed with so many vacancies on the bench. The president and the Senate could delay the confirmation process until this LW and his militia are captured."

"There it is," Evans said. "All right; it's on the table. Does anyone second Justice Dunlin's motion that we adjourn during these trying times?"

"I did not place a motion on the table, Mr. Chief Justice. I thought we were having informal discussion."

"All right then," the chief justice corrected himself, "does anyone wish to informally discuss further Justice Dunlin's idea of recessing early?"

Justice Sanders stabbed his notepad with his mechanical pencil. "I will oppose any effort for an early adjournment. Make no mistake, whether foreign or domestic, if madmen figure they can shut down the Court or any part of America we will get more terrorism, not less." A double pencil stab punctuated his comment.

Chief Justice Evans pointed his finger and thumb at Sanders as a child would mimic a pistol. "I agree, Sandy, but high principle is often easiest when one is not looking down the barrel of a gun." He then turned to his senior associate. "Justice Dunlin, do you wish to put your idea in the form of a motion?"

Dunlin stroked his pale, bony jaw. "No."

# CHAPTER 23

The president and the Senate are discussing
plans to fast-track the confirmations process.

—*FOX News, June 11*

Ms. Addiena Welch, the White House press secretary, sensed her
boss would be on the ground floor nearing the situation room
about now. She knew him to be a punctual man, even for press
conferences.

"Ladies and gentlemen," she said, standing on her toes so as not
to adjust the microphone that had been preset for the president, "a
few ground rules: This press conference is limited to the president's
statement and your questions related to the recent killings of government officials. No other subject will be discussed. A little later
the president will be joined by Senators Marshall Leland and Ruth
Ann Mitchell, the chairs of the Senate's Judiciary and Banking Committees, respectively, the confirming committees for nominees to the
Supreme Court and the Federal Reserve Board of governors."

She paused and blotted her forehead with a tissue. The maintenance staff had failed again in their effort to lower the temperature in the pressroom to offset the heat generated by the television
lights and cameras.

There was a slight disturbance behind her. She glanced over her
right shoulder and saw the president in the wings. She stepped back.

President Schroeder moved into position in front of the soft blue
backdrop and stood at the microphone. He drank from the glass of

room-temperature water left on the shelf just below the top of the lectern and began.

"Thank you for coming with so little notice. Under the circumstances it is important that the American people hear from their government."

He paused and then read from a prepared document: "As you all know, we have lost three U.S. Supreme Court justices, Adam Monroe, Herbert Clarkson Montgomery, and Donald Quincy Breen, as well as two Federal Reserve governors, John Santee and Charles Taylor. All of them were good men who believed in and practiced public service. To their families, friends, and all of you, I offer my deepest, heartfelt condolences. They will be missed."

After a somber look into the cameras, he continued reading his statement. "Their positions will be filled by other capable, patriotic men and women. We are a nation of many such individuals. The business of this government will continue. No other position is consistent with the strength of this country. No other position is consistent with the responsibilities of governance. No other position is consistent with the examples set by our forefathers, and the legacy we must leave for those who come later. I will now take your questions."

Unlike most presidents in the past, Samuel Schroeder often moved out from behind the lectern after finishing his prepared statement. He did so now and pointed toward the *New York Times*'s Washington correspondent. "Ms. Liotta."

Her bleached teeth matched the white collar on her taupe blouse. "Mr. President, what's being done to protect the eleven remaining members of these two institutions?"

"It would be inappropriate for me or any member of the government to reveal the security measures in place and please, ladies and gentlemen, we have to assume whoever is behind these killings listens to press conferences, watches television, listens to the radio, and reads your papers. Let's all do what we can to catch this . . . this . . . LW," the president said, clearly suppressing other words he would rather have used. He then called on the reporter from the *Baltimore Sun*, Arthur McDonald.

"Mr. President, our observer at the Court reported that the justices vacated the courthouse this morning shortly after nine. Is the Supreme Court standing down as LW has demanded?"

The president moved forward so that he was looking directly at McDonald, who was sitting in the front row.

"Your sources are reliable. The Court has a long history of recessing for various periods of time, for various reasons. I'm confident that tomorrow your observer will confirm that the justices have returned to their duties."

President Schroeder gestured toward the *Washington Post's* plump White House correspondent, whose constant wearing of heavy earrings had elongated her earlobes enough that some of the catty members of the press called her Dumbo.

"Mr. President, what can you tell us about the efforts to identify and stop this Commander LW and his militia?"

"As you are aware, we have assembled a multiagency task force under the leadership of Jack McCall, a special deputy to Harriet Miller, the director of Central Intelligence. Mr. McCall has a long and distinguished career as an American intelligence officer." The president spread his hands. "I have complete faith in Jack McCall."

"Mr. President, is this LW an American Carlos—a killer extraordinaire?" asked the reporter from CNN, making reference to the world's most famous assassin, now in jail in Europe.

"No." The president fixed her with a stern stare. "There'll be no cult status for this fellow."

Then the president pointed to Ms. Little, a local newscaster.

"Mr. President, the Court is now three justices short. The Federal Reserve two governors short. It would seem the normal pace of dealing with replacements is slower than what is needed. Please tell us about your plans for processing nominees through the Senate's confirmations committees."

At that moment, Senators Marshall Leland and Ruth Ann Mitchell, whose appearance the president had expected, stepped onto the rostrum.

"You're quite correct, Ms. Little," the president replied. "The ordinary course, a reasonable pace under normal conditions, is inadequate in the current circumstance. Before dawn this morning, I met with Senators Leland and Mitchell." The president gestured toward each as he said their names. "The leadership from both parties also attended that meeting. We reached unanimous agreement to fast-track the confirmations process. Let me emphasize that the nominees will all be worthy Americans who would graduate under the normal process. In no way will the Senate shirk its responsibility."

For the last question, in a bold move the president selected Ellen Sherman, the newest reporter on the White House beat. Talk was, she asked incisive questions.

"Is it possible, Mr. President, that while his methods are deplorable, Commander LW may have a valid point in light of the absence of an election process for selecting these officials?"

As if an unseen hand had twisted an invisible knob, the volume in the room went quiet.

"Ms. Sherman," the president began, "all of you, both here and listening everywhere, including LW, let me remind you that the people's elected congressional representatives passed the Federal Reserve Act of 1913, and an elected president signed it into law. The government of the people, by the people, and for the people that LW speaks of, enacted the Federal Reserve System.

"Government does many good things. It also lives with the pressures of elections. Things such as lower interest rates and larger margins for buying traded securities could be very tempting ways to appeal to voters. We are fortunate to have the Federal Reserve Board making those decisions independent of the vicissitudes of politics.

"As for what LW calls the 'unelected Supreme Court,' it is crucial these judges remain independent of politics, and, I might add, the Court has never exceeded its constitutional authority.

"Thank you ladies and gentlemen. Senators Leland and Mitchell have agreed to remain to answer your questions regarding the work of their respective committees and the expedited process for confirmations. But please remember the committees chaired by these senators are very busy with this matter, so do keep your questions limited."

LW had watched the president's press conference while eating his microwaved TV dinner. Tonight's choice: meatloaf with mashed potatoes and green beans.

He had heard what he had expected, the arrogance of power. Despite his avoidance of a direct answer, the president had been obvious. Steps were being taken to further protect the rats he planned to fumigate out of America's house.

He wedged the last slice of meatloaf into his small mouth without bothering to cut it, and then haphazardly stacked the sectioned plastic tray on top of the one from last night's Salisbury steak, which sat balanced at an odd angle atop the one from the prior night's southern fried chicken.

Over recent days, the press had reviewed the top choices for nomination to the Supreme Court: Gerald Garfield, Sophia Washington, and William Ladd. For the Federal Reserve Board, the Senate's Banking Committee had reported scheduling hearings for Dr. Manuel Acosta and Charlene Hancock.

For over a year, Gerald Garfield had been strongly rumored to fill the next opening on the Court. As a result, LW had chosen Garfield for the honor of being the first nominee to make the ultimate sacrifice for his country.

# CHAPTER 24

President Schroeder's reported list of
nominees includes few surprises.

—A.P. *Wire, June 11*

Rachel asked Jack to call everyone to the table so she could tell them
about her intruder. Before she did, Jack told them all about his latest call from LW, steeling himself to remain calm while repeating
the part about the death of his brother, Nick.

Then Rachel gave them an overview, ending with, "After I found
Jingles, I called in an FBI evidence team. I just got off the phone
with them. Other than my dead cat, there's nothing that proves anyone had come in."

"Had someone been in your home before last night?" Jack asked
her.

"I didn't think so. Well, maybe I suspected, but now I'd say yes.
What made you ask?"

"Last night I found this propped against my front door." He
reached down and brought up a large manilla envelope. "It's from
LW. The lab found nothing that could help us."

"What was in the envelope?" Colin asked.

"I hope this doesn't embarrass you, Rachel," Jack said, "but all of
us need to know everything."

Rachel stroked her throat softly and nodded, then sat quietly with
a questioning look on her face.

Jack straightened the little prongs of the envelope's metal clasp, pulled the flap up over them, and dumped a brassiere onto the table.

"Son of a bitch," Rachel said. "I thought I had put the bra on my bed but I didn't see it after I showered. I have several just alike, so I blew it off after I found one on top in the hamper."

"Jack," Colin asked, "how did you know LW sent the envelope and that the bra belonged to Rachel?"

Jack reached inside the envelope and pulled out a sheet of plain white paper.

"The words were clipped from magazines," he said, "and attached with Elmer's glue available in a zillion stores. The lab said he did not lick the envelope or touch the top of the glue bottle before applying it."

"Read the note, Jack," Rachel said, her face now expressionless. He read:

You might want to put this back where it came from, Jack. A nice size. I'm sure you agree.

*LW*

P.S.: I kept her panties for my own amusement. Maybe one of my militiamen will wear them as a mask.

Rachel's voice went husky. "I never missed my panties."

She didn't give a damn about the bra. LW could hang his balls in the cups and hook it behind his waist, but her panties were personal. It sickened her to know that asshole possessed her scent as would a man with whom she had shared her love. She startled when Jack spoke again.

"After I got that envelope, I ordered personal protection details for all of you. Next time Nora or Frank calls in, tell them. And let Frank know that protection is also set up for his ex-wife and his children. The same as is set up for the families of the targets."

"No," said Millet. "No way. My house has the best security system in America. Set it up myself. I don't want nobody messing around my place."

Jack pointed at the eccentric genius. "That's it or you move into a CIA safe house and they'll transport you back and forth daily. Take your pick. End of discussion."

"Crap! You always get your way don't you, Mr. McCall?"

"Yes, Millet, I do. Now which will it be?"

"Shit. Have them come to my door tonight so I can familiarize them with my system before they set it off and embarrass themselves." Millet slammed his chair against the wall and stormed over to the beverage area.

"LW is telling us we aren't off limits," Jack said, paying no attention to the departure of the unruly Millet Yorke. "He's telling us he knows who we are and where we live, and we don't know him. Be careful. Don't relax until you're inside your homes and have checked the premises. The reporters who cover Metro PD reported that Frank and Nora had been assigned to us, but to date, neither Millet's name nor Colin's has been reported. Still, we can't assume just because the media doesn't know about them, that LW doesn't."

Millet stuck his head out of the kitchen door. "What about you, Jack?"

"I get the same thing as the rest of you."

Rachel kicked off her shoes. "Let's get our focus back on catching him. Millet and I stayed late last night. We're organized. Before we quit today, we should have a decent guess at how big a list of air passengers we're going to end up with."

"I've got good news," Jack said. "Frank and Nora found a witness at the Resort at Depoe Bay, Oregon, one the locals didn't have. There was a gardener working in some shrubbery about seventy-five yards away at the corner of the parking lot. He saw a van drive up and park. A man got out with flowers and headed up the path toward the honeymoon cottage. The gardener described him as white, medium height, about thirty years of age, an average build, wearing a red baseball cap. The gardener remembered the cap matched the roses."

"Did he see his face?" Colin asked.

"No. When the deliveryman came back, he had the flowers in front of his face."

"He brought the flowers back?" Nora asked.

"Odd, isn't it. But the gardener was sure. The delivery guy brought the flowers back with him, and no flowers were found in the cottage."

"What about the van?" Rachel asked.

"No company name and the gardener did not know the make. He only remembered a dark color and that it was quite new. The front desk had no knowledge of the flower delivery."

Jack glanced down at the notes he had taken while he had talked with Frank. "Neither the victims' families nor their office staffs knew who sent the flowers. Nora found a florist in Newport a few miles south of the resort that made a sale of two dozen red roses arranged in a vase. A man picked them up. The clerk's general description agreed with the gardener's. The buyer came in at closing time and the store was busy. He doesn't really remember the guy. Millet checked the statistics from the Florist Association and learned the overwhelming majority of flower purchases are paid with a credit card. This buyer paid cash. It doesn't give us much, but at least the guy's not invisible."

Rachel turned to Millet. "We need to concentrate on flights out of West Coast airports. Ask each airport's security and the local police about abandoned dark vans. We can start with the airport in Portland, Oregon."

Jack pulled close a map of Oregon, found Depoe Bay, and ran his finger first to the north and then to the south.

"Start with the airports in the San Francisco area and work north."

"Why start with the airport that's farthest away?" Rachel asked.

"Not because it's farthest away, but because it's to the south. For now, let's assume the flower buyer in Newport and the deliveryman at the resort was our man. If he had been coming from the Portland

Airport, he would likely have used a florist in Lincoln City to the north of Depoe Bay. But he bought the roses south of the resort."

Rachel shook her head easily and smiled, obviously impressed with Jack's perception.

"We believe LW has preceded each of his killings with thorough surveillance," Jack continued. "The Breens had planned to honeymoon in Hawaii. Their D.C. security detail stayed with them until they went through airport security. The FBI office in Hawaii had agents at the airport on Maui. When the Breens didn't show, Hawaii informed the bureau who learned of their flight to Oregon and began tracking from there. About that same time the locals in Depoe Bay ID'd the Breens and called it in."

"Why would Breen mislead the FBI?" Millet asked.

"We can't know for certain," Jack said. "Perhaps to get away and be alone. Avoid the local media. Probably figured it would be more romantic. That if they told no one, not even the FBI, and didn't use Justice Breen's name or position they'd be safe by being anonymous. Truth is, judges are rarely recognized anywhere."

"But somehow LW tracked them," Nora said.

"Mrs. Breen's mother, Mrs. Ashcroft, told the bureau her daughter informed her about Oregon by e-mail a week before the wedding and swore her to secrecy." Jack went on. "Both the mother and father insist they told no one. That e-mail had to be the *how* LW knew. LW or someone in his militia must be a skilled hacker."

"Yeah, yeah," said an impatient Millet, running his fingers through his already tousled hair. "We get all that, but how does that make you give priority to the airports around San Francisco?"

Jack swivelled his chair to face Millet. "We've reasoned that LW did surveillance on all his targets, so he had a San Francisco plan for William Powers, the Fed governor from that district. His plan for Powers likely included getting in and out of Frisco."

"So he used Frisco." Rachel raised her eyebrows. "Even though it meant he had to drive to Oregon. Hey. Wait a minute. He sent his communiqué with FedEx in Redding, California, which he could pass through on the way back to San Francisco."

"Correct. But don't fall in love with it," Jack cautioned. "It's still an educated guess. I just don't see him leaving the place he had researched, San Francisco, to go through an area he probably had not researched, Portland. How do you guys react to this?"

"It's full of supposition," Colin said, "but hey, we got nothing better."

Rachel pushed back her chair. "Let's get on it."

There was, Jack realized, a refreshed sense of urgency in Rachel's manner. And why not? She had become a target of LW's twisted mind.

Jack put up his hand. "If it isn't looking right as you proceed, drop it, Millet." Then Jack moved his attention to Colin. "What's the latest on the lists of violent military people and agents?"

"I spoke to the agencies an hour ago. They said tonight."

"That'll have to do," Jack muttered. "Hey, Millet. Can you work without Rachel?"

Millet shrugged. "It'll add some hours."

"Understood. You're flying solo today then, at least for a while."

"Then leave me alone." Millet abruptly turned and walked toward his desk.

Jack looked at Rachel. "I'm sorry about . . . you know, having to discuss your bra and—"

"No sweat. Now, what do you want me doing?"

"Get with that great profiler lady at the FBI's behavioral analysis unit. I want you, her, and the best here at the CIA to put your heads together and get us a preliminary psychological and physical profile of LW."

# CHAPTER 25

A *Wall Street Journal* article refers to Jack McCall
as a shadowy figure of international intrigue.

— *Mel Carsten, D.C. Talk, June 12*

From an article in the *Wall Street Journal*, June 12:

**Jack McCall**: A combination of official records and unofficial accounts disclose a muddled picture of the man President Schroeder has put in charge of the investigation into
the deaths, and continuing threats to the safety of our
Supreme Court justices and the governors of the Federal Reserve Bank Board.

The first account, albeit it unofficial, states that a young
McCall, after several years of Middle East postings, worked
as the middleman between President-elect Ronald Reagan
and a spokesman for the Ayatollah Ruhollah Khomeini who
led the overthrow of then Iranian shah, Mohammad Reza
Pahlavi. The sixty-six American hostages at the U.S. Embassy
in Tehran were released twenty minutes after President
Ronald Reagan finished his inaugural address to the nation.
McCall's rumored role in that quick release has never been
confirmed.

The official records show McCall played an active role in
formulating the plan for the possible removal of American

personnel from the U.S. Embassy in Kuwait, following Saddam Hussein's invasion of that country.

In 1994, several years after al-Qaeda's failed attempt to blow up the World Trade Center in New York, McCall was the on-the-ground leader in a covert operation reported to have corralled Osama bin Laden in Afghanistan. The mission ended after the Taliban-ruled Afghan government publicly disclosed the planned American effort, demanding that U.S. troops be withdrawn from their soil.

In the mid-to-late 1990s, McCall functioned as the liaison officer for George Tenet, the director of Central Intelligence, in his dealings with Saudi Arabia's Intelligence director, Prince Turki al-Faisal. During those years the Saudi government's intelligence agency tried unsuccessfully to capture Osama bin Laden.

Jack McCall is rumored to have led a failed black operation in 2000, undertaken to bring back proof of Saddam Hussein's weapons of mass destruction. That failure led to the establishment of a board of inquiry to determine whether or not McCall had been culpable in the failure. Two men died in the fiasco, including McCall's younger brother, Nick. The board cleared McCall of all charges. The findings of that board concluded that the failure resulted from a leak traced to an intelligence officer in a Middle East country that had agreed to let the American force use its soil to stage the operation. After the hearing ended, McCall requested and received a sixty-day bereavement leave of absence. During that time, our sources report that the foreign officer who betrayed the operation was found dead.

"We'll be landing at Cleveland's Hopkins Airport in ten minutes," the Air Force captain announced. "Please fasten your seat belts low and tight across your middle and return your tray tables to their full upright and locked positions. We know you have a choice when you travel, so we thank you for flying with your United States Air Force."

During the flight, both Frank and Nora had remained in the foggy void between sleep and wakefulness. Before deplaning, Nora asked the pilot to keep his cell phone on so she could call him when they were ready to leave.

A tall, thin man with a sharply receding hairline waited on the tarmac while Nora descended the stairs. After looking her up and down, his gaze roosted on her chest.

"I'm Lieutenant Wes Hamilton, Cleveland PD, homicide. You Sergeant Nora Burke?"

"Yes."

Nora briskly introduced Hamilton to her linebacker-sized partner. "This is Lieutenant Frank Wade." When they got to Hamilton's car, she made certain that Frank got in the front seat with the Cleveland lieutenant.

"So, how'd you two get stuck working with the feds?" Hamilton asked looking back over the seat.

"Just lucky, I guess," she answered without bothering to mask her irritation. "Let's talk about your investigation into the death of Charles Taylor and his family."

Hamilton eyed her in the rearview mirror. "Whenever you two're ready," he replied. "The chief said to give you our full cooperation."

"I faxed you the FBI report," Nora said. "Assuming you read it, did you disagree with anything you saw in it?"

Hamilton shrugged. "No. We agreed with the FBI. The killer used plastic explosive."

"Have you come up with anything further?" Frank asked.

"We backed off when Special Agent Rex Smith got here," Hamilton told him. "We figured the feds had it and, hey, we got plenty of our own."

"What had you done before the FBI arrived?" Nora asked.

Hamilton's voice turned stern. "Sergeant Art Benson and I

started canvassing the neighborhood. Bottom line, nobody saw nothing before they heard the blast. Benson should be there waiting." After turning right, Hamilton told them they had just entered the Pepper Pike development.

Nora watched as they drove through an affluent neighborhood of gracious houses set back on well-groomed lawns. A moment later, Hamilton slowed the car in front of a yard scattered with fallen debris, a blackened chimney standing vigil beside a charred hole.

"There's Benson," Hamilton said, pulling tight to the curb.

Sergeant Benson, as broad as Hamilton was tall, greeted them with an outstretched hand.

"I'm sure Lieutenant Hamilton told you he'd ordered a stop to our investigation when it became a federal case," Benson told Frank.

"We know that," Frank said with an abrupt nod. "Please show us which houses you interviewed at before Lieutenant Hamilton stopped the canvass."

Hamilton put a hand on Benson's arm, stifling his partner, and pointed a dirty fingernail. "We saw people at those two houses. They knew nothing," Hamilton said, "but the man who lives over there told us that he was in bed and only heard the explosion, but that his wife had stayed up later. His old lady wasn't home at the time we interviewed him."

Frank pointed at the same house. "In that case, go interview the lady," Frank said to Hamilton. "And then continue to the end of the street. Here's my cell number. Call whenever you get something. Detective Benson, please do the same on the other side of the street."

"Where will you two be?" Hamilton demanded, clearly uncomfortable at having been put, so abruptly, in a subordinate position.

"Sergeant Burke and I will be doing the same thing around the corner on the side street and the next street over," Frank answered, his voice now even.

As they walked away, Nora asked, "Why did you give them the street Taylor lived on and us the side and back streets?"

"This LW may be a nut, but he's no dummy. Rex's report described Taylor's house as a two story with the bedrooms upstairs in the back. The houses behind Taylor's are one story. From the back street, the killer would have a clear view of the upstairs rear. He may have used that look as his last checkpoint to be sure he had Taylor at home. If I'm right, once the bomber turned onto Taylor's street all systems were go."

"The back street's your idea," Nora said. " You work it. I'll take the side street."

An hour later Frank and Nora met at an intersection.

"I found a man who saw a guy on a bike around ten that night," Nora said. "He had taken his dog out the side door for his evening walk. He described the rider as young and average size. That's all. You get anything?"

"Was the bike red?"

Nora shaded her eyes from the sun to look up at Frank. "Too dark. He couldn't see any colors."

"Guess at the man's age."

"The rider?"

"No. The man who saw the rider."

"Early seventies. Why?"

"Older citizens often describe people in their thirties, even their forties, as young."

"Why did you ask if the bike was red?"

Frank turned and pointed. "The widow who lives over there behind Taylor's house, her name's Constance Harding, saw a rider on a red bike dressed in a black outfit stop at the curb. At first the lady thought he was staring at her. Then she realized he was looking over her home at the back of Taylor's. When the biker started up again, he passed under that streetlight. That's when Ms. Harding saw the colors and, get this, he wore a red baseball cap. The woman described him as about the age of her grandson and about his size. Her grandson is thirty-two and weighs a hundred seventy pounds. With him on the bike, she couldn't guess at his height."

"What time did she see him?" Nora asked.

"Ten fifteen."

"That fits," she told him. "My guy saw the biker a little after ten. How'd the lady know the exact time?"

"She hates the news, so she sits outside between ten and eleven. She hadn't been outside long."

"She hates the news?"

"Her protest. I listened to the whole spiel. Believe me, you don't wanna know. But she's sure about what she saw. I believe her."

"A bike rider here in Cleveland and a flower-delivery person in Oregon, both wearing a red baseball cap," Nora mused, poking Frank in the chest. "That can't just be coincidence."

Frank hopped up on the curb and walked with his arms out for balance. "Maybe her grandson is LW?"

Nora punched Frank on the arm. He faked a teeter, and stepped off the curb.

"What kept the rider from seeing the Harding woman?" she asked.

"She has a screened-in porch and sits in the dark, finds it relaxing. She's lived there for decades and she'd never seen the red bike or the rider before, and not again since. Tell you what. Let's finish this street and one more block on each side. And ask if they know anyone in the neighborhood with a red bicycle. Don't mention the red cap. Let's keep that on the QT."

"We've got a lead," Nora said, showing her excitement. "I'll keep going while you call Jack, and then go find Detectives Harpo and Zeppo, so they'll know to ask about a red bicycle."

"Unless you'd like to go back, that way you can spend a few more minutes with Hamilton?"

"You want I should punch you again?" She held up a clenched fist.

Nora watched as Frank walked away a little faster. The red cap wasn't much, but it matched with what they learned in Depoe Bay. Now, the question was, where would the red cap take them?

# CHAPTER 26

LW watched Gerald and Martha Garfield through silver-mirrored
sunglasses. The Supreme Court nominee and his wife had just
finished an early dinner out and were taking a meandering walk in
downtown Washington, D.C. They had the tired gait of the elderly
and the roving eye of the tourist. He followed them inside the Washington Marriott on Twenty-Second Street and up to their room.

On the ninth floor he took off his sunglasses, placed an antacid
on his tongue, and used the shiny frame around the elevator door to
curve the brim on the red baseball cap he took out from under his
windbreaker. He slowed his pace while a room service waiter pushed
a serving cart into a room down the hall. He stopped outside
Garfield's room, adjusted the fit of the stun gun tucked in his waistband, knocked, and stood back from the peephole. In his hand was
a large brown envelope, the kind that came with a red string wrapped
around a paper disk to secure its flap.

The door opened with the safety chain still in place.

"Mr. Garfield?" The crow's-feet beside LW's eyes added inno-
cence to his still boyish smile. "I have a package from the president's
chief of staff, Mr. Clarence Stafford. I'm required to have you sign
for it, sir. My pen ran out of ink at my last delivery. Do you have
something you could use to sign for this, please?"

Garfield released the chain and opened the door. "One you can keep young man. Come in." Garfield, a sallow-complected man, turned his back on the deliveryman and walked into the room. LW followed. The automatic closer brought the hotel door shut behind them.

Mrs. Garfield sat knitting next to a lamp, her feet on an ottoman, her legs covered by the room's spare blanket. She smiled at the courier and returned her attention to her handiwork.

Mr. Garfield picked up a hotel pen, but before he could turn, LW held the stun gun against the side of his neck. The 100,000 volts of low-amperage electricity mimicked Garfield's body's natural electrical signals. The old man went into temporary paralysis, lost muscle control, and fell to the floor, his tongue protruding between his bluish lips.

Mrs. Garfield's knuckles paled white as her fists tightened around her knitting needles. "Who are you? What do you w—?"

While she had been speaking, LW tossed the stun gun to his left hand and jammed it against her breast. Her rigid body rose from the electrical trauma. After several seconds, LW took the stun gun away, and Mrs. Garfield's head flopped sideways onto the chair's overstuffed arm.

In her convulsive reaction, Mrs. Garfield had thrust her arms upward. This action had driven one of her knitting needles into the underside of LW's forearm.

LW pushed up the sleeve on his windbreaker. His skin had been punctured, and the blunt hole felt hot, but he saw no blood. He slid the offending needle partway inside the back of his pants and lowered his windbreaker over the top end.

He checked the elderly Garfields. They were dead.

After taking out a penknife, he finished the job.

Jack stepped out of the shower to answer his phone.

"Jack. Fred Hampton here."

They could say what they wanted about the obese FBI director, like the crack about the president getting two FBI directors for the price of one, but at five thirty in the morning Hampton was already on the job.

"LW has struck again."

Jack stood dripping water onto his bedroom carpet. "Who? And where the hell was the surveillance?"

"The victims were not being protected. They were Gerald Garfield, a nominee for the Supreme Court, and his wife. They were here in town for his appearance before the Senate's confirmation committee."

"Shit. I never thought about nominees." Jack sat on his bed. "It's logical. Damn it. Fred. It's logical as hell. It does him no good if the government keeps replacing his victims. He'd kill some nominees hoping to discourage others."

"I've already started the ball rolling to extend protection to all the nominees and their families."

"Can we be certain LW was the killer? Where did it happen?"

"At the Marriott on Twenty-Second. The bastard carved LW in their foreheads. Rex Smith is in charge at the scene."

"I'll go over myself, Fred."

"I'll let Rex know you're coming. Are you making any progress?"

"LW knows where he's going," Jack told Hampton. "We don't. Tell Rex to be alert for witnesses who might have seen someone wearing a red baseball cap. Could be a delivery person or a courier, maybe a hotel handyman. Make sure that doesn't get out to the media."

After he hung up, Jack called Rachel and discovered that she had planned to spend the day with the experts developing their first, sketchy LW profile. He decided not to take her off that, and called Nora to meet him.

Jack left his house while still fussing with his tie knot on the way to his car.

●　　　●　　　●

Nora got to the Marriott before Jack, and found Agent Rex Smith alone on the ninth floor wearing an open-collar, rusty-red shirt and tan slacks. "Hello, Rex." She smiled. "You look like you were somewhere other than at home when the call came in."

"You got that right." He stepped toward her. "But I always look forward to seeing you so I'm not complaining."

Nora swivelled her hips. "All you Fed hardbodies, and so little time."

They had just stopped laughing when Jack stepped out of the elevator. "I understand LW initialed his work?"

"That he did. Carved in their foreheads," Rex said, as they entered room 914. "Given the positions of the bodies and the blood blurring the letters, I doubt the hotel workers who found them looked closely. Hotel security agreed to sit on the information about the initials."

Mrs. Garfield's fleshy white arms were decorated with four bracelets. They didn't look gaudy and they were not expensive. She was simply someone's grandmother who would not get any older. She looked at peace, unlike her husband. His mouth was agape. One arm stretched toward his wife. His feet twisted in the opposite direction from his arm, an uncomfortable looking position he no longer felt.

"Any witnesses?"

Rex shook his head. "Not yet."

"What's that smell?" Nora asked.

"The hotel employee who found the Garfields barfed." Rex grinned. "We've spoken to the hotel guests who are still here. None of them saw or heard anything. Agent Amanda Walker is talking with the other employees."

Nora knelt beside Mrs. Garfield. "She was knitting what looks like a blanket for a bassinet."

Jack put his lips inside his mouth, then released them making a popping sound. "Doesn't crocheting require two needles?"

"Yes. One is kept free much of the time to pull yarn into the pattern."

"Where's the other one?" Jack asked.

After several minutes they concluded the other needle was missing.

"Could she have stabbed LW?" Nora asked.

"Tell me about knitting needles." Jack asked.

"The points taper, but are blunted."

"That means, if she did stab him, that the wound would not be serious," Rex interjected. "Mrs. Garfield doesn't appear to have been a strong woman. Still, I'll let the evidence team know to be especially careful looking for blood."

"If he bled, it might've dripped onto the blanket she was knitting."

Rex nodded.

"What time were the Garfields found?" Nora asked.

"Around six thirty this morning."

"Why did someone from the hotel go to Garfield's room at that hour?"

"The White House had called to ask Garfield some question in preparation for an early meeting on the hill. When they got no answer, the hotel's front desk was asked to send someone up to Garfield's room. A young girl working the shift behind the counter offered to go up as she went on break. She's the one who barfed."

A stout woman approached.

"Tell me you've got something, Amanda?" asked Rex.

She nodded. "Maybe I do. Time will tell how significant it is. A room service waiter said he delivered an order to room nine thirty-two. When he came out of that room, he saw a man carrying a large envelope going into a room down the hall. He described the wearer as average height, medium build, and not too old. Oh, yes. He says he was wearing a red cap. He says he could have been going into room nine fourteen. He's not sure. He only got a glance."

Nora looked at Jack.

"I want to talk to that waiter, Rex," Jack said, before turning to Nora. "Check with the guests in the three rooms on each side of nine fourteen and the three nearest rooms across the hall. Unless the waiter is hallucinating, either nine fourteen or one of those nearby rooms had a visit from someone wearing a red baseball cap."

Rachel had just put the last pin in the picture of nominee Gerald Garfield, adding him to their graveyard section, when Jack and Nora returned from the Marriott. They joined the others at the table to report on the Garfield murder scene. After they finished, Rachel began passing out copies of the LW profile.

"This report rests on the sightings of a man or men we're assuming were the killers in Oregon and Cleveland," she said. "The descriptions in both cases are about the same: average height, average weight, what appeared to be short hair under the cap, and about thirty to thirty-five years of age. The vagueness of this reflects LW's ability to blend in. This description also matches the one Jack and Nora just got for the courier seen entering Garfield's room in the Marriott. The red baseball cap remains the single feature that stuck in the minds of the witnesses."

Jack noticed that everyone on his squad was sitting up straight, most jotting notes while Rachel talked about the profile. He didn't know where the profile would lead them, but he felt they were finding traction.

"The psychological profile," Rachel continued, "and this is flimsy, is of a person who reads comic books. We took that from the tone in his communiqué in which he portrayed himself as a superhero out to save America. Despite the juvenile overtones, the skill and ingenuity with which he's carried out these murders suggests lengthy, patient surveillance and planning. These are the tools of an intelligent, calculating killer. We must now assume he has also been tracking nominees for the Court and the Fed. Garfield had been rumored to be a nominee for months even though it was only formalized a few days ago. The killer knows weapons, computers, and explosives which suggests LW may have received training from the military or in law enforcement.

"Our boldest guess is that LW operates alone, or at least is the only killer. That is, unless he's limited his militia to average-sized men in their thirties with clean-shaven faces who wear red baseball caps. And I don't believe he would have enough recruits to pick from that he could be that particular. Also, the red cap could be the militia's subtle uniform, or simply something intended to draw people's eyes so they don't focus on his face."

After Rachel finished, Jack thanked her and told Frank and Nora to go home and get some rest. "I don't want to see you two again before tomorrow morning."

"We're okay, Jack," Frank protested.

"You've just been to Oregon and Cleveland and since you got back you haven't stopped. When we get closer, it'll be twenty-four-seven. You won't be any help then if you're dead on your feet. It's not just physical. I need your minds. Now get out of here. That's an order."

On the way out Nora stopped at the coffee corner where Colin had just finished pouring a fresh cup. "Is your invitation still open for breakfast with a coworker?" she asked.

"You've been thinking about me!" He grinned. "This is good."

"Jetting across the country gives one plenty of time to think," she said. "You may have come to mind a time or two. It helped cut the boredom."

"You want me to call you in the morning to remind you?"

"Why don't you just nudge me?"

"You changed your mind!"

She smiled. "Come over after you get out of here."

"I don't know what time that'll be," Colin said. "I'll call first and pick up some Chinese."

Nora was walking out when Rachel said, "Jack. I need you to call the White House and get the identities of any nominees not yet reported by the media. We can't assume that LW doesn't know about them."

LW shouted in jubilation when he heard it announced on MSNBC that beginning tomorrow the station would begin round-the-clock special coverage of the hunt for LW and his militia.

To fill those hours they'll have to cut into the meat of all this, he thought. They'll discover these aristocrats are running amok, and alert the country. It's working, Father. My plan is working.

The hit program *D.C. Talk*, hosted by Mel Carsten, would be the hub for the special coverage, including interviews with political leaders and guest experts on matters relevant to the hunt. Their first announced guest would be Charles Nesbit, the counterterrorism expert, who had appeared yesterday on the regular version of *D.C. Talk*.

*Mr. Carsten, you'll be needing a replacement.*

# CHAPTER 27

Ten are dead. McCall reports no progress.
—*The D.C. Tattler, June 13*

The sidewalks were crowded with men with fat stomachs, women in shoes with fat heels, young workers rushing to catch the subway, nannies pushing baby carriages, and old people walking their dogs, all of them mere plankton floating through the sea of life.

LW mouthed another antacid tablet.

It would be too dangerous to be seen wearing his red baseball cap across from Charles Nesbit's apartment building. He had worn the cap the night before while attaching the explosive to Nesbit's car after he parked on a side street near Blues Alley, a D.C. jazz club on Wisconsin Avenue, NW. Nesbit had entered the club with a statuesque woman in a tight white sweater and a dark skirt who had arrived in a separate car. After dinner she had followed Nesbit back to his apartment and not left until an hour ago.

The startling clanks from the metal lattice gate rising over the exit from the parking level under Nesbit's building, drew the attention of everyone nearby. A moment later a car began its climb from the concrete tomb. The early morning sun reflecting off its windshield prevented LW from seeing the driver. The car topped out at the street. The glare died. The driver was Nesbit.

LW casually reached inside the pocket of his lightweight jacket, his fingers curling around the remote. Then he pressed its only button. The explosion incinerated the car, transforming Nesbit from a lying sack of shit into a squirming stalk of fire.

When he got home, LW shut the door to the room he thought of as his hideout, plopped onto the couch, and turned on the TV to see that MSNBC had already reported what they were calling the tragic death of Charles Nesbit.

"We have another message from Commander LW," Carsten was saying as the camera panned in on his expressionless face. "The authorities have approved our reading it."

LW's lip synced as Mel Carsten read his words on national TV:

### A Communiqué from the American Militia to Restore Representative Government:

President Schroeder was a fool to ignore my order. Since our demands were not met, the eliminations will continue without further delay. The greatness of our fathers can no longer be ignored.

Mr. Nesbit spoke of our cause as one led by a madman, and he has been punished for his arrogance.

It's time to revolt against the tyranny of a government ruled by unelected aristocrats.

I advise Mr. Carsten to use his program to showcase something more than the ignorance of seeing this issue in the context of a few deaths. All meaningful change in the history of the world has required killing. Use your program to explore and discuss the deterioration of America's representative government.

*Commander LW*

Hearing his own words read on television excited him. His father's ideals carried forward with his words and tactics.

*Stay tuned America. There will be more.*

• • •

"That fuckhead," Millet bellowed. "When we get him, let's cut off his balls and hang him up in the town square."

"Easy, Millet," Jack said, "let's not lose sight of what he is and who we are."

Nora, who was standing behind Millet, put her hands on his shoulders. "Our revenge comes when we stop him."

Millet hurled a wadded piece of paper at his wastebasket. He missed, swore, took a deep breath, and challenged the others. "Did you notice that bastard used 'fathers' not forefathers. Wouldn't you say that means that his father was a force in his life?"

Rachel exhaled slowly. "Could be? We just don't know enough yet."

"I can think of no reason why Charlie Nesbit would have been among LW's targets," Jack said, looking at the pictures of Charlie Nesbit that came on each of the three televisions in the Bullpen.

"Godspeed, Nessy," Jack said before turning to the others. "The president wants to introduce me at a press conference. He's hoping it will help calm the public and the financial markets. 'Let America meet the man on the job,' is how he put it. I had hoped to avoid it, but I promised I would if he thought it necessary."

"Let's hope the attention doesn't make you a target like it did Charles Nesbit," Rachel said, avoiding Jack's eyes.

Nora asked Jack why he was in favor of Carsten reading LW's communiqué. "Why give this jerkoff another audience?" she asked.

"LW is itching to talk about what compels him to do what he's doing," Jack said. "Every time he shows himself, we get another piece for the puzzle."

Jack moved through a strand of Princeton elms across from his house.

He had been coming home on foot from different directions each night since LW had left Rachel's bra in the envelope on his porch. He hadn't liked lying to the others, but he had not ordered protection for himself. This cat-and-mouse game could go on until all the targets had been killed. Jack needed to try everything, including setting himself up as a target.

He held his position near a tree until another cloud again dimmed the moon, then crossed to the front yard of his neighbor, Janet Parker. He loitered in the bushes between their two properties, and used a remote to turn on two of his lamps. He had positioned the lamps to make it impossible for a person to be in his living room without casting a shadow on one of the front window shades. There were no shadows, but the light spilling from the moon reflecting off the wings of moths circulating outside the illuminated window shades, gave the appearance of swirling snowflakes. He drew his SIG, held it along the side of his thigh, and moved toward the make-believe snow.

Once inside he checked the other rooms, then the phone rang. It was Rachel.

"You were really sharp today," she said, "with that observation about LW flying to San Francisco and driving to Oregon."

"Not bad for a spook, eh?" he asked, keeping it light.

She laughed. "No. Not bad for a spook. You want to talk about what we've learned? Maybe I should say, what we're guessing we've learned. Also, what we're going to do tomorrow."

After they had reviewed the last two days in detail, she asked, "Did you really remember me from that time years ago?"

"Yes, ma'am," he told her. "I never forgot your blue eyes."

"I'll bet you say that to all the girls with blue eyes and cleavage."

"We were on the carrier *John Stennis* in the Persian Gulf. I remember your eyes kept changing. Inside they were a deep blue. Outside they matched the blue-green of the Persian Sea."

"Have a bowl of your ice cream and no insomnia tonight. I'll see you in the morning." She hung up.

Atypical for Jack, he fell asleep rather quickly. His clock said he had been asleep an hour when the ringing phone woke him.

"Hello, friend. I'm the guy who brought you Rachel's bra."

"If you're calling to get more underwear, I can leave a pair of my shorts on the porch." Jack looked at caller ID. It hadn't been blocked so LW was probably calling from a pay phone.

"Cute, Jack. You can't make me angry. We're a lot alike, you know."

Jack swung his legs over the edge of the bed and got to his feet. "Just how do you figure that?" He picked up the drink on his nightstand. The ice cubes were mostly melted, the outside of the glass wet. Then he heard a faint scrape, perhaps his caller's unshaven cheek dragging across the mouthpiece.

"You hunt me, Jack. I hunt the aristocrats. You've done covert operations. I'm doing a covert operation."

"It's not the same," Jack said. "When I kill you, the murders will stop."

"We are also alike because we're both protecting something. You're trying to protect America's unelected government. I'm trying to protect the future of our country. Without a cause, there can be no true greatness. I offer you that cause. Join me, Jack. Together we can resurrect America and achieve immortality."

"Sounds right to me. You know where I live. Come on over. Ring the doorbell." Jack sipped his diluted drink.

"Not so fast, Jack. We can meet later. You know who the targets are. Earn your stripes. Take out a few. Then we'll meet."

"Starting tomorrow, you keep a keen watch over your shoulder. The footsteps you'll hear will be mine."

"I haven't told you the main reason why we're so much alike."

Jack heard traffic in the background. "Go ahead," he said, "then I'm hanging up. If you want to talk more, come over."

"You want to fuck Rachel Johnstone. So do I. A friendly wager says I'll be in her panties before you." He laughed. "In fact, I've already won. I'm in her panties right now. I wonder why we call panties plural? Yes, there are two leg holes, but a brassiere has two cups and they are named in the singular. Strange isn't it? Anyway, I've got the flesh-colored sheer ones I took from her apartment pulled over my head. With each breath, I inhale her fragrance. My tongue tastes her. Now I want the whopper, not just the wrapper."

"You aren't kidding me for a moment. You're not interested in America, only in having an excuse to kill. You're a coward. You kill women and unsuspecting men who have no chance to defend themselves."

"Fuck you, Jack McCall. At least I wasn't inept enough to get my own brother killed."

Jack fought to hang onto his composure. He rolled his cold drink glass across his forehead. "Charles Nesbit had you pegged," Jack said. "You're one wacky psycho and I'm guessing your father was nuttier than you are."

"Gotta go. Time is nearly up. One more thing. We are not friends anymore, Mr. McCall."

Jack heard a loud slam and the phone went dead. He immediately called the tracing center at the FBI. LW had known how long the trace would take. The bureau had only been able to narrow it down to a D.C. pay phone within a few downtown square blocks.

At least, the call had likely confirmed their theory that LW was locally based.

Jack called the protective squad covering Rachel, then called Rachel.

# CHAPTER 28

President Schroeder's popularity drops to below
60 percent for the first time in his first term.

—*A.P. Wire Service, June 14*

President Schroeder entered the room in the White House that had
been set up for today's press conference. He began by stating that
after his opening remarks he would introduce Jack McCall. He also
confirmed the rumor that Associate Justice James Dunlin had resigned from the U.S. Supreme Court. The president sipped from
the glass of water that had been left for him.

"To assuage any rumors before they start, I'm going to read Justice Dunlin's letter of resignation. Justice Dunlin has approved my
doing so. As you've already been informed, there will be no follow-
up questions."

Dear Mr. President:

As you know, my son, James Dunlin, Jr., died in the military engagement known as Desert Storm. My wife, Rebecca,
and I are raising our grandchildren. The recent murders of
Supreme Court justices and a nominee for that great office,
together with the continuing threats of more, no longer permit me to enjoy the honor of serving as a U.S. Supreme
Court associate justice. We cannot put our grandchildren at
further risk through the loss of their grandparents. Therefore,
I tender my resignation, effective this date, with deepest

thanks to our nation and you, Mr. President. I also wish to thank Chief Justice Thomas Evans for his excellent leadership, and my fellow associate justices for their understanding and support. I offer my apology for exacerbating the problem of a Court short of justices. Under different personal circumstances, I would stand my office.

Respectfully, *James Dunlin*

President Schroeder then announced that Sophia Washington had withdrawn her name as a nominee for the bench, and that Dr. Manuel Acosta had declined his nomination to the Federal Reserve Board.

"I understand and respect the decisions of each of these loyal Americans and thank them for their lifetimes of service to our country," he continued. "I assure everyone within the sound of my voice that we have many fine Americans on the lists of nominees. Men and women who stand ready to accept and are qualified to serve."

The president rested his hands on each side of the lectern. "And now, inadequate as I may be at it, I'm going to introduce Jack McCall. Until only a short time ago, few Americans had ever heard his name so let me share a brief and, I assure you, understated résumé.

"For more than twenty years, Jack McCall has headed up numerous special operations. The life of every American has been made safer by Jack McCall. He has stopped terrorists, saved the lives of Americans held hostage, and rescued embassy personnel under threat.

"On a personal note, I worked with Jack McCall during my foreign service for the State Department. At all times he carried out his duties as a capable and resourceful patriot. Your government continues to support Jack McCall as the right man for this job. And let me describe the job we have given Mr. McCall. We asked him to find a person who calls himself Commander LW and who claims to head an organization called the American Militia to Restore Representative Government. Here and now, I confess that none of our law enforcement and intelligence agencies at the federal or state level have ever heard of LW or his militia. The same is true for the world's friendly governments.

"As you can see, Mr. McCall has taken on quite a task, a job at which he has been working for only a matter of days. Anyone expressing impatience with his results is either playing politics or being wholly unrealistic. Ladies and gentlemen, Mr. Jack McCall."

The president shook Jack's hand and moved to the back of the rostrum.

While reminding himself not to squint into the television lights, Jack stepped to the microphone. "Thank you, Mr. President, for your kind introduction. I know many of you from your work, but not by sight. Please state your name when I call on you so I may acknowledge you when I answer."

He pointed at a rail-thin lady in the center of the front row. "Yes?"

"My name is Gloria Powell from the *San Francisco Chronicle.* Mr. McCall, please tell us what you can about your progress."

"Thank you, Ms. Powell. We have cleared a few people who at one time or another, on some preliminary level, were considered suspects. Naturally, I can't comment on those on whom we are currently focused, but the effort continues."

In accordance with the stated rule for this meeting with the media, Jack ignored Ms. Powell's efforts at a follow-up and called instead on a gentleman whose bushy mustache hid his upper lip.

"I'm Eric Dunn, a freelance national columnist. Mr. McCall, please identify those who have been eliminated from suspicion"

"It would be inappropriate to identify people who have been cleared. I'm sure you understand."

"But America has a right to know, Mr. McCall."

"All right. We have eliminated one serious suspect, a man with the freedom of movement to obfuscate his appearances in the locations of the killings. His name is Eric Dunn."

Jack waited while the murmurs quieted, Dunn's face turning red. Then he held his palms outward.

"Mr. Dunn, you are not and never was a suspect. I only wished to illustrate the point you refused to accept. It would be unfair to name people who have been cleared. My career has required the analysis of a situation and a quick effective thrust to get the job done or, in this case, the point made. I trust you'll forgive me for appearing insensitive."

"Mr. McCall, Mr. McCall."

"Yes?" Jack pointed to a round sturdy gentleman in the back row.

"Sal Ramirez from CNN. Mr. McCall, how did LW get past your security to kill Court nominee Gerald Garfield and his wife?"

"I failed to consider protection for the nominees."

The president cleared his throat and stepped forward. Jack moved to the side.

"Mr. Ramirez," Schroeder said, "if you knew Jack McCall as I do, you'd know he makes no excuses and deflects no accountability. In fairness, it should be acknowledged that Mr. McCall's job has been to identify and stop this LW and his militia. Providing security is not part of his assignment."

The president stepped back and Jack gestured to his right, calling on a female member of the press corp. "The lady on the end in the third row."

A plump woman in a bright red dress stood and spoke through matching colored lips. "I'm Agnes Patterson from the *Detroit Ledger*. Mr. McCall, you've told us that you cannot identify suspects and the specifics of the progress of your investigation. Can you tell us how soon you anticipate ending this terrorizing of America?"

"Another valid question," Jack replied. "I only wish that I could answer it. The truth is we just don't know. We believe we're making progress, but an investigation cannot fool itself, and I will not attempt to fool you. The lady in the center of the room."

"My name is Marian Little from local NewsCentral Seven," she said. "Do you have a comment on LW's killing of counterterrorism expert Charles Nesbit?"

There it was. The opening. The reason Jack was doing the press conference. He squared his shoulders and looked straight into the cameras.

"Men like Charles Nesbit have kept America free and safe for even the likes of you, Commander LW. Mr. Nesbit did nothing but speak his mind when asked a question. Free speech is essential to the representative government you claim to espouse. But your idea of representative government is that it must be what you dictate. America will never follow a dictator. So tonight I warn you: if you're smart, surrender, because we're coming for you."

The audience of media, having never heard a press conference used to deliver a direct threat, sat stunned. Then a gray-haired man with a slight hunchback stood without being called on and broke the silence.

"Kenneth George. *Los Angeles Times.* Mr. McCall, may I say I find your forthrightness refreshing. What can you tell us about this LW? What makes his kind tick?"

I'd rather parachute behind enemy lines, Jack thought, than do any more of these press conferences. In special ops, the enemy was often both easier to identify and to anticipate. And, he knew how to treat that enemy.

"It's a complicated world, Mr. George. To answer your question, I'm no psychiatrist. The furthest thing from it, but for me people like LW are a mutation. They believe they have the ultimate wisdom, but they lack the courage and commitment to work within the American system. They cloak their cowardice in violence, rationalizing that their violence is necessary to remedy the injustice they perceive. I feel sorry for LW."

The reporters were all on the fronts of their chairs, edgy in trying to time the moment when they might start their question to be heard first, in just the right tone to capture the audience.

"My father loved America," Jack continued. "He would have

helped LW learn how to serve, not try to destroy, our country. We believe LW's father may have been a sexual deviant, perhaps an abuser of drugs, some combination of human deficiencies that denied LW a proper role model."

Jack stood stone still and silent, then went for the jugular of the only viewer in whom he held an interest. "LW is a murderer, no more honorable than any other vicious killer. Violence is the last resort of weak men holding failed ideals."

When it was over, Jack walked out beside the president. As they hurried out the door, Jack reminded himself that LW had killed Charlie Nesbitt within a day or so of Nessy's comments on television. If this public insult of LW's father worked, Jack knew the assassin would soon be coming for him.

# CHAPTER 29

McCall warns LW: ready or not, here I come.

*—Sal Ramirez, CNN, June 14*

After Jack's press conference, the president took the elevator up to the fitness room, changed into a pair of sweats, and did fifteen minutes on the stair stepper, then moved to the treadmill. He could not get his mind off what Jack had said toward the end of his meeting with the press. After only ten minutes of his usual thirty-minute walk, he hit the stop button, got off and picked up the phone to buzz his chief of staff.

"Clancy, I trust you heard the press conference?"

"Yes, Mr. President, I watched with Harriet, Fred, and General Crook. We found Jack very effective. At the end he appeared to be taunting LW."

"You're damn right. I want to confirm that there's a protective detail on Jack."

"Mr. President, it's on all the members of Jack's squad, but not Jack. He refused protection for himself."

"What? And you didn't do it anyway?"

"Your order was that we were to give Jack our full cooperation. So we did what he asked."

The president rested his forehead in the palm of his hand. "Jesus Christ," he muttered.

"Mr. President, Jack is apparently setting himself up as bait. If so, he doesn't wish to chance LW seeing our people and backing off."

"I'm countermanding Jack's order. Get some top personnel on him. I want it operational tonight."

"Yes, sir. Right away. Anything else, Mr. President?"

"Yeah. Damn it. Have them give Jack some space. Tell your people to back off enough so that Jack doesn't know they're there. If he can't tell, LW won't know. I want good men, close enough to come on strong if he needs help."

The president slammed down the phone, turned off his desk lamp, and prayed he had not just put Jack's neck in a noose.

Jack returned to the Bullpen after the press conference to find the room unoccupied except for Rachel, who had fallen asleep at her desk. Her head next to a partially eaten apple balanced on the end of its core. Her clothes were disheveled and her hair a mess. He moved closer and stood quietly listening to her soft breathing. She was beautiful.

He gently canoodled her shoulder. "Rachel," he whispered, "wake up."

Her eyelids lifted. Her hand bumped the uneven apple. It rolled away with a strange wobble.

"Oh, Jack. I guess I dozed off after watching your press conference. I thought you might come back here."

He shook his head. "You've gotten to know me pretty well, haven't you, Ms. Johnstone?"

She touched his arm. "A lady gets to know her coworkers."

"So I'm not Spook anymore?"

"Oh, I think we've worn that one out, don't you? Why don't you drive me home? I can leave my car here if you'll stop to pick me up in the morning."

"It would be my pleasure," he said.

Rachel looked at Jack as he drove. His button-down shirt had long ago lost its morning look, his tie knot yanked crooked to one side, and a five-o'clock shadow darkened his cheeks and chin. He was sexy in an earthy way. Then she glanced down at her own outfit and saw a fully qualified candidate for the take-me-to-the-dry-cleaners stack. If things went according to plan, she'd soon have it off. The FBI had taught Rachel that a lack of sleep can lower a suspect's resistence during an interrogation. She planned to find out if it would do the same during a seduction.

While driving across the Key Bridge, Jack told her about his most recent call from LW. As he steered his Chrysler out of the Sheridan Circle onto Twenty-Fourth Street near the Woodrow Wilson House, she casually said, "That Marian Little from channel seven is hot."

"I didn't notice."

"Come on now. Women notice shoes, clothes, hairstyles, everything other women wear, even jewelry and handbags. Men only notice BL&T, breasts, legs and tush, and Ms. Little has 'em all."

"You couldn't see her butt on television."

"I'd seen it before."

"Is there a side to you I don't know?"

"Don't try to fog the issue. For men a woman's outfit is only relevant to the extent that it aids or detracts noticing the body. Admit it."

Jack glanced over and grinned.

Rachel knew her plan for Jack would provide titillation for the protective detail watching her place, but the hell with them. Tonight she planned to finish some old business.

He pulled to the curb in front of her apartment, a middle-class building that was home for a scattering of executive secretaries and others who helped run the machinery of the nation's government.

"I'm sorry about your cat," he said. "Jingles, right?"

"Yes. Thank you. That crazy cat would always meet me at the door when I got home and bug me nonstop until I filled his food bowl, even if it was already full. Funny, isn't it, how we remember the silly things."

"Yeah."

"Here's another silly thing," she said, putting her hand on his arm. "I promised Jingles we'd get the bastard." She turned toward him and looked into his eyes. "Come on in, Jack. We're both tired, but sometimes there are things that are more important to rest than sleep alone."

The brain is an amazing thing—the body's only analytical, reasoning organ. And Jack's screamed, "Watch out. You work with this woman." At the same time man's reactionary organ silently screamed, *Go on in and get laid.*

On the way up the stairs, she said, "Cover your eyes at the top of the landing or the streetlight will blind you." She unlocked and opened the door and flipped on the light. "This is it. The bathroom's off the hall, if you need it."

"Yes. I do."

When he came out, she was in the kitchen. "I'm opening a Zinfandel," she called out. "Sit down. Make yourself comfortable."

When she brought in the bottle and two glasses, he was looking at the titles of the books on the shelves of her entertainment center. "The spines on the novels haven't been creased," he said.

"I know. But I keep buying them." She set the glasses on the coffee table in front of the couch. "I just can't find the time to read them."

She poured the glasses halfway, sat beside him, and handed him one. "I don't know how you guys wear those infernal ties all day. Take it off. Get comfortable."

"Habit, I guess." Jack pulled off the tie and pushed off his shoes. Then he put his feet on the table, sipped his wine, and enjoyed the surrounding solitude with his eyes closed.

After a few minutes their breathing fell into a matching rhythm, as if guided by an invisible metronome.

"Millet and I finished our first run-through of the list of passengers," she told him. "We still have about a hundred whose flights fit at least one of the murders. We're examining passenger descriptions and backgrounds and flight itineraries. Hopefully, we'll knock it below fifty tomorrow."

He opened his eyes and nodded. "Good. What's the latest on the violent agents and military personnel?"

She reached over and casually touched his thigh. "It came in midday." She moved her hand and took another sip of her wine. "We eliminated a whole bunch based on their confirmed postings on the dates of the murders. We hung onto the information on the ones we threw out on appearance, just in case we later get a different description."

"That sounds like progress. I told the country we were making some." He let the empty glass dangle from his fingertips, and closed his eyes.

"Had you ever done a press conference before?"

Even tired as he was, he enjoyed being with her. Just sharing his weariness helped.

"No," he admitted. "I hope the press gives me a break. But I doubt that'll happen. I put one of them on the spot."

"You mean Eric Dunn?" Rachel laughed. "The TV camera showed a lot of faces. They were all giggling. I think you made your point, then pulled back and showed humility by apologizing. At the end even Dunn appeared to think it was funny."

"Sal Ramirez from CNN hit the nail on the head," Jack said, yawning. "The Garfields are dead because I made an error."

"That's bull," she said, kicking off her shoes. "Damn it, Jack. You are not responsible for protective surveillance—the president left that to the agencies."

She was right. Still, Jack said, "I should have thought of the nominees."

She halted her glass in midair. "Now listen here, Mr. McCall."

"So we're back to Mr. McCall, are we?"

"For the moment, yes, you are not the entire government, Mr. McCall, and you are not in charge of everything associated with LW. You told the president that others could become targets. The killing of the Garfields is tragic, but you are not responsible and you can't afford the distraction that comes with carrying the blame."

"You're right," he told her. Then yawned again. "But I can't help wondering what else I'm missing?"

"Sleep, Jack. You're missing sleep." She took his hand and pulled him up from the couch, walked him into her bedroom, and pushed him onto her bed. "You're in no condition to drive home. I'll see you in the morning."

The last thought he remembered was hoping they would do this again, under better circumstances. When there was not a protective squad outside.

# CHAPTER 30

Meet Jack McCall, a direct and capable American agent.

—*Eric Dunn, freelance columnist, June 15*

Jack woke at four and after a moment of confusion realized he was in Rachel Johnstone's bed. Alone. He thought about his evening with her and somewhere in those thoughts Wee Willie snapped to attention and took on its secret identity, Sir William.

Next time, he thought, damn the regulations. Sir William is a nobleman and his orders must be obeyed.

Last night he had skipped his nightly bout with insomnia, never even thought about it. And this morning he felt more rested than he could remember. He pulled the covers up to his neck, clamping them down with intertwined fingers, and stared at a lithograph of a home in the mountains hanging on the wall across from the foot of Rachel's bed.

The aroma of fresh coffee entered the room ahead of Rachel, a cup in her hand, steam rising from it.

"Good morning," she said bubbly. "I took the liberty of going to your place last night to get your dopp kit and a fresh change of clothes. I know it was a bit forward of me, but I wanted to let you sleep as late as possible. Don't worry. I called my protective detail and one of them went with me. I hope you approve of what I picked out."

He reached out and took her hand. "You didn't need to do that, but, well, the sleep was great. Thanks."

"Breakfast in forty minutes," she told him.

After she'd left, he cradled the hot coffee in both hands, absorbing its warmth. For a moment he felt like a man in one of those stories where the couple lives happily ever after. But in a little while he and Rachel would be putting happiness aside to continue their efforts to stop some lunatic hell-bent on putting America on tilt.

He had known what Rachel had on her mind last night, and what had been on the mind of Sir William, but the moment she had brought in the coffee, Jack knew last night had turned out right. Still, that realization didn't make him smile.

He put his face in the pillow and inhaled Rachel's fragrance, then showered and got dressed. On the way to the kitchen he saw a blanket folded on her couch.

"You didn't need to give up your bed. I could've slept out—"

"Are you feeling comfortable with me right now?" she interrupted.

Her tone of voice sounded a warning that told Jack what would follow would not be as pleasant as the soft fragrance of her pillow.

"Because I wanted to kick your ass last night after watching your press conference. You challenged LW. You insulted him. His father. His cause. The kindest word I can think of to describe your actions is foolish."

He broke the yoke in his egg with the corner of a piece of toast. "He might not have even been watching?"

"Don't patronize me, Mr. McCall."

*So, we're back to that, again.*

"Even if LW didn't see it live, your comments have been rerun all morning on all the news and talk programs," she told him. "You knew the networks would do that. You called him out and don't try to pretend you didn't."

"We need him to make a mistake, okay," Jack said somewhat defensively. "Nessy, angered him—"

"You knew Nesbit pretty well, didn't you?"

"We were friends for fifteen years, in some tight spots together. I was trying to say, Nessy made LW mad and he lost his operational discipline. I want to do the same thing. Knock him off his plan again. Get LW to focus on me. Maybe that'll make him more vulnerable."

"That could also make you a target."

She picked at her breakfast while Jack finished his eggs, smearing the yoke puddle with his last piece of toast, and washing it down with the rest of his coffee.

*My God. We're doing morning after stuff without the night before. Sir William, next time you're in charge.*

A little after six, Jack and Rachel walked into the Bullpen to find that the others had already arrived. A minute later Lana Kindar brought in one of her proprietary coffee blends and pastries, fresh strawberries, and sliced mangoes. Nessy had been with Jack and Colin when they had saved Lana and Zaro. Before leaving, the old woman cradled Jack's face in the palm of her open hand. Her coarse skin felt as warm as her smile.

"Jack," Millet called out. "There's a Michele Browning from Phoenix on the phone. Says she's your sister."

Michele had probably watched the press conference. The day always seemed to run out of time, but he should have let her know about it.

"Hi, sis. Everything okay?"

"I'm not quite sure, bro," Michele answered. "I just learned my brother is an imposter. The president of the United States told me. At the same time he told the rest of the world. You've been lying to me for twenty years."

"Michele, I can explain."

"Just hold on, Mr. McCall."

*Christ. She's doing the Mr. McCall bit too. My own sister.*

"I've got more to say, bro, a lot more. For days I've been seeing your name in the newspaper and hearing it on the news. I just assumed it was another man with the same name. After all, my brother worked security for the State Department, and my brother wouldn't lie to me. Not gullible me!"

Jack held the phone a few inches from his ear and continued to listen.

"I suppose you're going to tell me that you had to live your cover, that your superiors ordered you to lie. That you didn't want to put me in jeopardy or make us worry—"

"All that, sis," Jack interrupted calmly. "I'm glad you understand. I was worried you'd be mad."

"I was! I am! I'm trying not to be. Why shouldn't I be? I called your house this morning and got no answer. If I'd reached you then, well, it wouldn't have been pleasant. Dick tried to calm me down before he left for work, but he wasn't all that successful."

"Your husband's a good man." Jack told her while loosening his tie.

"Damn it," she said, turning her volume button back up. Then, sounding more hurt than angry, she huffed, "You couldn't even tell the truth to your only sister?"

Noting that the others in the Bullpen were all staring at him, grinning, Jack smiled and waved them off. It didn't work.

"What would have been accomplished if I had told you?" he said, switching the phone to his other hand and giving his team a mind-your-own-business glare, which they also ignored. "You'd have worried and had the additional burden of keeping the secret."

Jack sat forward and spun a ballpoint pen on his desk. "These things go with the job. Tell me you really understand?"

"Oh, I understand. I guess. You're right. I would have worried then, like I'm worried now. Are you okay? Can you catch this LW?"

"I've got a great team and President Schroeder is giving me full support."

"When I saw you walk forward after the president said your name, I almost fell off my chair."

"How is your family?"

"Did you learn to change the subject in spy school? We're all fine. Really. Don't worry about us. Call me when this is over. We'll all get on the phone and you can tell us the behind-the-scenes story."

"Michele, I had planned to call you this morning, a little later when it wouldn't be so early on your end of the country. We don't know where these killers will try to strike next. The government has round-the-clock protection in place for the justices and the Federal Reserve governors, including their families, and mine."

"But you're not—you mean us don't you?"

"You should know that all three of you are under twenty-four-hour protective surveillance. You won't see them so don't look. The chance of anything happening is remote, but you need to know." He gave her his current cell phone number, and the number for her protective detail. "I keep my cell phone with me day and night," he continued, "but call the detail if you sense an immediate danger. They're close. Then, when you can, call me."

The mere fact that she had not tried to interrupt him, let him know she was taking what he said seriously.

"Don't stop to help strangers or give directions. Keep your place locked up all the time and don't open your door to anyone you don't know. If something happens and you don't have time to call, scream your head off. Start screaming at the slightest hint of a threat. Don't stop to try and reason with whomever it is. Just scream and keep screaming. The protective detail will hear you."

"Oh that makes me feel so much better," she said.

"We'll get him, sis," Jack promised. "Soon."

Soon. He wanted soon. The president wanted soon. The whole damn country wanted soon. But he knew he was far from being as confident as he had sounded, and wondered if Michele had sensed that, too.

# CHAPTER 31

Unconfirmed report out of Europe: LW is a member
of Hezbollah, trained as an assassin in Iran.

*World News Report, June 15*

"Who is it?" Jenny Robinson called from behind the front door of
her condo.

"Harold's Plumbing."

She opened her door, leaving the flimsy slide chain in place.

"The building manager sent me to replace the washers in your
faucets." The plumber was wearing denim bib overalls and held his
hands behind his back.

"I've got no leaks," she told him.

"I unnerstand, ma'am, but the boss man has us change 'em all
ever three years whether or not they're leaking. He wants to avoid a
bunch of service calls when one a you gets a drip. Five minutes, lady,
that's all I need."

"Come back tomorrow," she said, starting to close her door.

He spoke quickly through the narrowing crack. "You're my last
one today, lady. Please. I gotta work on the other side of town to-
morrah. Honest, lady, I'll be out of your hair in five minutes."

In forty-five minutes Jenny expected U.S. Supreme Court Associate Justice Michael Roberts, the benefactor of half her rent, to visit
and she was in no mood to argue.

"All right. All right!" She said, releasing the chain. "Come in.
But I need you gone in fifteen minutes."

"Won't take me more'n five minutes. That's my guarantee, Ms. Robinson."

Jenny closed the door and, after turning back toward him, saw the black gun looking even darker in the plumber's white latex gloved hand.

Her reaction was to draw back in alarm. Then her basic instincts took over and her eyes softened, her mouth curling into a coquettish smile.

"Please don't hurt me," she cooed. "If you want sex, it's okay. I'm an escort girl." She had always preferred that title to hooker. "Whatever you want—just don't hurt me."

"Anything?"

"Name it, honey. Just don't hurt me. My appearance is how I survive."

He grinned. "Put on a thong and high heels. Then lay face down on your couch."

He watched as she stripped down to the black thong and heels she already wore, and strutted toward the couch on incredibly long legs. Her jugs were as big as Kitt's in San Francisco, and even bigger when she used her arms to accentuate her cleavage. Her bleached hair flowed over her shoulders to cascade down the sides of her well-tanned arms.

*She's enjoying this. She wants it.*

He watched her walk while his mind altered the words from a story his mother used to read at Christmas: she shook like a bowl of jelly, only, Momma, it's not her belly.

He wanted to touch her smooth skin, but as had been the case with Judith Breen at the Resort at Depoe Bay, he couldn't chance it. He just couldn't. He couldn't endanger his mission.

"Okay, Jenny darling," he said in a voice dripping with sarcasm, "lay butt up on the couch and put your face toward the backrest."

When she did, he squatted like a baseball catcher next to her expensive, overstuffed couch.

"Hey, whore," he said, "did one of your sugar daddies buy this couch for you?"

Her answer was muffled by the cushions.

He slowly brought his hands up her calves, the latex dragging against her skin. Then up her thighs, his stroke slowing as it climbed the crown of her butt. Then slowly up her back, his shirt bunching over his shoulders and along the backs of his arms, until he grasped her neck and tightened his grasp. Moisture beaded on his forehead. Then a sudden snap, and she went limp.

Justice Roberts would find her precisely as she looked at this moment. The plumber smiled, pleased with his design of the scene.

It had been back in March when he first followed Justice Roberts to this little love nest in condo 1214 in the exclusive Capitol Arms, a twenty-minute walk from the courthouse. He had returned to follow Roberts in April and May to reconfirm Roberts still visited Jenny Robinson, and still walked to get there. A week ago, using the skills he'd learned courtesy of the U.S. government, he had tapped Jenny's phone at the phone company's box in the building's basement and heard Roberts tell Jenny he would arrive at his regular time, three in the afternoon.

"I'll walk out with the tourists," he had said, "wearing a different coat than the one I'll wear in that morning. And I'll wear a hat, something I never do. When I get there, I'll use my key. You can wait inside to surprise me. I'm not going to miss an afternoon with my Jenny."

The old widower had sounded like a school kid bragging about sneaking out of the house after his parents went to bed.

*The horny old fool.*

LW stood watching from Jenny Robinson's window until Roberts suddenly appeared at the corner of Fifth and F streets, a cigarette dangling from the edge of his mouth. He had not been followed.

Three minutes later, standing near the door, LW heard light footfalls on the carpeted hallway. He held the ends of his fingers loose against the lock and through the latex felt the stuttering friction of a metal key nesting into the grooves.

The knob turned.

The door swung inward.

"Sweetpea!" Justice Roberts called. "Daddy's home!"

# CHAPTER 32

President Schroeder meets with retired Senator Wilson Fowler,
former chairman of the Senate Intelligence Committee.
Is he the rumored replacement for Jack McCall?

—*New York Daily News, June 16*

Ms. Lurleen Grissom's fuzzy slippers sopped the water on her hardwood floor as she slogged her way into the kitchen where she departed from her normal morning routine of turning on the coffeepot. She picked up her phone.

"This is Ms. Grissom in eleven fourteen," she told Joe Carter, the building manager. "I have water dripping into my living room. It's coming from that harlot's penthouse above me. My expensive new Persian hallway runner is ruined, not to mention my slippers. I'm standing in water right now. I demand the building pay for my losses. You get up here, Mr. Carter. I expect you to do something about this. Fast. The water just keeps dripping from my ceiling!"

Joe took his time getting up to the crotchety old busybody's condo. It annoyed him that this time Gripey Grissom might have a legit beef.

Ms. Grissom wasted no words. "My apartment is a damn swimming pool," she said as soon as she opened her door. "Just look. Look at that." Her hands roosted on her hips when she finished pointing.

After an apology and a bit of groveling, Carter called the tenant in 1214, a woman he thought of as Ms. Jenny Sweetmeat. When Sweetmeat didn't answer, he dashed upstairs, the chain of keys suspended on his belt loop jangling against his leg, Gripey Grissom audibly panting as she waddled up the stairs after him.

His knock went unanswered. "Ms. Robinson. Ms. Robinson. It's Joe Carter, Ms. Robinson. Please open your door."

When Ms. Robinson didn't open her door, Carter used his passkey and upon stepping inside he heard a squish, looked down and saw water rising around his canvas shoes. Then he saw Sweetmeat. Face down on her couch. Butt up, wearing a black thong.

Ms. Jenny had asked him to help her slide that couch into position as a room divider. It remained his favorite help-me-with-this-will-you-Carter chore. When she had leaned to push, he had gotten his best look ever at her big knockers.

Sweetmeat must have tied one on and passed out, he thought. I'll probably need to put my hands on her to wake her.

It took great fortitude for him to stop looking at Sweetmeat, but he did and went into the master bath to see water flowing over the rim of her old-fashioned tub, its brass claw feet standing ankle deep in water. He had often fantasized how she might look in that tub with bubbles clinging to the ends of her nipples. After turning off the water, he rolled up his sleeve, plunged his arm to the bottom, and pulled the drain plug.

When he came out of the bath, on the dining room side of the couch, he saw a man's body. A large knife handle appeared to be balanced on his chest, and blood from his forehead had pooled and dried in one eye socket.

Carter didn't know who the gent was, but he had the sinking feeling he would never realize his fantasy with Ms. Jenny Sweetmeat.

"LW task force. Nora Burke."

"Nora. Paul Suggs. How are you?"

She remembered Suggs as a steady detective whose grin often revealed that brushing and flossing could not be part of his morning ritual. "I'm staying busy, Paul. What's up at Metro?"

"We have Supreme Court Justice Michael Roberts dead in condo twelve fourteen of the Capitol Arms on Fifth Street. Initial estimate about twelve to eighteen hours. The cause of death appears to be the knife sticking in his heart. Ain't all this talk about 'alleged' and 'appears' a bunch of crap? The damn attorneys are taken over the cop business. Anyway, the killer carved LW in Justice Robert's forehead, so, yeah, this here's the work of your guy."

Nora propped her elbow on her desk, and cradled her chin in her open hand. "What the fuck happened to his surveillance?"

"Search me. I'm just glad Metro PD didn't have that job."

Nora snapped her fingers twice to get the attention of the others. "Run it down for me, Paul."

"We got a dead young woman in the same unit, a Ms. Jennifer Robinson. It's her condo. The front desk described the owner as a quiet resident who lived well without any known means of support. The doorman knew Justice Roberts as Mr. Smith, one of a number of gentlemen who regularly visited Ms. Robinson a few hours a month. I'm telling ya, this gal's a centerfold so you can fill in the blank about what she did for a living. Nobody recalls seeing anyone unfamiliar enter or leave the building. We found signs of a lock having been forcibly picked on the outside door leading into the basement equipment room. A work elevator comes up from there to all the floors."

Suggs went on to describe how the bodies were found.

"You got anything suggesting who left the water running in the tub?" Jack and Rachel were now standing next to Nora's desk.

"No," Suggs said. Nora shook her head for the others. "I'm guessing LW surprised the babe while she was filling her tub."

"Is it possible that LW used the tub as a crude timing device to trigger the discovery?" Nora asked.

"I hadn't considered that, but, sure, it could've went down like that. I mean it's possible. Yeah, it might've been."

"I'll advise the bureau. They'll be coming out to take control of the crime scene. If the media gets to you before that, tell 'em to sit tight and wait for the FBI. Okay?"

"Okay, Nora. Catch this jerkoff, will ya? Our cases are stacking up and we're short a couple of detectives. I won't mention any names, but they're Wade and Burke."

By the time Nora hung up, Frank and Millet had also come to her desk. She turned the notepad on which she had scribbled and underlined: Justice Michael Roberts and Ms. Jennifer Robinson.

Rachel quickly called FBI Director Hampton. While she was on the phone, the director dispatched a senior agent and an evidence response team.

Jack knew that the bureau would get things started at the Capitol Arms, and he planned to send Frank and Nora over, but before they left he called everyone to the table.

"We often ask victims and witnesses to tell their stories more than once. Let's do that for the same reason: sometimes something comes out on the retelling. Frank, start us off."

Jack could see that Frank was clearly antsy to get to the murder scene, but he did what Jack asked.

"The Oregon gardener and local florist, and the two neighbors close to Chip Taylor's home in Cleveland, as well as the room service waiter at the Marriott gave us very similar descriptions. Male. Age thirty, thirty-five. Normal length hair. Eye color unknown. Build, medium to light. Height, about five ten. Each time he's been seen he wore a red baseball cap. No names, other than what may later be suggested by the lists Millet and Rachel are developing. It's not likely but his initials could be LW. Now, can I get going?"

"When we're finished, Frank. There are capable people already on their way," Jack said. "It won't be long."

Rachel sat forward with the backs of her hands stacked under her chin. "His psychological profile characterizes him as delusional, someone who thinks he can change the authority structure of America. He plans far in advance. Apparently there's nothing frightening about his physical manner. People are opening their doors to him. His communiqués suggest he's either a college grad or highly self-educated. His latest writing hinted that his father, in some way, contributed to perverting him."

"What do we have that tells us anything about any other member of his militia?" Jack asked. "Anybody?"

"Nothing," Frank answered, adding squirming to his fidgeting. "Nothing at any of the crime scenes suggested anyone with a different description. And the manner in which each of his victims was murdered would not require an accomplice."

"Nothing we have supports there being more than one killer," Millet added in support of what Frank had said.

Everyone nodded, except Colin.

"Isn't it possible," Frank asked Colin, "that the idea of his having a militia is a red herring? Couldn't this be the work of one psycho?"

"I just can't see it that way," Colin answered. "The assassinations so far have been from coast to coast. Oregon and Cleveland were on two consecutive days."

"But the Breens in Oregon were dead a couple of days before they were found," Rachel said, correcting the impression of what Colin had said. "The findings of the bodies, not the killings themselves, were on consecutive days."

Jack put down his coffee cup. "Anyone agree with Colin that there must be more than one killer?"

"Consider this," Nora said, taking off her earrings and massaging her earlobes. "In Oregon and Cleveland we have witnesses who gave almost the same description. Is it reasonable to think the members of this so-called militia all have the same physical basics?"

"That argument relies on the assumption the sightings in Oregon and Cleveland were the killers," Colin said in defense of his position. "It remains possible all we have is an innocent fellow riding a bike and another guy delivering flowers."

"But the local FBI offices," Rachel said coming back at Colin, "have been unable to find either an Oregon florist with a delivery to the honeymoon cottage, or someone in the Pepper Pike neighborhood of Cleveland who owns a red bicycle and rode it near Taylor's home. When we rely on the presumption these sightings were the killers, the question becomes do we have several killers or is this LW character working overtime?"

"We need to decide whether we believe LW has a militia or is a lone wolf," Jack told them. "Whatever we decide, that decision will remain open to constant reassessment."

"Jack!" Frank exclaimed. "Could that be the LW? Lone Wolf! Telling us, he's operating alone? Is he toying with us? Like he did when he went inside Rachel's place. Teasing us?"

"Maybe," Jack said reflectively. "That could certainly fit a guy who thinks he's smarter than the rest of the country. Colin, your first priority is to develop a rolling timeline. Find out if it's possible for one man to have committed all these murders. Be sure to include the times and the locations from which the communiqués were FedExed. I want you to prove your argument that one person couldn't do it, or find out that one could."

"You got it," Colin said, pushing his chair back from the table.

"Rachel and Millet, you keep working your lists. Prioritize as you see fit. You know what we're looking for. We need some passengers whose flights will fit the timeline Colin's developing, so you three co-ordinate."

"Now, Jack?"

"Now, Frank. You and Nora get over to the Capitol Arms. Me, I'm going to play a long shot. I'll fill you in when I get back."

Ten minutes later, Jack had FBI Supervisory Agent Rex Smith on the phone, asking him about one house in the report on the canvassing of the neighborhood in which Chief Justice Thomas Evans lived.

"That house sits directly across from the home of the chief justice," Agent Smith said. "The neighbors say it's empty, and the couple next door saw a car there a month or so ago, but not again since.

And before you ask, no, they never saw anybody, just the car. The man thought it was a dark-colored SUV."

"I know all that, Rex. That's what the report said. It's time to play a hunch. Give me the address. Find out who owns that house, and if there's been any changes in ownership within the past few years, and so on. Contact the owner to get permission for us to enter the house. When you have it, bring an FBI SWAT team. Be sure they include specialized medical advanced response personnel. And get a chopper in the air as near as possible without being heard. I'll meet you there."

Jack poked the end button with his finger, and pressed the accelerator with his foot.

# CHAPTER 33

Several Federal Reserve governors are
reported to be considering resigning.

—A.P. *Wire, June 16*

"Jack. Rex. I'm in the back of the SWAT van. We're ten to fifteen
minutes out. Where are you?"

"More like fifteen. What have you got on the mystery house?"

"It should be coming on the screen in a moment. I've got you on
a headset. Here! Here it is. The house is owned by a Mr. and Mrs.
Harrelson of New York City. We reached Mrs. Harrelson. They
rarely use the home. It's rented out through a D.C. rental agent.
Mrs. Harrelson has authorized us to enter and search the house in
whatever manner we deem necessary. We're still trying to reach the
rental agent. I'll get back to you when more comes through."

Jack tossed his agency cell phone on the passenger seat and focused on making up the minutes he was behind Rex. A dark sedan
in his rearview mirror drew his attention as it moved behind him
three cars back. He changed lanes. The sedan changed lanes. When
he cut between cars and switched back to the left lane, his tail passed
another vehicle using the lane to its right, holding its position three
car lengths behind.

Jack grabbed his CIA cell, then put it down and used his personal cell phone to dial the direct line the president had given him
to reach FBI Director Hampton. "Director. Jack McCall. I'm on my

way to meet Agent Smith. Someone's pinned a tail on me. Tell me it wasn't you."

"The president countermanded your refusal of protection."

When his CIA phone on the seat started ringing, Jack had no choice but to hang up on Hampton.

"We spoke to the rental agent," Rex said right away. "It's scrolling now. He rented the house sixty days ago to a Barry Jones. The rental was arranged by phone and Jones paid in advance by wire transfer for six months and requested the agent send the key to an Arlington PO box. The wire transfer came from a cash transaction by Barry Jones at the counter in a small bank branch—one with no video. The bank told us wire transfers at the counter from noncustomers are rare. So far that's—wait. Something else is coming. The street address Jones gave the rental agent in a suburb of Chicago is an empty lot."

"What else?"

"The phone company shows no active number at the Harrelson house. The electric company shows usage at maintenance levels for a vacancy. We're six minutes out. What's your ETA?"

"I'm still a minute or so behind you," Jack said. "Call back if you need to talk."

He glanced in the rearview mirror. The tail car had not broken off.


After attaching the velcro straps on an aramid fiber vest, Jack took a position beside Rex Smith at the front door of the Harrelson house. Jack knocked. Four members of an FBI SWAT team were with them. The SWAT agents took up positions near the door, and after Rex checked and found no outside trips or alarms, Jack knocked hard. Again.

"Stop!" Jack shouted when two members of the SWAT team swung back a battering ram to take down the door. "Pick the lock. We want everything here to look as normal as possible in case he returns."

Rex picked the lock, drew his 9-mm Sig Sauer from his belt and stepped back, standard procedure dictating that the SWAT team enters first. The four in the lead held either a Springfield semiautomatic handgun or an HK MP 5/10 machine gun. Once inside the squad took line-of-sight positions to cover all interior doorways, fanned out, and went into every room.

"Mr. McCall. Agent Smith," one of them called, "upstairs, the first bedroom on your right."

Jack and Rex took the stairs two at a time. An AM-180 machine gun bolted to the floor, loaded with a full magazine, quietly aimed through the window directly at the chief justice's white colonial across the street. From that position the 180 could rip through a small crowd like a scythe cutting down spring wheat.

Jack let out a low whistle. "Get your top forensic guys in here, Rex. This is the one place we've found where LW has been. I want every conceivable test run on this gun, the room, the toilets, showers, sinks, faucets, knobs, window sliders, the contents of the drains, everything in the kitchen. And don't miss the trash."

"They know what to do," Rex said.

"Mr. McCall," another agent called out. "There's a note taped behind the door. Your name's on it."

Jack holstered his Sig Sauer, pulled on latex gloves, and carefully peeled the note off the door. It had been composed, like the note left at Jack's house with Rachel's bra, using words cut from magazines and newspapers. Before reading, he turned to Rex.

"LW could be watching us right now. Call in the chopper to search the neighborhood. Assign your squad for ground support."

Before leaving, Rex told one of the SWAT guys to stay with Jack. Jack read the note twice.

Dear Jack:

It's good to know you're hard at work. I have eliminated the chief justice. It appears you continue to be a day late and a dollar short. I took extreme care to prevent leaving any forensic evidence. I doubt you'll find anything useful. I never used the toilet or the kitchen. I wore gloves when I assembled the gun and I sprayed it to dissolve any traces that may have somehow slipped by my careful attention.

You cannot stop my militia. We will restore representative government in America.

Commander LW


"Damn," Jack muttered, handing the note to Rex, who had just came back.

"With your permission," Rex said, "I'll let the ERT read the note. I want them to see that this asshole is thumbing his nose at them."

Jack glared at Rex, his face still tight. "Do it. But remember, other than that the content, even the existence of this note is a secret."

"I'll get back to you after they're finished," Rex said. "May I make another suggestion?"

Jack took a deep breath and eased it out. He had never been sure which was emotionally harder, an assault that became a firefight or one that turned out to be a dry hole.

"I need all the ideas I can get," he said.

"We ought to stake this place out," Rex said. "LW has a reason to come back."

"Do it." Jack said with enough emphasis to add some of his saliva to the crime scene. "I want agents set up with line of sight. Get 'em within a block. Don't use the chief justice's house. LW will be watching that one. Maybe one of the neighbors has a garage we can use. Use a cover story so they won't connect this to LW. Coordinate the effort with the protective detail moving with the chief justice. Let me know as soon as it's up and running."

Rex turned to go. Jack grabbed his shoulder.

"Leave this place like we found it. Order your squad to not speak

of this to anyone. You make the report. Give it only to Director
Hampton. Tell him I want it held, not filed in accordance with normal procedure."

On the way back to the CIA, Jack found himself falling into a
funk. Rex would challenge the FBI's forensics experts, but what had
an hour before appeared to be a trove of leads, now had the cold feel
of a damp, dead-end alley.

# CHAPTER 34

McCall is hanging by his chinny chin chin.
He will be replaced if the LW case is not
solved within seventy-two hours.

—*Washington Web Rumors, June 16*

Jack had just gotten got back to the Bullpen when he received a call
from Director Hampton. Jack started to explain why he had hung up
on him earlier, but Hampton interrupted him.

"Listen," Hampton said, "I just got a call from the producer of
*D.C. Talk.* They've received another communiqué from LW and
Carsten's people want him to read it on the air. I've faxed you a copy.
It should be there. I'm having the original picked up."

"Rachel just brought it to me," Jack said. "Give me a minute."
Rachel read over his shoulder. "I don't see a problem. Let them read
it."

"I agree. We want to keep this bastard talking," Hampton said,
"and that if MSNBC doesn't read them, LW will just find an alter-
native messenger—maybe one of those—"

"You just recapped why I want it read," Jack said. "The communiqués are becoming more frequent. We've got to keep him talking.
He's going to slip up and tell us something that will nail him."

"Jack. I agree, except that I doubt Justice Budson wants a threat
to her family reported on national television."

Jack exhaled slowly. "I see your point. How about we approve

Carsten reading all but the part about Budson's family?" With that agreed, they both hung up.

Fred had been right, Jack realized. He wouldn't want the details for his sister's family to be read on television.

Rachel laid the LW communiqué in the center of the table and read the message aloud.

### A Communiqué from the American Militia to Restore Representative Government:

During his press conference McCall attempted to bait me into coming after him. Did you get that idea from a movie, Jack? No dice. I didn't like your nasty comments, but I understand what you were attempting to do, so I forgive you. In your press conference you said you had a great father. I wish you'd met mine so you'd realize that your father could not have measured up.

Let me take this opportunity to say good night to Justices Budson, Huckaby, and Sanders, as well as Mr. Chief Justice Thomas Evans, also Federal Reserve Governors Nelson, Powers, Capone, Jones, and Busch.

You should all follow the lead of Justice Dunlin and resign. When you do, I will take your name off the list for elimination. If you don't care about your safety, think of your families. I know everything about each of you. An example. Penelope Budson: You have three children, from oldest to youngest, Martha, Bradley, and David. Martha, thirty-two, is married to John Coleman, and they reside on Olive Street in Detroit, together with Budson's grandchildren, Erin and Sharon, ages seven and four. The government cannot indefinitely protect you. They cannot even protect you tomorrow and the next day. The best solution for all of you is to immediately stand down and support representative government.

*Commander LW*

"Notice that he again used the term, 'stand down,'" Colin said, poking the page.

Millet poked the copy as had Colin. "He's saying his daddy can beat up Jack's daddy, as if they were schoolkids. That's what this jerkoff is doing."

"What strikes you about this, Rachel?" Jack asked.

"He's finding the protective surveillance difficult." She wrinkled her brow. "Sure, he's bragging like a schoolboy. But, more important, he's ratcheting up the level of fear and terror, hoping to bully a few into early retirement."

"I'm not done with the timeline yet," Colin said after stopping Jack on the way back to his desk. "But it is looking like one person could be doing it all. I'll know pretty soon."

Before sunrise the next morning, LW was sitting on the ground leaning against the back of his father's headstone, the dark sky pocked with stars. More stars than all the gravestones in all the cemeteries in this great country. Despite the chill from the stone, he always felt safe when he was here. He stared at his black tennis shoes, bit his fingernails, and listened to the crickets. After a while, he spoke aloud to his father.

"The protection around these aristocrats is tight. Late yesterday I walked by the house I'd set up across from Chief Justice Evans. I'd taken a dog I bought at a pet store for a walk on a leash, then turned it loose after it provided my cover. Just as I got there, the FBI was pulling away from the curb. I had planned to save the chief justice for last. I admit that was foolish and melodramatic. It won't happen again, sir."

He ripped out some of the scraggly strands of grass that were growing over the gravestone at an angle that kept them below the blades of the lawnmower.

"Perhaps, we should lie low for six months, Father. They can't keep up around-the-clock protection forever. On the other hand, by then they'll have the vacancies filled, our surveillance would need updating, and they'll have new security procedures in place.

"Their moves. Our countermoves. This is very much like the chess you taught me. I still play you know. I entered the Golden Knights' correspondence tournament you used to play in. I'm into my sixth match. My opponent is really quite good, but not as good as you, Father. Without being under a threat, I recently used the king-side castle move you taught me to reposition my opponent's focus. I expect to win with a few more moves. The victory points from this match will qualify me for the finals."

He sat there another hour, without speaking further. After a while his eyes began tracking the large branches of one of the old gnarly trees whose roots he imagined snaked down into the very coffins. Then he stood and moved around to face his father's name. "You're right, Father. I will stay the course. Like you always taught me, if it goes bad, stand up straight and don't cry."

Colin pinned his completed timeline and map next to their paper graveyard. The squad gathered around.

"It fits!" Colin declared. "These red pins are the sites of the murders. The yellow ones are the locations where LW sent his communiqués."

"Okay," Jack said. "Colin's timeline proves one person could have done it, not that one person did. Should we assume we're looking for only one person? That LW has no militia?"

Frank massaged his chin thoughtfully. "Ever since Nora and I went to Oregon and Cleveland, my instincts have said that LW's a loner. The timing of the killings in Oregon and Cleveland allowed for one person to travel between them, and the descriptions we've gotten are too similar. Ringo's timeline removes any doubts I had."

"In the note LW left at the Harrelson house and in his most recent communiqué, he spoke in the singular," Jack observed. "Saying 'I,' not 'we,' took care to avoid leaving forensic evidence. 'I,' not 'we' have this kind of detail on all the justices. If he had a militia, at least one member would've been with him to help set up that big AM-180, yet he spoke of the assembly in the first person."

Colin scooted back to sit on the table. "I'm the one who has been resisting the idea, but no more. This dude's on his own."

Jack made eye contact with each member of his squad. "Is anyone opposed to assuming LW is a one-man militia?"

"Still," Rachel said, "we need to keep an open mind in case we find something that does suggest he's got help."

"Okay then," Jack summarized, "for now, no militia. We have a serial killer of high government officials who has conned himself into thinking he serves some noble purpose."

Rachel reported that she and Millet had narrowed the list to fewer than twenty passengers.

After the meeting broke, Jack stood in front of the paper graveyard of dead officials that he had been looking at off and on all day. Something kept squirming in some dark place at the back of his mind, but he just couldn't bring it into the light. He kept staring, but the lurking thought stayed just out of reach.

"Most of the murders were here in D.C. or within a day's drive," Jack said to Rachel who had come over to stand with him. "I'm guessing that the D.C. murders didn't require LW to travel."

They rearranged the pictures so that the photos of the victims killed within driving distance of D.C. were in one row, pinning the others off to one side.

"If LW lives near here only Taylor in Cleveland and Breen in Oregon would have required him to travel. We're assuming he flew."

Rachel moved the idea forward. "Living here would have also simplified the surveillance of his targets."

"Makes sense," said Millet, who sneezed and wiped his nose on his shirtsleeve. "And it would explain why we found phony passengers on just the flights that fit what you're calling the-out-of-town murders. It's not rock hard but it's more than a guess."

"Can you go back and see if any of your remaining twenty took an earlier flight to Cleveland or the West Coast within the prior year?" Jack asked Millet. "It could've been LW on surveillance trips."

"What we're doing now with the flights is all within a known time span, framed by the dates of the murders. To do what you're asking now would have no time frame. LW could have made those trips weeks or even months before the murders. Think number of passengers times all those flights, over all those months, even years, and the jobs gets too big unless you can get us access to the airline's master computer. If the airlines will cooperate, they could search the names we give them to see if they have ever had a passenger with those names."

Rachel agreed to speak with the FBI Director to see if there was a precedent for the cooperation of the airlines without a court order. It would take a few days at least to get that clearance, and they all knew that if they did get it, they would need to share parts of their investigation with a broad group of people untrained in detection.

They were bogged down with paper pushing. Right now, that was their best choice, but Jack didn't like it.

# CHAPTER 35

The president's political opponents are pressuring him
to appoint an independent commission to look
into McCall's mishandling of the LW case.

—*Washington Post, June 17*

On June seventeenth, with the early sun coloring the gray morning sky, LW left home. He spent a good part of the morning driving to Pittsburgh where he caught a plane for Dallas, the home of Federal Reserve Governor Harold Capone. Harry wasn't related to the late Alphonse "Scarface" Capone of Chicago fame but, of the two, LW believed the man he called squinty-eyed Texas Harry to be the bigger criminal.

Capone had first been appointed to complete the remaining twelve years of a retiring Fed governor's term and, after that had expired, he accepted his own full fourteen-year appointment to the board. LW was infuriated that someone never elected by the people could wield such great power for so long over the financial health of the nation.

For two weeks, earlier in the year, LW watched Harry Capone. During that time he discovered that Capone was a man of decidedly regular habits. When in Dallas, he always arrived home by five, and immediately walked for forty-five minutes on the treadmill in his exercise room. After that he swam for thirty minutes in his backyard pool. This behavior had also been written about by a Dallas newspaper.

LW had also found the perfect venue, a hill five hundred yards behind Capone's house. For the shot he selected the pool rather than the exercise room. In the house Capone would go down under the window sill, but in the pool his scope would allow confirmation of the kill.

For this operation, LW carried a driver's license identifying himself as George Marks from Sharon, Pennsylvania. He had studied maps of Sharon and researched the name of its newspaper, main stores, banks, and schools so that he could appear highly familiar with the town. He even carried a marked-up golf scorecard from the Sharon Country Club.

After a reduced-price early dinner in Dallas, a tip for frugal consumers he had learned from his mother during their inseparable years after his father died, he paid cash and left the restaurant at four thirty.

His first stop was a you-store-it, you-lock-it storage garage where he had previously rented a unit that couldn't be seen from the office, but could be seen from across the street. He donned latex gloves, opened the storage unit, and removed two guns and a boom box with a remote control, all rolled inside a blanket.

He had outfitted a Tango 51 with a threaded suppressor and .308 Winchester cartridges. He also carried an Ingram MAC-10, .45-caliber rapid-fire submachine gun. The plan was to leave the Tango 51 on the hill, but keep the Ingram until he had safely cleared the area, then dispose of it before returning to the airport.

A street on the back side of the hill provided a quiet, private place to park. From there he walked up the hill carrying the guns rolled in their storage blanket to a point where he could see over Capone's back fence.

The view into Capone's yard reminded him that the grass, nourished by the chemicals that polluted America's ground water, was always greener in the yards of the rich.

Capone was already swimming his laps, with two suits, probably FBI agents, continually circling the pool. LW had expected agents to be watching Capone up close. To date LW had given the authorities no reason to anticipate he could strike from distance.

LW believed that most people working for the FBI were devoted to America. He didn't wish to kill agents. Not unless it became necessary, and if it came to that it would be their own fault. Next, he inserted a tape of sporadic gunfire into the boom box, and slid it into a bush on Capone's side of the knoll. He then moved fifty yards to the north, got on the ground, and rolled over the crest to behind a patch of scrub brush. He would take the shot from Capone's side of the hill so his silhouette would be against the hill, not the horizon.

Next, he unrolled the blanket, assembled his Tango, and brought the scope to his face. The view through the scope suddenly darkened. His heart raced. He lowered the scope. *Shit. It's only a cloud passing in front of the sun. Get a grip, asshole.*

He understood feeling a bit jumpy. After all, there were people trying to prevent him from completing his historic mission. People who, like the shadows from the clouds, were sneaking up on him, people being led by Jack McCall. He had tried to befriend McCall, even gave him a chance to join him, a chance to be a patriot and help save America. But Jack had hurled insults at his father and his cause. He knew right then, that he would kill McCall.

The thought of having resolved the dilemma of Jack McCall calmed his nerves. After reversing his red baseball cap, putting the bill to the back, he continued watching through the scope as Capone swam back and forth from one end of his pool to the other. Back and forth, back and forth like a bloated dolphin without the fluid grace.

When Capone finished his laps, he stood in the shallow end, tilted his head back, and ran his hands hard over his wet hair, plastering the remaining strands to his scalp.

Capone stepped onto the first step on the pool. Now. LW brought the rifle to his shoulder, the scope to his eye.

One of the agents threw Capone a towel. He stood on the step drying himself, then blotted his face and tossed the towel onto the nearest pool chair.

LW squeezed off a single round that blossomed into a small red boutonniere on Capone's forehead.

The justice spun around in an uncoordinated ballet of death. His arms lashed out as he fell back into the pool, a jagged red stain coloring the water as it refilled the hole Capone's ruined face had smashed into its surface.

The two agents immediately drew their guns and began scurrying about like Keystone Kops on a flickering silent silver screen. Two more agents ran out from the house, the first restrained Mrs. Capone while the other jumped into the pool to remove her limp husband.

When the agents were looking in his general direction LW pressed the button on the remote. Upon an unexpected sound, people instinctively turn their heads toward that sound.

At that moment, LW dropped the Tango 51 and rolled back over the crest of the hill, stood, brushed himself off quickly, and trotted down toward his car. The gunfire tape went silent just as he reached the road.

Ten minutes later, LW tossed the Ingram in a Dumpster behind a Taco Bell. Inside the fast food restaurant, he flushed his surgical gloves in their bathroom, using a paper towel to push the flusher and turn the knob. After five minutes of driving at the speed limit, he turned onto Interstate 45 south.

Later, he pulled off the highway at the exit for Huntsville, a small town approximately three quarters of the way to Houston. There, in a vacant lot he set fire to the car he had stolen from the long-term parking lot at the airport in Dallas. It had rained the night before and the car had been clean. The owner would likely not return for several more days. After walking a few blocks, he flagged down one of Huntsville's few taxis to take him the rest of the way to the Houston Airport.

*Where are you Jack McCall? You told the nation you were coming for me.*

LW laughed, leaned back, and closed his eyes.

# CHAPTER 36

Fed Governor Harold Capone has been shot dead at his Dallas home.
The world waits to confirm the obvious: LW has struck again.

—*Mel Carsten, D.C. Talk, June 17*

Frank leaned against the Bullpen wall and spoke to Jack. "I'm not so sure we should've authorized Carsten to read this newest communiqué. It stinks of a recruiting message."

"His story is burning a hole in his gut," Jack replied. "He's longing for people to say they understand. That they agree. That he should keep killing. We learn something more every time this sick bastard runs his mouth. We must trust the American people to take what they hear for what it is, the rambling of a lunatic."

"Listen up," Rachel said, turning up the volume on their television as *D.C. Talk* returned from a commercial break.

Carsten stood in front of the cameras holding a sheet of paper. He began to read:

### A Communiqué from the American Militia to Restore Representative Government:

I'm proud to announce the ranks of the American Militia to Restore Representative Government continue to grow. Today, another right-thinking American became our newest volunteer by eliminating the unelected aristocrat Harry Capone.

The recruit is apparently a crack shot. Welcome to the militia, whoever you are. I'm not sure when we will meet, but for now it's okay if we don't. You know our mission.

To my friend Jack McCall: this makes your job harder, doesn't it? I'm beginning to enjoy our little game. Will America continue on the path to an aristocracy or return to the representative government envisioned by our fathers? Which of us is America rooting for now?

*Commander LW*


Jack turned the volume off and called the FBI detail that had been protecting Capone. After he hung up, he brought his squad together and told them what he had learned about the shooting.

"The shot that killed Capone required considerable skill. Let's brainstorm the possibilities of who might have been the shooter and then qualify them on their merits."

Rachel turned from the pinboard. "In my mind, there's no doubt that LW was the shooter," she said while moving the picture of Harold Capone to the row of victims, their working hypothesis said would have required LW to fly. "LW did it." After a deep breath, she lowered her voice. "He's using his sharpshooting skills now because the increased security keeps him from getting close to his targets."

"It may not have been either LW or a recruit," Colin said. "It could've been someone else with a grudge against Capone, using LW for cover. His wife, a lover, somebody he owed a gambling debt. Any of the reasons Americans kill each other every day."

"It's also possible," Frank said while refilling their coffee cups, the handle of the pot lost in his massive hand, "he's really got a militia or at least a few cuckoos willing to do his bidding. The sharpshooter might have already been a member of his militia. If so, his communiqué is either misdirection or a solicitation for more recruits."

Nora stood while Jack furiously wrote on the flip chart, then said,

"The shooter could've just been some wacko copycat wanting to see his killing on the front page."

Jack scribbled, "copycat," also adding "recruit" to their growing list of possibilities. Then said, "It's possible some moron could have joined him."

Millet quit scratching himself. "It could have been someone with a rage against some ruling by the Federal Reserve. There are those who blame the economic slowdowns on the Fed's fucking obsession with inflation—including me. Productivity gains resulting from technological advances would have continued to offset inflationary pressures. The economy had been running so good for so long the Fed just couldn't keep their fingers in their butts."

"For the sake of argument we should include the possibility that the killer simply got the wrong house and intended to kill someone else. The backs of houses don't show addresses." Jack stepped back to the flip chart and wrote: wrong victim.

"Okay, we've got the possibles. Let's trim them down to the probables. We need this investigation to continue as a rifle shot." After a grin, he added, "No pun intended. Come on. Come on. Talk it out. Knock out one of these theories."

"I think we can eliminate the likelihood of someone shooting the wrong person."

"Why, Colin?"

"This killer chose a good rifle, dedicated himself to develop the skill to hit a man's head from five hundred yards, even included the use of a boom box to aid his escape. All this suggests a careful, intelligent professional. Shooting the wrong person at a wrong house after using a scope to get a good look suggests an idiot. I can't see this shooter being both brilliant and stupid. Is there anyone who disagrees?"

When no one spoke, Jack drew a broad line through what he knew had been the weakest choice on the chart—wrong victim.

Rachel kicked off her black flats. Jack had noticed she often did this when she was deep in thought. Then she proposed they reject Colin's contribution of a personal grudge killing.

"The FBI report indicated the Capones were a loving couple," she said. "The background check didn't indicate either had any problems."

"Does anyone disagree with Rachel?"

"Except for not being married, Justice Roberts had that same image until we found him dead in his mistress's condo," Colin reminded them.

"Everyone knows that we have these officials under tight security," Frank said. "Few hit men would have taken this job at any price. Let's toss that theory, but ask the FBI to check for a meaningful change in Mrs. Capone's finances."

"How does that sit with you, Colin?" Jack asked.

"I'll go along."

Jack tapped the flip chart. "What about these others?"

Rachel repeated her position. "We had good reason to conclude LW worked alone. I've heard nothing that argues to the contrary other than LW's own claim."

Rachel moved to an empty chair near the flip chart, and sat on one shoeless foot. With the motion of leaning in, her breasts swelled to fill the opening at the top of her blouse. "Is there any support for any of these other possibilities?"

"Let's talk some more about why it's reasonable to conclude LW has no militia," Frank suggested. "I know we talked before about the descriptions we got in Cleveland, in Oregon, and elsewhere, but our conclusions weren't solid then, they still aren't. Our thinking on this has been like nailing Jell-O to the wall. Is there something else that supports LW being a loner?"

Millet stood and scratched his belly with both hands. "Can I take over for a minute?"

"It's all yours, Millet." Jack put down his marking pen and sat at the table.

"You guys are the investigators," Millet began. "Let me throw out a question and you all react to it. Okay, here's the deal: each of you is LW and you have a militia."

Millet began prowling around the table, talking faster as he circled. "Your self-appointed mission is to eliminate the justices of the U.S. Supreme Court and the governors of the Federal Reserve System. Are you going to dink along as LW has, killing one every week or so? If not, what's your plan?"

Millet stopped circling near the head of the table and fixed them with a professorial glare. "Come on! Participate! Think out loud. You're LW! You've got a militia! What's your MO?"

"I would've used my militia to shorten the early-stage surveillance work," Colin said to start the discussion. "That would also make the information from each surveillance more current when I needed it. Once the killing plans were set, I'd proceed like the American Mafia did to eliminate the old Sicilian Mustache Petes. I'd kill them all within a couple of days, if possible the same day. I'd assign each target to the member of my militia who surveilled that target."

"That'd shut them both down immediately, Frank added. "The Fed and the Court. And all the killing would be done before—"

"Before security could be enhanced," Colin said, to finish the thought.

"Exactly," Frank said. "I don't need to call for these officials to stand down. I could send one communiqué with my demands, threatening to kill any replacements."

Both Frank and Colin, who had tag teamed the theory, threw Millet self-satisfied looks.

"And," Nora added, "I'd be out of the country before Jack McCall has been appointed to catch me."

Rachel, who had sat quietly nodding her head like a bobble doll, said, "We know LW is intelligent. If he had a militia and he didn't do it that way, he'd have to be a fool. LW is a lone wolf, whatever the hell the initials stand for."

"Anybody?" Jack asked.

No one spoke.

"Okay, we continue to treat LW as a lone wolf until we have a reason to think otherwise. And when and if we have a reason, it will be our reason and not something LW puts out."

It was nearly midnight when LW grabbed a pair of scissors and a flashlight, and left his home. Despite the hour, he knew where he had to go before he could sleep. Thirty minutes later, he was kneeling beside his father's gravestone.

"I thought you'd like to know that we've eliminated seven aristocrats and forced one to resign. That's eight down and eight remaining. The other casualties were necessary to dial up the terror. The protection around the aristocrats has increased. If they don't start resigning soon, I'll kick up the terror by adding in some of their grand kiddies."

He set the lighted flashlight on the ground and began using the scissors to clip the unruly blades of grass that were assaulting the base of his father's grave marker. His previous hand pulling of the rebellious strands had left a clumpy look. Mom had always kept the house neat for Dad.

Before he left, he stooped, struck a match and cremated the fake identification of George Marks, the assassin of Fed Governor Harry Capone.

*Your birthday's coming soon, Father. I have something special planned. A surprise.*

# CHAPTER 37

LW has Wall Street in a free fall, the Dow has
dropped over 400 points since his first killing.

—CNBC

It had been another early morning followed by a long day, and Jack
saw fatigue on the faces of his squad. Colin had dark circles under
his eyes. Rachel's hair had the look that came from trading styling
time for a few extra minutes in bed. Only Millet, who always looked
disheveled, looked normal—normal for Millet.

As for himself, when Jack felt exhausted, the lines in his face that
had developed from a lifetime of laughter and sorrow, deepened. His
sexy neighbor, Janet Parker, had once told him that lines on a man's
face added character, while on a woman they were simply wrinkles.

Millet and Rachel continued to work their passenger lists while
Colin brought his timeline current to include the Capone killing
and the place from which LW had sent his most recent communiqué. The logistics still supported the thesis that this was a one-man
operation.

It was after seven, and Jack stood at their paper graveyard, challenging himself to figure another way to configure the victim's pictures to suggest a different chain of thought.

Rachel came over to tell him that Frank and Nora were on their
way back from Texas. "They landed at Bolling," she said. "They're on
the George Washington Parkway right now."

"Shit," Millet said, "they just left late last night."

"I didn't even know they'd gone," said Colin. "I walked out last night with Nora. I thought she went home."

"Frank called me last night," Jack explained. "He suggested they fly to Dallas so they could be at Capone's house first thing this morning."

Thirty minutes later, Frank and Nora were reporting on their trip to Dallas.

"Capone was taken out by a rifle shot from about five hundred yards," Nora said. "For obvious reasons no initials were carved in his forehead, but we found no reason to conclude other than what we did yesterday: LW shot Capone."

"Did you find anybody who saw anything?" Jack asked.

"We spoke to a Mr. and Mrs. Converse," Frank told them. "The Converses live in a house across the street from the back side of the hill from which Capone had been shot. They saw a man coming down the hill carrying what looked like a blanket."

"We separated Mr. and Mrs. Converse," Nora added. "Each of their descriptions agreed with what we had from our earlier witnesses."

"Bingo," Rachel said. "He's a loner."

"Not to change the subject," asked Frank, "but what's happening at the Harrelson house?"

"Forensics called from the bureau," Jack said. "They've finished, and found nothing. Another dead end. The observation team remains in place watching both the chief justice's home and the Harrelson house in the hope that LW returns."

"Let's not get off Dallas just yet," Colin protested. "Did the guy who was carrying the blanket walk off or drive? What about the make of the car?"

"He drove away, all right," Frank said. "But neither Mr. nor Mrs. Converse are car buffs. They could only remember that it was a dark-color, not new, but not more than a few years old. Mr. Converse thought it was a coupe."

Colin scowled. "Great. That narrows it to only a couple million cars in Dallas. Did the agents at Capone's see anything?"

Frank shook his head. But before he could open his mouth, Nora interrupted. "One more thing," she said, grinning. "Both the Converses said the man coming down off the hill wore . . . anybody?"

"A red baseball cap!" the team chorused.

"Bingo!" Both Frank and Nora said at once.

Frank said, "The Dallas FBI office is trying to trace the Tango and the Winchester shell case. They had both been wiped clean. The Dallas Police Department and the FBI are coordinating an effort to check the retail stores hoping to find a clerk who sold a boom box with a remote control. A buyer with a different description would suggest LW has some kind of help."

"What's been going on here?" Nora asked, taking off her earrings.

Pointing his water bottle at Millet, Jack said, "Update us on your lists."

"Rachel and I are walking on his shadow," Millet began. "Ain't that a cool way of saying it? I heard that last night watching one of those old movies you dig so much, Jackman."

"Millet. The lists."

"Okay. Okay. Lighten up. We've shaved the passenger lists for the Oregon and Cleveland killings down to six and eight."

He passed a copy to each of them. "Those passengers made this list based on two things: The height, weight, and age details we found for these passengers generally fit the sketchy details we've gotten from the witnesses, and we have been unable to confirm their whereabouts at the times of the killings. The names with asterisks appear to be phonies."

Colin glanced up, "Any names on both lists?"

"No, but each list has one passenger we suspect is bogus."

Colin pointed, "These two? Kimble in Oregon and Campbell flying into Cleveland?"

"Way to go, Superfly," Millet said. "I just told you the phonies are the ones with the asterisks!"

Jack turned to Nora, "Call that reservations woman you spoke to at the resort on the Oregon coast. Find out if she recognizes the name John Kimble."

Colin and Millet watched Nora as she walked to her desk, her jacket draped back over one shoulder. Jack cleared his throat loudly to recapture their attention.

While Nora made the call, Jack had Colin call Rex Smith to report the twelve remaining names, including the times for establishing their whereabouts. Also the two phony names to see if the bureau could scare up anything that would establish those two were real people.

"We've got a winner," Nora declared hustling back to join the others. "Peggy Fallow says that a John Kimble called her a couple of times. Kimble told her he lived in Southern California and wanted the honeymoon cottage the same days the Breens had it reser— "

"Yeah," said Colin, "sure, he wanted to confirm the Breens had arrived."

"You got that right," Nora said. "This Kimble told Peggy Fallow he'd come to see the honeymoon cottage, but he never showed. She has no phone number for him. She'd chalked him up to just another sales lead that petered out. She promised not to repeat our conversation to anyone."

"That gives us three aliases," Rachel said. "Barry Jones rents the house across from Chief Justice Evans, John Kimble in Oregon where Mr. and Mrs. Breen were killed, and Robert Campbell in Cleveland when the hit was made on Taylor and his family."

"Let's not get too proud of ourselves just yet," Jack cautioned. "This only means something if we can parlay these aliases into one real man. Colin, have Rex Smith check California and Oregon for a marriage license or a wedding announcement for a John Kimble to marry anyone. This could be a coincidence and Kimble could be legit."

Jack looked into the bleary eyes of each member of his team.

"We're creeping up on this guy. We've got to suck it up and stay in our full-court press."

There was no need to go into any detail about what might happen if they didn't. They all knew. He could see it in their faces, and he was also aware that in the end, everything depended on him.

A little after six, Rex Smith stormed through the door and joined the others at the table. "Turns out the forensic guys did find something at the Harrelson house," he said. "LW had applied a heat-generating chemical around the jambs of the front and back doors. When we opened the door, we disturbed it. He could have only seen that stuff through an infrared scope."

"The army developed that scope for our special forces," Colin explained. "The planners called it FLIR for forward-looking infrared. It's part of the equipment package being developed for the digital soldier of the future."

Rex frowned. "Do you want me to shut down the stakeout of the Harrelson house? We could always—"

Jack interrupted him. "What's the current status?"

"We've applied new chemical to try and make it look like it did before," Rex answered. "With the cooperation of a second neighbor we've established sight lines to the areas LW would need to be positioned to check that chemical using a FLIR scope. Given his trip to Dallas, LW may have been too busy to recheck the Harrelson house since we found it."

"Stay with it. Give him no avenue of escape."

"That's how it is now."

"Good work, Rex. We were about to call Director Hampton. Colin's got the details on another assignment I'd like you to ramrod. It'll require the help of some FBI research people for a few hours."

"Already approved. My orders are that you're my only assignment. I have high-priority access to whatever resources I might need to carry out your orders."

It occurred to Jack that having the president as your blocking back certainly opened the holes. It also eliminated all the excuses if he didn't get the ball into the end zone.

Colin and Rex headed for the sitting area in the middle of the room.

"Rachel," Jack said, "get with the folks down the hall. We need to contact every shooting range within a hundred miles of Dallas, and two hundred miles of D.C. It takes lots of practice to hit the back of a man's head at five hundred yards. Have each range give us a list of all their members. If they keep a list of their nonmember shooters, we want that as well."

"How far back?"

"We need current memberships and a list of members who have dropped out within the past ten years. Do the same for nonmembers. We'll pick up the lists. See Rex for manpower. Get those lists combined into one master list broken down into subcategories: members, former members, and nonmembers. Show names and the dates each used the range. Group them by years. I want full names, not just first initials. LW should be somewhere on those lists."

"What do you want us to do?" Frank asked.

"You two have flown to Oregon and Cleveland, then last night to Dallas, go home. Sleep. Keep your cell phones close. I'll let you know if anything pops."

"We're okay, Jack." Frank protested.

"Jack's right," Nora told her partner. "We'll be more productive." She grabbed Frank's arm and started him toward the door.

"I've got Rex off on his assignment," Colin said after coming back into the Bullpen and approaching Jack. "What next?"

Jack held up two fingers. "Contact General Crook to find out if it's feasible to trace the sales of FLIR scopes. It's military technology so the general should be able to tell us if that trail can be followed. And catch up with Rachel. We also need lists of public figures, college professors, politicians, entertainers, and candidates for national office with a history of railing against the Fed or the

Supreme Court." He held Colin's forearm while he thought, then added, "Say five or more times. Have the lists grouped according to the number of times each spoke out. I also want a copy of their articles or speeches."

"Over what period of time?"

"What do you suggest?"

"Well, we're putting LW's age at thirty to thirty-five years old," Colin mused. "Impressionable years for intellectual subject matter start around age ten. Let's go back thirty years just in case he's a bit older than we're thinking."

"Do it. I want an estimate of how long it will take to develop that list. If more manpower or resources are needed, tell Rachel to get them. If she needs me to pull strings, have her tell me."

Jack returned to his gray, government-issue chair, leaned back, and stared at the ceiling.

*We're getting closer, you son of a bitch.*

# CHAPTER 38

LW toys with McCall in a macabre game in
which he sees America's future as the spoils.

—*Mel Carsten, D.C. Talk*

Jack gave up on sleep, brewed some coffee, and sat down at his chessboard. His opponent, Harry, had posted his next move. It appeared
that Harry was attempting to checkmate Jack's black king within the
next five moves. Jack's own planned checkmate on Harry could take
only four moves. Jack took his next move, and posted it as Nb4 on
the Chess Forum.

Before the sun came up, Jack pushed through the door into the
Bullpen and found Millet hunched over his computer. For the next
several hours the whiz worked in silence except for periodically
swearing at one of the cups of hot chocolate that had betrayed him
by turning cold.

Jack had chosen Millet in part because of his intellectual tenac-
ity. The man would not stop once a computer project captured his
mind.

At five thirty, Jack heard someone come in and looked up to see
Rachel. She mumbled good morning, dropped her purse on her
desk, and went back out the door, assumedly to check on the round-
the-clock development of the lists of shooters and dissidents.

A little after six, the phone rang. Clancy Stafford, the president's
chief of staff, had a deep, rich voice smooth enough to play the lead
in Rodgers and Hammerstein's *Oklahoma*.

Clancy's message was simple. "The president wants to see you at four thirty this afternoon."

"Go right in," Ms. Gruber said, opening the door. "The president and the others are already inside."

*Others?*

President Schroeder's bloodshot eyes told Jack that he, too, had been putting in long hours. Clancy Stafford and the directors of the four primary federal intelligence agencies, Miller, Hampton, Quartz, and General Crook were seated. The president was already pacing.

NSA Director Quartz, who always dressed to the nines, wore a black suit with gray pinstripes, a gray display hanky peaking from his breast pocket like a cautious mouse about to leave its hole. General Crook looked as if he had skipped the morning trim that usually kept his wiry mustache as precise as the edge on a bayonet.

The always tight, slick-looking bun in CIA Director Harriet Miller's hair had more than the usual number of escaped strands.

"Thanks for coming on such short notice, Jack," the president said. "We need an update. I know about your finding LW's setup across from the home of Chief Justice Evans. The Supreme Court is being held together by little more than the strength of his personality. His loss may well have shut down the Court in a more profound way than a temporary inability to seat six for the required quorum. Bring it all together for us, Jack."

"The bottom line, sir, we think we're close. We don't yet know LW's real name. We have a few aliases he has used, but that does little more than confirm we're on his trail."

General Crook, his voice dry as beach sand, said, "What supports the view that you've cut his trail?"

President Schroeder stopped pacing and stood with his hands clasped behind him.

"We believe LW is operating alone," Jack said. "No militia. To us, LW means Lone Wolf." Then he reviewed the physical description they had for LW.

"You've just described a good percentage of the men who walk past the White House every day," Fred Hampton said, after Jack had finished.

"True. Still, it does eliminate other descriptions. Since he killed Capone in Dallas, we've added that LW is an accomplished marksman."

"So you believe his claim of a volunteer recruit is bogus?" Quartz asked, scoffingly. "You see this LW as one man dashing back and forth across the country alone killing officials? I don't know about the rest of you, but for me that dog don't hunt."

"For a long time I shared your hesitance, Director Quartz," Jack told him. "That's why, at the start, we assumed the militia existed, but over time our thinking changed. The manner of each assassination required only one person, and Colin Stewart has developed a timeline that allows for one man to have committed all the killings. We've found air passengers flying alone under aliases that fit that timeline. We've reduced the number of uncleared passengers to a little over a dozen, including those aliases."

"Why don't we just pick up the whole lot and shake 'em out later?" Quartz persisted, before poking his mouse hanky deeper into his breast pocket. "We've got to stop these killings."

The president ignored Quartz and kept his focus on Jack.

"We could do that," Jack replied, "but I doubt we'd find our guy. We're all but certain the male passengers with phony names was LW. We need to stop him not scare him off so he can come back later.

"We believe LW lives within a reasonable drive of D.C.," Jack went on. "We also believe his background includes military, intelligence, or law enforcement training. This is consistent with his use of the term 'stand down,' his sharpshooting skill, and his ability to get black market guns, explosives, and fake identification. Various police departments and federal agencies, including Alcohol, Tobacco and Firearms, are pressuring their snitches for the sellers of these items. Given the time needed for the surveillance of his targets, we estimate LW has been planning all this at least two years. Assuming that's true, any leads about his purchasing weapons and false identification are probably cold. Still, those efforts continue."

Jack could feel the doubt coming from these leaders of the intelligence community. From the start, Quartz had been strongly opposed to Jack being in charge of this investigation. Harriet and the general remained supportive, but the pressure had grown intense. Fred Hampton, a team player who hated the politics of it all, would do his job properly, but otherwise remained somewhat aloof after the FBI had not been the lead. To stay in the saddle, Jack had to sell the president. Having said that, politics were fickle, and television had convinced the American people that any problem should be solved in an hour, two at the most. Without clear results soon, someone's head would have to roll. Someone's? Hell. It would be Jack's head and he knew it.

"Your agencies are putting together lists of current and former agents and military personnel who have shown a pattern or tendency for violent behavior," Jack continued. "Current personnel are being eliminated through confirming their whereabouts at the times of the killings. Former personnel are taking longer."

Quartz leaned down to rub out a smear on the polished toe of his wingtip. "Are you suggesting this LW is a federal agent or a member of our armed forces?"

"We hope not, but we can't dismiss it on blind pride. LW is knowledgeable about things that could well have been learned through such service."

Jack uncrossed his legs and sat back, pausing to meet the eyes of the president and each of the directors before going on. "We believe LW has been negatively influenced by his father. We had just begun developing that angle when Clancy called to arrange this meeting."

"It seems," Bob Quartz said through a carnivore grin, "that you're making a lot of assumptions about weapons and ID, that he has no militia, and so on and so forth, without a full investigation."

Jack fought off his rising irritation with Quartz's condescending tone.

"None of us want this to settle into a multiyear investigation," Jack replied, straining to keep his voice even. "We're doing just what the president ordered. We leave procedural leads and heavy manpower tasks to the FBI. My squad follows our instincts. That requires we make assumptions, but we do not fall in love with them. To the contrary, we continue to reassess and refine as we go. In general terms, our efforts are more like that of a small covert foreign operation than a full-blown domestic investigation."

"Could this be the work of foreign terrorists?" Harriet Miller asked.

"It's always possible. Early on we all assumed that, but we quickly put the thought on the back burner."

"And why is that?"

"Because none of your agencies or those of our international friends have heard the increased electronic chatter we commonly experience either just before or after major acts of terrorism. Neither the profiles we've developed of LW nor the analysis of his communiqués suggest someone from the Middle East or any other region of the world. Furthermore, the wording of the note LW left in the Harrelson house across from the chief justice's residence reflects a decidedly American sense of humor."

Jack turned to address the president, whose facial features sagged enough to show the demands of his office. "As you said, Mr. President, we started out knowing nothing about this LW or his militia. We've used instincts and assumptions to narrow the field. We think we're on the right track, but I cannot report that with certainty."

Schroeder rubbed his hands together. "Everything you've told us seems well thought out. I know you're still looking for a needle in a haystack, but it sounds as if you're reducing the size of the haystack. What can we do to help?"

"Continue to have your agencies do what they're already doing, Mr. President. If we can keep the targets safe for the next week or so, we may be able to get this job finished without any more deaths. This is far from a promise, but another week or so may do it."

"Some of these folks here think the country could use some reassurance that we're making progress," the president said. "That it might take the jitters out of the market. We've been discussing the benefits of having you do another press conference."

Silence hung in the air like hot breath on a cold day.

"If you order it, sir," Jack said after a pause. "I'll do it, but if you're asking for my opin—"

"That's exactly what I'm doing." Schroeder's eyes were intent on Jack's. "What's your opinion?"

"A press conference would not be wise from the perspective of catching LW, as for the politics of it, that's not my area."

Clancy Stafford rested his head back into his interlaced fingers. His speech still smacked more of his self-made industrialist background than his later-in-life college years. "Why would a little old press conference keep us from catching this guy?"

Jack had feared from the start that the hunt for LW could turn into a massive political sideshow which would become the Achilles' heel of his investigation. He quickly gathered his thoughts before replying.

"First, it would deflect my focus at a critical time when things are happening fast. Second, to give a press conference and not tell America we're close would accomplish little in the way of what you're after. Third, to hold a press conference to assure America we are getting close would also warn LW to exercise more caution at a time when it appears his success may be making him cocky and, hopefully, careless."

Sam Schroeder had always been a man strong enough to stand against the shrill voices of partisanship. Jack's confidence was growing that the president would continue to stand with him. He also knew that time had become as much the enemy as LW.

"We don't want LW closing up shop." Jack turned back to the president. "We don't need another Carlos the Jackal to chase around the world for God knows how long. I want this madman feeling safe, feeling superior. If in the short run we look inept, so be it. I want

LW to think we aren't getting close until he puts his nose on the cheese and we spring the trap."

"But—"

"No buts, Clancy." The president said, interrupting his chief of staff. "Politics is our concern, not Jack's. There'll be no press conference for him. If the heat goes up, we'll grin and bear it. Ultimately, the best politics will be to catch this guy." The president turned his gaze from Clancy Stafford back to Jack. "You look like you're chewing on something else. Let's have it."

Jack had been close to saying it several times. Now he did. "Mr. President, right at the start, CNN reported that the six of you met to decide to form my squad. Even my name and Rachel Johnstone's were reported. Today, I have shared everything we know. It will damage our efforts if any part of what we have been discussing appears in the media."

Bob Quartz slapped the arm of the couch. "McCall, are you accusing us of leaking stories to the media?"

"Quartz, I'm a little fed up with your—"

"You can't talk to me like that. I'm the national security advisor."

"Bob," General Crook said, "all Jack is saying is that the six of us met and the next morning CNN reported some of the content of our meeting. That is a fact, not an accusation."

"True enough, General," the president said. "The fact remains that CNN got something only we had. Bob, from the beginning your actions and some of your public statements have put you at odds with the rest of us on this matter. Contrarian views can be healthy. But people who hold those views can be too zealous. I think we're ready to adjourn. Bob, on the way out tell Gruber to schedule you to come back in later today."

Director Quartz stood, snorted audibly, and started toward the door.

"Hold on Bob," the president said. "Before any of you leave, let me say this: None of you are to speak of this meeting to anyone in your agencies or families. There are to be no notes from the meeting. No exceptions! Director Quartz, I am deadly serious about this. If a comma from this meeting is reported by the media, I will launch a relentless investigation to identify which of you to castrate. Or a similar fate if it's you, Harriet."

The president smiled, but Jack knew he had just witnessed a clear threat of political reprisal. And, he knew the president meant the threat.

# CHAPTER 39

It's been reported that McCall has talked President
Schroeder into giving him more time.

—CNN

Jack left the White House and, despite the hour, went back to Langley. The short drive through the trees off Dolly Madison Boulevard made the route into the CIA headquarters seem like the entrance to a different world. A world always preparing for a life-and-death situation, or experiencing one, or recovering from one, or being called to Capitol Hill to explain the agency's actions, or to receive a tongue lashing from senators striving to extract political points from the hides of the intelligence community.

He found Frank Wade sitting alone with his feet on his desk.

"Rachel sent everyone home at seven," Frank said. "The latest estimate for our list of shooters is tomorrow mid-afternoon, so she figured we ought to try to get some sleep."

"What about the lists of dissidents?"

"Those will take longer, but hopefully we'll also get them tomorrow." Frank swung his feet off his desk and stood. "I know you're tired, so blow me off if you wanna head home and crash, but I thought you might like to get a beer and relax for a while."

"Let's do it," Jack told him. "I never get to sleep before about midnight no matter how tired I am."

Jack followed Frank to a classy, quiet lounge on the D.C. side of the Potomac River. The place had a comfortable feel with canned lighting and booths covered in padded burgundy, the air dense with the smell of popcorn and the songs of Sinatra.

"The usual," Frank hollered toward the barkeep.

"Damn good idea," Jack said, "I needed this."

"Figured you might."

"You and Nora have been just incredible."

"We appreciate your not treating us as peons because we're locals."

"You're still here 'cause you're doing the job." Jack reached over and tapped mugs with Frank. "How long you two been partners?"

Frank grinned. "I've been a homicide detective for fifteen years. Nowadays our division's more than just homicides. A few years ago the guys upstairs gave us a new name. We're the Violent Crimes Unit. About a year after Nora made detective, my former partner, Max Logan, retired. I ruffled a few feathers among the good old boys when I asked for Nora. I've never regretted the choice. A woman brings a different way of looking at some things, and I enjoy working with her. She's a good detective."

"You're divorced, right?" When Frank nodded, Jack asked, "Any kids?"

"Two. My ex, Sharon, is an administrative assistant in the DA's office. We still care about each other." He shrugged. "She just couldn't handle the hours and stress of my work. She's right. The job sucks, but it's in my blood. We still do some things together with our two children."

Jack licked beer froth from his upper lip. "How old are the kids?"

"Becky, Rebecca, is thirteen." Frank opened his wallet and showed her picture. Then he flipped over to the next plastic sheath. "William turned fourteen last month. The teen years! Sharon and I are scared to death, but so far it's been fine. They're still my life, other than police work. You ever marry?"

Jack seldom talked about himself this way, but he found that, after listening to Frank, he was in the mood. He told Frank about his sister in Phoenix and even showed him a snapshot of his niece, Amy.

Then he brought the subject back to Frank and Sharon by suggesting that the two of them might get together again some day.

"There'd still be problems," Frank said. "A few weeks before I joined your squad she told me she still cared and still worried, but because I don't live with them anymore, at least she doesn't get pissed nights sitting home alone."

"Maybe when the kids are older," Jack said.

The waiter stopped to check their table. "Can I get you two something to eat?"

"I haven't eaten all day." Jack picked up the table tent card promoting spicy chicken wings and held it up. Frank nodded. "Bring us a big order of these," Jack told the waiter.

"Anybody serious in your life?" Frank asked.

Jack shrugged. "Sometimes I date a divorcee who lives next door, and there's an old college sweetheart who lives in Alexandria. We've had a long on and off relationship. No pun intended," he added with a wry grin.

"That's a lot of years for it not to be serious?"

"We care about one another, but we've agreed it's nothing more than a safe physical convenience. She's a lobbyist here in D.C. Her life is her career—like mine, I guess."

When the wings arrived, they munched in silence for a few minutes.

"Truth is I'd like to get married someday," Jack admitted. "But as you know it's a hard mix with the job. Have you ever thought about not being a cop?"

"Nora and I have talked about a private agency. Neither of us wants to give up being a detective, but we'd give up the department. That was a hard decision for Nora. She's a third-generation D.C. cop."

"I've never worked for a PD. What're the problems?"

"I think the thing that frustrates us most is the politics in a big city police department. A private firm might also allow a more normal home life."

"What's stopping you?" Jack asked.

"That's easy. Funds. We both know it's more dream than plan, but we drift into the talk sometimes when the frustrations pile up. And for me there's the issue of benefits and health care. The department provides good coverage for the kids."

Listening to Frank, Jack thought that maybe a private agency might be right for him. He liked a lot of things about the work he had done for the government, just not the lack of roots.

"After we stop LW," Jack said, "I've got some decisions to make along those lines. I'm forty-six. It's time to either get my life in order and take a shot at a family or accept that it's not in the cards."

"I'll keep my fingers crossed for you," Frank said. "How'd it go at the White House? That part of this case you've had to carry alone. Are the politicos pushing you?"

"They're in a hurry, but then who isn't?" Jack lowered his voice. "If we don't stop this guy soon, President Schroeder won't have a second term and that would be a great loss for America."

"You believe in the guy don't you?"

"I do. He's a good man with a fine mind and a tremendous sense of right and wrong."

"You're doing all that can be done. Quit beating yourself up. We started with nothing and in a little more than two weeks you've led us onto his trail. I feel it."

"I do, too," Jack agreed. "But the devil of it is, we're at the point where we may soon find we're following a false trail."

"Maybe the lists tomorrow will bring the piece we need."

Jack knew it had better be more than a maybe. The president had not said it, but Jack left the White House knowing his time was limited. Those opposed to him were gaining ground with the president.

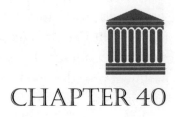

# CHAPTER 40

President Schroeder has asked for a letter of resignation
from National Security Advisor Robert Quartz.

*—Sal Ramirez, CNN, June 19*

"Mom, are you going to give up your job at the fed?"

Federal Reserve Governor Deirdre Jones looked up from her
kitchen table where she sat having breakfast with her husband,
Christian, and their two teenage children.

"Why, sweetie? Do you think I should?"

"Yes, Mom," the fifteen-year-old said, "and Ben agrees with me."

Mary Ellen often assigned her views to her younger brother, Benjamin. In this instance, however, thirteen-year-old Ben did agree and
said so. "Yeah, Mom, you should quit."

"Did you put them up to this?" Deirdre asked her husband.

"Actually, I didn't," Christian told her. "But, I agree with them.
You're under great stress and in danger. We don't need the money,
so why do you choose for all of us to live in harm's way?"

She turned to her children. "Why do you want me to quit?"

"I agree with Dad," Mary Ellen said. "Besides, it's a bummer having FBI agents following me."

Deirdre left the table, and got a paper from her built-in kitchen
desk.

"A few days ago, George Nelson, one of the other Federal Reserve governors, brought me a copy of something he received in his
e-mail. Nelson's hobby is colonial history. He said that he didn't

know its source, but he considered it substantially accurate. Please listen while I read it aloud. And then we'll vote, as a family, to decide whether or not I resign."

## Would You Have Signed the Declaration of Independence?

The signers of the Declaration of Independence numbered fifty-six men. What were their fates? Five signers were captured by the British. Twelve had their homes destroyed. The sons of three were either killed or captured. Nine died, directly or indirectly, as a result of the hardships of the Revolutionary War. What kind of men were they? Twenty-four were lawyers and judges. Eleven were merchants. Nine were farmers and owners of large plantations. They were all wealthy, well-educated men. They signed the Declaration of Independence knowing they would receive the penalty of death in the event they were captured. Most of the ships of Carter Braxton of Virginia, a wealthy planter and trader, were destroyed by the British Navy. He sold his home and lands to pay his debts, and died of a stroke. Thomas McKean served in the Congress without being paid. His family hid. His properties were taken and poverty became his reward. The British government confiscated the property of Lyman Hall and charged him with treason. In early 1776, the British placed a reward on the head of John Hancock. The British General Cornwallis confiscated the home of Thomas Nelson, Jr. General George Washington, with the consent of Nelson, opened fire and destroyed his home. Nelson died bankrupt. Thomas Lynch, Jr., died with his wife when the ship on which they were sailing to the West Indies in 1776, disappeared. The British threw the wife of Francis Lewis in jail and destroyed his home. John Hart was forced to leave the bedside of his dying wife, and his thirteen children fled for their lives. For more than a year he lived in forests and caves, returning home to find his wife dead and his children gone. A few weeks later he died. Others suffered similar fates. These were men of wealth, yet they valued liberty more. Together they took a pledge: "For the support of this declaration, with firm reliance on the protection of the Divine Providence, we pledge to each other, our lives, our fortunes, and our sacred honor." They gave you and me a free and independent America.

Deirdre Jones, her husband, Christian, and their teenage children, Mary Ellen and Benjamin, discussed what they'd heard and what it meant. Then they took a vote and shared a family hug before Federal Reserve Governor Deirdre Jones left for work.

# CHAPTER 41

Unnamed sources: NSA Director Quartz has resigned.
The official announcement is expected at any time.

—D.C. *Talk*, Mel Carsten

Jack walked into the Bullpen at seven in the morning and saw his disheveled computer expert heading into the small kitchen area, a cup in hand. "Millet," he said, "what about that list of air passengers for the Capone killing?"

"Good morning to you, too, Jack," Millet snapped. "Let me get my fucking hot chocolate, okay?"

Millet's outburst quieted the others in the Bullpen.

"Talk while you stir. How's it coming?"

"During the night I eliminated those who didn't meet the description and those I could confirm or deduce were elsewhere," Millet said wearily. "Three need fieldwork and we have another phony."

"Tell me about the phony."

"Might be two dudes, but he's looking like just one. A passenger using the name G. Marks flew from Houston to Pittsburgh. On an earlier flight a George Marks flew from Pittsburgh into Dallas. I factored in the time of the shooting and the time to drive from Dallas to Houston for the return flight—looks like the same dude."

Nora came over and took Millet's cup of hot chocolate from his hand, set it on the counter, and hugged him. "What a guy. We may have another LW alias."

He blushed. "Oh, it's no big deal. I just stayed here listening to the Dodgers game and before you guys got here this morning, I had Marks."

Jack took his position at the flip chart as the others gathered around the table. "Assume Marks is LW. Based on the times of the two flights, he had about two hours on the ground in Dallas. How does he get access to a special rifle with a muzzle suppressor and scope when he lands in Dallas? First the possibilities."

"He could have bought it on the black market in Dallas," Nora suggested.

Jack wrote: "black market," while Millet was saying, "he could have bought it from a gun dealer in Dallas or maybe at a trade show."

"I would've obtained the gun during my prior surveillance trip and stashed it in Dallas," Colin said. "The same for the boom box. That's why the police haven't found a retailer who remembers the sale."

"We should include the possibility that he's got a local accomplice or militia member," Frank said.

Rex Smith, who had not participated in any of their previous brainstorm sessions, said, "He brought the gun with him on the airplane. Properly shipped in the cargo hole, this can be done."

Rachel said, "If he shipped it to Dallas and he only had two hours there, he couldn't risk waiting for the rifle to be delivered. That would mean, if he shipped it he had a place for it to go, a place where it would wait for him. Could be to a package service, or an accomplice, or a dead drop? Maybe a rental house like he arranged across from the home of Chief Justice Evans."

After writing feverishly, Jack stepped back from the flip chart. "Okay, let's qualify them."

Rachel began the attack. "The Harrelson house proved LW will rent a house for several months. If we're assuming he lives near D.C. then the rental of the Harrelson house had been local. If LW rented in Dallas, he would've had to rent from long distance. And, if the authorities detected a sniping rifle in transit, LW had to be concerned that we might arrive with the package. So, let's drop my idea. And, unless we're ready to give up the assumption that LW's a loner, we can also eliminate Frank's contribution."

Jack asked, "Anybody want to argue for him having an accomplice or shipping the gun to Dallas?"

No one spoke until Frank said, "Cross them both off."

Millet spoke next. "I don't like the idea of his buying it when he arrives. The timing is too close to the murder. It risks the availability of the right gun, or silencer, or scope as well as the likelihood of the seller remembering his face after the media reported the kind of weapon used in the killing."

"I agree with Millet," Colin said, "but for a different reason."

Colin had several sniper kills at distances up to two thousand meters, and those were just the ones Jack knew about. He particularly wanted to hear Colin's views.

"What's your reasoning?" Jack asked Colin.

"However he got the rifle, he would've needed time to calibrate the scope at the approximate distance. Five hundred yards is not a real long shot, but it's long enough that without adequate time to calibrate properly, even a top marksman would likely miss a head shot. If Marks is LW, he didn't have time on the ground in Dallas to both obtain the rifle and test for the shot."

"Arguments?" Jack asked.

When no one spoke, he drew a line through "black market" and "across the counter." Although, they all realized, he could have gotten his shooting rig either of those ways during an earlier trip to Dallas.

"Isn't it risky to check a rifle as baggage on the airplane?" Nora asked. "He would have chanced the bag being lost or delayed. The rate of lost airline baggage is high enough for him to be concerned it might not arrive. At the least this would've meant he wouldn't have the rifle, and at worst that the bag would be x-rayed or opened."

They were left with Colin's theory that LW must have bought both the rifle and the boom box on a prior trip and hidden them in Dallas.

"Check the name George Marks and the other fictitious names we have with all the places you can think of where he might have cached the gun in Dallas without an accomplice," Jack told Rex. "Maybe one of those self-storage units, but don't stop there. To cover all the bases, get ATF to check for reported Texas retail or trade show sales of a Tango 51, regardless of what accessories were sold with it."

Jack went over to their paper graveyard where he had written John Kimble's name in red on the card below the pictures of the honeymooners, Mr. and Mrs. Breen, and Robert Campbell below the pictures of Chip Taylor, his wife and mother. He picked up the pen and wrote George Marks below Capone's picture.

*You do live near D.C., don't you?*

# CHAPTER 42

The Supreme Court's information office states
that it's business as usual, but the empty wing
chairs sitting behind the bench in the Court's
chamber remain as a silent,ghastly reminder
that nothing here is, as usual.

—*Fox News*

During the weeks LW had been watching Thomas Evans, the chief justice of the United States had twice gone to his dentist, Dr. Jonathan Eberhard, whose office was on Sixth Street north of F Street, about ten blocks from the Supreme Court. Evans had walked to both appointments.

After hacking into the appointments log in Dr. Eberhard's computer, LW saw that the chief justice had an appointment set for tomorrow at two forty-five in the afternoon. Expecting that Eberhard's staff, like the staffs of dentists the world over, had the annoying habit of calling the day prior to confirm appointments, LW decided that he would hack in again tonight to verify that the appointment had been confirmed.

For the shot, LW had selected the roof of the Oriental Building Association building. The OBA, built in 1861, stood empty and boarded up on the southwest corner of Sixth and F Streets. Evans, a creature of habit, turned at that intersection each time he walked to his dentist.

The MCI Center, across from the OBA on the northwest corner, had no event scheduled tomorrow. Directly across Sixth to the east, was Engine Company No. 2, a fire department substation. The backside of a Washington Metropolitan Rapid Transit building sat catty-corner, with nearly no aboveground sight lines to the top of the OBA. The taller building to the immediate south near the corner of Sixth and E Streets had no windows on the side that faced the OBA.

A border of cement pylons separated the F Street sidewalk from an empty lot on the west side of the OBA. That lot hooked around behind the building until an eight-foot block wall partitioned the lot from the Sixth Street sidewalk. The wall, which continued a good part of the way to E Street, for some inexplicable reason had a locked door, a lock which LW had picked as part of planning this mission, and then relocked until early this morning when he picked it again and left it unlocked. The wall jutted in such a way that he could walk the Sixth Street sidewalk to E Street without being seen from the intersection where he would leave the dead chief justice of the United States.

An air duct ran down the OBA's rear southwest corner from its roof to within a few feet of the empty lot behind the wall. He had hidden a knotted rope inside that air duct. He would be blocks away by the time the agents reacted to the source of the shot.

The roof on this five-story building provided a perfect field of fire in every way possible. The afternoon sun would be at his back, angling into the eyes of anyone looking up from the street, and the rooftop's equipment shed gave enough cover to prevent his being seen from a helicopter.

*A perfect set up.*


Jack and Rachel were sitting in two brown occasional chairs in the Bullpen when Frank drifted over to join them. Then Rex came to sit on the arm of the chair across from Jack.

"The Dallas PD found a storage unit rented by George Marks," Rex told them. "Marks paid cash and the address he gave the manager is a vacant house. The Dallas FBI evidence response team found nothing that pointed to LW's identity."

"Did they find anything that tells us this Marks is definitely LW?" Frank asked.

"I'll give you one guess as to what they found around the door of the storage unit."

Rachel squeezed the bridge of her nose with her eyes closed. "More of his heat-emitting chemical."

"Give the lady a kewpie doll!" Rex grinned and slid off the arm down into the seat of the chair. "That particular storage unit could be seen from the street. My guess is he picked that one so he could check it with his FLIR scope before entering the facility."

"Did they find anything that might give him a reason to go back?" Jack asked.

"The storage unit has served his purpose." Rex shrugged. "It's empty."

"What about when he rented the space?" Rachel asked.

"The manager remembered that Marks had his hands bandaged, but the manager's general description of the guy matched what we have. The manager completed the forms for Marks and, because of the bandages, they didn't ask him to try to sign."

Rex opened his notepad and thumbed over a couple of pages.

"The manager said that he watched Marks struggle to move a rolled-up blanket from his car's trunk to inside the storage unit. He came across as too proud to accept help. He left saying he would be back with more in a few weeks when his hands had healed."

"How did he pay?" Jack asked.

"Cash. He couldn't write a check or sign a credit card voucher. The manager remembered nothing more, other than he wore a red cap."

"The bastard certainly pays attention to the details," Jack said.

Colin ran his hand through his black, wavy hair. "I finally reached General Crook. Portable night-vision equipment, both image enhancement and thermal, is very popular. You can buy it in some retail outlets, most war surplus stores, and over the Internet. So, following that lead would be a long chase. What's the latest on the lists?"

Rachel shrugged. "They're supposed to be ready in a few hours, and once they get here we won't have much time for anything else so let's get some lunch now."

"That sounds better than this cold croissant," Colin said, tossing it into the wastebasket, "cafeteria or off campus?"

Millet said, "How 'bout Friendly's off Old Dominion?"

"Let's eat in the cafeteria," Rachel said, "just in case the lists come early. I'll leave a note for Nora. She should be back any minute."

*Who will be the next target?* Jack wondered. *And how much time do we have?*

# CHAPTER 43

Within D.C. legal circles, Chief Justice Evans is
known as "Walking Justice," for his habit of
going for walks during private deliberations.

—*Parade Sunday Supplement Magazine, June 20*

Samuel Blackmer, the flamboyant freelance writer and longtime
watcher of the U.S. Senate, loved to poke fun at the establishment.
For his appearance on Carsten's *D.C. Talk,* he had dressed splen-
diferously in a black long-sleeved shirt and yellow suspenders, ac-
cessorized with a black and yellow polka-dotted bow tie that on
television appeared as wide as his handlebar mustache.

"The Fed board is down to four governors," the show's host, Mel
Carsten, began as the camera zoomed in on his somber face. "The
board does not have a critical meeting scheduled until their open-
market committee meets on June twenty-seventh. As for the Supreme
Court, they have not issued a ruling or heard oral arguments since
James Dunlin's resignation dropped the Court to five justices."

"What's the latest on this continuing story?" Carsten asked Blackmer.

"Both the Judiciary Committee and the Banking Committee have
nominees, but the nominees are moving with all the haste of the
race between a tortoise and a snail." Blackmer punctuated his sim-
ile by stretching out his suspenders, then leaving them to snap back
against his global figure.

"Why is that?" Carsten asked. "We have the president, the chairs of both committees, and the congressional leadership all on record favoring expedited confirmations."

Blackmer twisted his mustache. "Some nominees are delaying their response when asked to schedule an appearance."

Mel Carsten stood erect, his feet at shoulders width. "A recent news poll asked Americans: If you were a nominee for the Supreme Court or the Federal Reserve Board, would you (a) promptly continue the process; (b) withdraw your name from consideration; or (c) drag out the process hoping LW is caught before you're called to appear at a confirmation hearing? Less than one-third of those polled said, they would move forward promptly. It would appear the responses of the nominees are right in line with public opinion."

Blackmer's eyes twinkled as the camera came closer. "Senator Leland's Judiciary Committee had better get busy and confirm at least two nominees for the Court," he said. "Until then, LW has a de facto win. Without the six justices needed for a quorum, the Court is effectively standing down as this madman has demanded."

Carsten turned toward his second guest, sitting beside Blackmer, a thin man, dressed in a dark suit with a quiet tie. "What can you tell us about these persistent rumors that the president's advisors are pressuring him to replace Jack McCall?"

"Where there's smoke there's fire," said Matthew Gillis, a former undersecretary at the State Department. "The president, however, continues to stand steadfast behind McCall. And as long as that's the case, there will be no change."

Carsten turned to the camera. "Our next guest on *D.C. Talk* is Catherine Lee. Ms. Lee is a professor of political science and American government at Georgetown University."

He gestured for Ms. Lee to take the seat on his left so the conservatively dressed woman would not need to compete visually on camera with the colorful Samuel Blackmer.

"Thank you for joining us, Professor. Can you shed some light on LW's claim that the Supreme Court is exceeding its authority when it rules laws unconstitutional?"

"Yes, I can," she replied crisply. "LW's written public statements are based on a twisted and incorrect interpretation of the Constitution of the United States. Congress makes the laws and, assuming the president signs them, the agencies of the executive branch administer and enforce them. The Supreme Court, with an appropriate case before them, decides if the laws are constitutional, that is, whether a given law is consistent with the enumerated rights of the people and the states. In individual cases, the Court may also interpret the law to resolve specific disputes."

"Is this the separation of powers we learned about in school?" Carsten asked.

"Yes it is," Professor Lee replied. "Our founding fathers developed a system of checks and balances so that no single branch could dominate the others. We rely on the Supreme Court to interpret our laws and the Constitution for the good of the entire country. The justices do this by applying precedents from their previous rulings and by looking forward to how our principles should govern us. If the people's elected representatives do not like the Court's decisions, they are empowered to legislate a change in the law. And if they do not, the people, holding the ultimate power through voting, can change their elected representatives."

The camera panned in for a closeup of Carsten. "Catherine Lee, professor of American government at Georgetown University, with a civics lesson for LW and his militia, and for each of us."

LW sat at home, eating microwave popcorn, watching *D.C. Talk*, and growing more furious by the minute. Once again the program had failed an opportunity to bring the real issues to the forefront. They just kept saying the same things about him, Jack McCall, and the president, while ignoring the growing cancer that was devouring America. And, now this twit, masquerading as an expert, has misrepresented the role of the Supreme Court.

*The media is part of the conspiracy to steal our freedoms.*

•   •   •

After Jack learned that the lists from the shooting ranges and of the dissidents would not be ready until between seven and eight that night, he told everyone to take a few hours downtime.

"We need to stay after this guy," Colin said in halfhearted protest.

Jack threw his hands up in exasperation, "Doing what? I understand that we're all keyed up, but we have nowhere to go. Rachel, leave word with . . . what's her name? Marsha, Marsha White, to call me when the lists are one hour from being ready." He turned back to the group. "These lists will include details that apply to LW as a real person, not his aliases. When Marsha calls me, I'll call you and we'll meet back here, now get out of here. Everybody. Scram."

LW hacked back into Dr. Eberhard's computer and learned that Evans's law clerk had confirmed the chief justice's dental appointment for tomorrow. Next, he went to his chessboard. He didn't have a lot of time, but then he didn't need a lot of time.

Three days ago, his opponent had moved his bishop to the outside column, thus reducing its capacity to move from four directions to only two. He wondered how this lamebrain ever advanced this deep into the tournament? Now he's moved his second knight deep into my territory. He doesn't have enough pieces remaining to provide enough help to make this knight a meaningful threat. LW decided his opponent was going for a stalemate.

*No way, Jos. Two more moves and your ass is mine.*

He took his next move and posted it on the Internet. Then he took out his ironing board and pressed his special traveler's khakis that converted to a pair of shorts with a quick yank along a velcro strip. And pressed his sweatshirt. His mother used to also iron his underpants, but he had broken that habit.

Tomorrow would be special. To represent his own father and America's founding fathers, he wanted to look neat.

# CHAPTER 44

Is there progress on the LW front? Nobody's saying anything
for the record, but the mumbles are loud and clear: no.

—*Marian Little, NewsCentral 7*

The ringer on Jack's phone brought him around. Caller ID read
Rachel. He spoke before getting the phone up to his ear. "Did Marsha call you?" he asked, reaching into his shirt pocket for the pack
of cigarettes that wasn't there. It had been eight years, but still he
sometimes instinctively reached for his old habit.

"Marsha didn't call. I just wanted to talk for a few minutes before
we head back. Did I wake you?"

"I slept some. Dreamed some. Thought mostly."

"Tell me about the dream?"

"I'm on my knees looking for something. I don't know what or
where I was looking. It's all gone fuzzy. You know how dreams fade.
Is everything okay?"

"Everything but nailing shut LW's coffin," Rachel said. "But I think
we'll be doing that real soon."

"It can't be too soon for me." Jack carried the phone to the
kitchen to splash water on his face.

"You have your next assignment lined up?"

The question took him by surprise, Jack had become more than
just interested in Rachel, and sensed she had grown to care for him,
but to some degree such feelings were expected. People working

together on dangerous assignments develop a special caring based on the knowledge that, at any moment, one of them could hold in their hands the lives of the others. He had felt this on many assignments, for many comrades, but his feelings for Rachel were more than that.

"There's no next assignment," he told her. "This one'll be it for me. I had already decided to resign before, but I couldn't refuse Sam Schroeder."

"I haven't told anyone else, but I'm hanging it up, too," Rachel told him. "Listen, I gave you a ration of shit early on, but you've been just great. You're always there with direction and encouragement. Even the way you've put up with Millet. He's eccentric, but he knows you respect him so he gives you all he's got."

"Millet is different, but then we all are. He's just way more different, but he brings a lot to the table. Whatever we've accomplished would have been impossible without him and you, but the bottom line is we haven't accomplished much yet—and it'll stay that way until we stop this guy."

Jack opened his fridge and took out a beer, then slid it onto the shelf in the door and settled for a bottle of soda. He twisted the cap free and used his foot to swing the door shut.

"We'll get him, Jack. We'll get him."

"Thanks for the encouragement, but if these lists don't reveal LW's identity, we'll be left with chasing down violent ex-agents and military personnel one by one. And once we start that, the scuttlebutt will get to him and he'll run. Our only other option would be to try and capture him during one of his attempted assassinations."

He eased back the corner of his drawn drapes. At first glance the street looked okay. He widened the opening a little and used his vision as if it were a camera to take a series of pictures spanning the entire area. From a different window he repeated the process in the opposite direction.

"Regardless of how this turns out," he slanted the drape covering the next window, "this'll be it for me."

"I drove home going over what we have," she said. "He's had to have been practicing shooting for years. At some point in the past he practiced under his real name. The part about his father, well, we're reading some tea leaves on that, but I think it's got merit."

"I hope you're right." Jack sounded calmer than he felt. "What are your plans? Or did a rich boyfriend propose?"

"There's no rich boyfriend, and since I've grown accustomed to eating and sleeping indoors, I'll need to work. I just want to stop the bureau from being able to just up and transfer me to any old place, whenever they damn well feel like doing it."

"I know that feeling," Jack replied. "Since college I've spent more than half my life outside the U.S."

"I can't imagine how you've dealt with that as long as you have. At least my transfers have all been Stateside. You've been sent all over the world."

"What type of work do you see yourself doing?" he asked.

"Investigative work is okay. I enjoy the challenge. I just don't know what kind. It could be corporate security, or maybe some sort of computer work. I'll figure it out. I just want to have a life. Am I being selfish?"

"No. I want the same thing."

"I'd like to have a family. The doctors tell me I can't get pregnant. I'm okay with adopting, but first I need to get my life in order."

Jack understood that not being able to have children could make a woman feel inadequate.

"What happened?"

"The doctors say it's a birth defect in my reproductive system. I understood the high points. It has no effect on my health or life expectancy." Her voice seemed to be crawling out of somewhere deep inside her. "Just no little ones."

He could hear the hurt in her voice, and knew that for Rachel the subject was difficult to speak about. He was flattered that she had confided in him.

"There are lots of children who need loving homes," he said. "I've seen them all over the world."

"It kinda shook me at first," she admitted. "I'd like to get married some day, and I know men want children of their own."

"Most men probably," Jack assured, "not all of us."

"Listen to me, will you?" she said ruefully. "There's a million sad stories in the naked city, and you've just heard mine. Let's change the subject. What do you see in your future?"

"I'd like something that would allow some balance between my personal and professional life. I had a beer with Frank the other night. He and Nora have talked about opening a private agency. He's a good man and a fine detective."

"I'm very impressed with both Frank and Nor—"

"Hang on," he said, interrupting her. "My other line's ringing."

It was Marsha White calling to tell him the lists were done except for programing the commands that would allow them to manipulate the data. She expected to have it all wrapped up and to the Bullpen in an hour.

God. Jack wanted this LW mess over with. He wanted to tell Rachel how he felt. Hold her tight and then walk off with her into the sunset. But he had to put those thoughts out of his mind, for this new information might lead to failure.

Still, he was betting it all that the lists would be the answer. They just had to be.

# CHAPTER 45

Former NSA Director Robert Quartz has agreed
to appear on this show one week from today.

— *Mel Carsten, D.C. Talk*

Jack's running shoes squealed as he ran across the CIA emblem in-
laid into the marble floor just inside the agency's original headquarters building. The Bullpen was located on the ground floor of
one of the two six-story buildings, which together measured more
than one million of the two-and-a-half-million total square feet of
the CIA complex.

At this time of night he got little more than a nod from the security guards who all knew him. He dashed down one of the two
connecting corridors leading to the new headquarters building, past
the portrait gallery of former directors of the Central Intelligence
Agency, and beneath the model of the U-2 spy plane that hung in
the four-story atrium. As he slowed his pace before turning the final
corner that led to their squad room, he saw a young woman standing outside the Bullpen. She had a heart-shaped face, eyes the color
of old mahogany, a thin waist, and was busty enough to spread the
rib stitching in her turtleneck sweater.

"Hello, Mr. McCall. I'm Marsha White. I have your lists right
here." She held up her laptop case. "Both hard copy and CD."

"I'd like you to stay until the rest of my squad gets here," Jack
said as they shook hands. "Give us your overview. Answer questions
and make sure Millet's able to work with the data on your CD."

Her grasp was as firm as a man's. "Not everyone can be a data expert, Mr. McCall, and not everyone can lead the chase. I suspect your job's tougher than mine."

"I'm not so sure about that. Here's my group coming now. You've met Millet and Rachel, and I'll bet you know Colin Stewart. Colin seems to know every beautiful woman in the city."

"I surely don't feel very attractive right now," Marsha said. "I haven't bathed or changed my clothes in two days."

After Jack introduced Marsha all around, Frank mentioned that he and she had met two years before. "You gave a great presentation over at Metro on Internet research for police. The department adopted a lot of what you shared that day. We're lucky to have you on this."

"Marsha has been at this nonstop for more than forty hours," Jack said while his team came to the table. "We can all relate to that. She has agreed to stay with us for a while." He gestured to the newcomer. "Marsha, run with it. No one will interrupt until you've finished. Then you can expect questions."

"We were asked to work up two lists," she began. "The first to contain member and nonmember users of shooting ranges within a defined radius around D.C. and Dallas. The second list to consist of people with a public audience who have spoken out against the U.S. Supreme Court and/or the Federal Reserve System five or more times."

Jack felt himself growing tense. This was it. In the next hour or so he would know whether or not they were holding an empty bag.

"We found many more speeches and articles critical of the Federal Reserve than of the Supreme Court," Marsha continued. "Still, the shooting range lists are far longer, with just under seven hundred names. The lists of members are by club, showing the year each member joined with a notation of the year in which terminated members dropped out. We cross-referenced where we found a member dropped out of one club and joined another."

Seven hundred shooters. Jack clenched his teeth. He hadn't expected that many.

Marsha glanced toward Millet. "The CIA's database software will allow you to slice-and-dice the data any number of ways. There are two names that appeared on both the dissident list and the list of shooters. We poked around enough to tell you they both appear to be solid citizens. Those two have double asterisks."

"May I share some other observations?" Marsha asked. "I've spent a lot of time with these lists, but I don't wish to come off like I'm telling you how you should do your thing."

"Please do," Rachel said encouragingly.

Marsha fought down a rising yawn. "This afternoon Rachel told me LW may have been planning his killings for two years, perhaps even longer. With that guidance we assumed LW had frequented a shooting range using his real name before his decision to start killing and that after that decision he switched to a new range and a new name."

She pointed to one stack of papers "The shooters on that list dropped their memberships within the last five years; there are thirty-nine names. When we broke out the members who dropped within the past three years, the list was cut down to twenty-three names. May I also summarize the list of dissidents?"

"Take whatever time you need," Jack told her.

He admired Marsha for fighting through her exhaustion and making her presentation as professional as possible.

"The list of dissidents is much shorter," she told them. "We found thirty-one people who had used speeches, articles, columns, or public appearances to rail against the Fed or the Court more than four times. We ignored disagreements, even vehement ones, with a single ruling of the Court or financial decision of the Fed, and focused on attacks that were more institutional in nature. I'm holding those who did not meet your criteria of more than four times in a raw data file in case you want us to develop them later.

"We then grouped these dissidents by the number of occurrences. The quantities range from one energetic fellow who protested one hundred twelve times, to the stipulated minimum of five. You requested copies of their speeches or writings. We have about seventy-five percent in their full text. We've provided abstracts or news accounts sufficient to bring the total with some type of written record to ninety percent. We'll continue the effort to get the remainder under normal working schedules, that is, unless you instruct us to continue what Colin described as a balls-to-the-wall effort. We did not research the exact meaning of that description."

"Marsha, I've never heard an overview of a major research project presented better," Jack said when the team had stopped laughing. "Are you ready for questions?"

"I hope I'll be able to answer your questions."

"Marsha," Frank said immediately, "you indicated that one dissident attacked the Fed or Court more than a hundred times. What's the next largest quantity?"

"Seventeen."

Frank whistled before asking the obvious. "What's the name on the top of that list?"

"A man. Harry Dalton. I did a cursory reading of about a third of his hundred twelve. In the overwhelming majority he went after both the Court and the Fed. He accused them of destroying representative government in America. Stuff—"

Colin's posture came erect. "He used those exact words? Representative government?"

"Many times."

A crackle of energy rippled through all of them.

"Do you have anything on this Harry Dalton?" Jack asked without bothering to disguise the urgency in his voice.

Marsha grinned like a Cheshire cat. "I thought you might be interested in him so I dug around some. Give me a moment while I switch to a different doc in my laptop. Here it is. Harry Dalton was married to a Jane Styles, a woman twelve years younger than himself. Mr. Dalton died in nineteen eighty-two, Mrs. Dalton in nineteen ninety-five. In the seventies Harry Dalton worked as a college professor of political science. In seventy-eight, he retired after refusing his university's repeated demands that he end his vehement talks on the threats from within the government."

Rachel started to speak and then, apparently, thought better of it.

"Harry Dalton ran for the U.S. Congress in nineteen eighty," Marsha continued. "He filled his campaign with the same angry rhetoric that had poisoned his academic message. He lost in the primary with less than two percent of the vote. In eighty-two he committed suicide by shooting himself through the mouth.

"Mrs. Dalton died prematurely of cancer. She left a trust fund to care for their only child, a son, Isaac Dalton. The trust fund provides Isaac a hundred thousand dollars a year with annual cost of living increases. Mrs. Dalton also left Isaac a free and clear home. It appears the son still lives in that house. They moved there the year after Harry Dalton shot himself on June twenty-first—oh, that's tomorrow—in the Baltimore house where the family had lived when Isaac was born. The son found his father's body after the suicide. We have an address, phone number, and a social security number for Isaac Dalton."

"Millet, get on your computer," Jack blurted, no longer able to contain himself. "Now! Find out if Isaac Dalton shows up on the lists of people with a history of violent behavior who had been in the military or had worked in the intelligence community."

Millet had begun stroking his keyboard by the time Jack finished his instructions.

"Do you recall whether or not the name Isaac Dalton showed up anywhere on the lists from the shooting ranges?" Colin asked Marsha.

"Isaac Dalton is on one of the lists of people who dropped their memberships."

"Within the past three years, right?" Rachel asked.

"Isaac Dalton dropped out of the Baltimore Gun Club just about three years ago."

"And Isaac Dalton didn't use any other gun club after that?" Nora asked.

When Marsha shook her head, Rex slammed his fist on the table and exclaimed, "Isaac Dalton must be LW!"

Jack could feel the group's energy.

Millet's voice got back to the table before him. "Isaac Dalton joined the FBI in nineteen eighty. He resigned in ninety-five after his mother died. I called the Bureau. They're sending over his full jacket by helicopter. To hold down rumors I asked for the personnel files on all the ex-FBI agents with violence in their background. They still had them pulled from making the list for us. ETA, twenty minutes."

"Do you have anything more, Marsha?" Jack asked.

"No," she told him. "I just hope we aren't jumping to conclusions."

"Take a break everybody," Jack said. "Get some fresh coffee. Use the restroom. Stretch your legs, whatever until those FBI files get here. Think about what questions you still want to ask Marsha. Once those files arrive, I want to let her out of here."

The team scattered.

Marsha walked over to Jack. "I appreciate your concern for me, but I'm pumped. If you want me gone for security, I understand. But don't worry about my sleep. I had everyone working on this round the clock so I shut my section down for a few hours and staggered their comebacks. If you need anything, I should be here."

"Stay as long as you want. You can crash over there." He pointed to a brown leather couch.

She yawned. "I hoped you'd let me stay."

As Marsha had so aptly put it, he, too, was pumped. They all were. Jack went to the men's room. When he got back, Marsha was already asleep, the others having congregated in the kitchen area where, clearly not wanting to disturb her, they were talking in low voices. He turned off the lamp next to her head.

Jack recalled Marsha saying that tomorrow was Isaac Dalton's father's birthday. Something would happen tomorrow. He just knew it.

*Where's that damn Dalton file? Come on!*

# CHAPTER 46

The president told reporters during a news conference in
the Rose Garden, "There are no plans to replace Jack
McCall and there will not be any." Today's *New York
Times*'s editorial page, reports, "Our sources describe
McCall's progress in one word: zero."

—*Mel Carsten, D.C. Talk, MSNBC*

The hollow thumping of helicopter blades beating the night sky told
Jack that the FBI files on violent agents had arrived. Five minutes
later Millet took the box from the FBI's courier. Jack signed the re-
ceipt. The moment the door closed behind the courier, Millet slid
Dalton's jacket down the table.

Jack could feel his team's eyes fixed on him as he searched
through the file on Isaac Dalton. When he finished, he looked up,
grinned, and said, "I think we've found our man."

After the cheers quieted, Jack shared more details.

"His file shows the information Marsha obtained and more. Two
field offices had recommended he be removed from active duty and
put into therapy for his violent tendencies and antigovernment rhetoric. He resigned four months after the second recommendation,
never having gone into therapy."

Jack flipped back a couple of pages. "Here's a more complete
physical description, as well as a good picture." He held it up. "As
you can see, it's very consistent with the descriptions we've gotten
from witnesses. His eyes are brown."

He smiled at Marsha, who had joined them at the table. "Are you okay?" he asked. "Do you want to go home?"

"Quit worrying about me, Jack McCall, and tell me how I can help."

"How about making two hundred copies of his picture," he told her. "You can do it faster down the hall than in here."

"Is the FBI address from his resignation still good?" Frank asked.

"It's the same address as on Marsha's list," Rachel said.

"Rachel, Millet," Jack said, "I want everything current you can get on this guy. Fast. His credit report, driver's license, whatever. We need his address or verification that what we have is good. Get with Marsha for the names and addresses of all the shooting ranges within a reasonable distance of his home. What he drives. Does he have a police record? Check his bank accounts. Get a bank president out of bed if necessary. Oh, and find out where they buried his father. When you do, get a map of that cemetery and mark his father's grave."

"How cool," Millet said. "Are we gonna stake out a grave?"

"Colin, get to that cemetery," Jack said, ignoring Millet's question. "Find out if Isaac Dalton's been visiting his father's grave. If so, get back to me so we can come up with a plan."

"Rex, get a SWAT team ready to roll. Have them equipped and positioned as near as possible to Dalton's home. They have to be inconspicuous. If that can't happen, have them hang back until we call them in. Frank, Nora, what am I missing?"

"We should tell the protection squads to stay on their toes for the next forty-eight to seventy-two hours," Frank said. Then Nora added, "Tell them not to leave their charges alone anywhere—follow 'em into the can."

"We can tell them we had an anonymous tip that LW plans to strike soon," Nora added.

"Do it. Keep a log of the time and the agent you speak to in each squad."

Marsha returned with the copies of Dalton's pictures. "Jack," she said while handing the pictures to him. "I may know the fictitious name Dalton uses at the local shooting range."

"Talk to me," he said to her.

"We know when Isaac Dalton quit his membership at the Baltimore Gun Club. And I assumed he still lived in the house his mother left him."

"Yeah, yeah," Colin said. "Go on."

"The two ranges closest to his house had thirty-two new non-members who could be Dalton switching clubs and using a phony name. I excluded all shooters who shot on any of the dates of the killings. That dropped the list to fourteen. After running prelims we eliminated eleven whose physical descriptions didn't match up at all. That left three. I cross-referenced those three local shooters with the nonmember shooters on the lists from the Dallas ranges. One day in April one of those three, a Matthew Devine, used the Dallas Gun Range."

Jack closed his eyes and took a long breath. In every operation there was a turning point. Was this it? Did they have the right guy?

"That left me with the possibility," Marsh went on, "that someone named Matthew Devine started shooting using the gun club near Dalton's home the month after Dalton dropped his real-name membership. And, that same Devine or another person with the same name used the Dallas range in April. We found no Matthew Devine living near Dalton's home. However, we did find a Matthew Devine who had lived in the Dallas area for more than fifteen years. We figured if that real Devine were a shooter he would have shot at the Dallas range more than just that one day in April."

"Your conclusion?"

"If you ended up thinking Isaac Dalton could be LW, we should start out thinking that Isaac Dalton used the name Matthew Devine at both the Baltimore and Dallas ranges. We weren't able to discern a pattern as to when Devine shoots at the Baltimore South Range."

"Anything else?" Colin asked.

"I rechecked the dates Matthew Devine used the Baltimore

range and none of them clashed with any of the dates of the assassinations, or the immediately previous dates with respect to the murders you believe were his out-of-town killings."

*We gotcha!*

Jack swivelled his chair to face the other end of the Bullpen. "Listen up," he said. "This amazing woman has the name LW uses when he practices shooting: Matthew Devine, D-E-V-I-N-E. She also has identified the range in the Baltimore area where he shoots under that name. There's no use pattern, but also no reason to think he won't continue to shoot there."

Colin shot his fist into the air and they all broke into applause. Marsha blushed.

"Rex, put together an FBI Special Operations Group to watch that range every hour it's open until we've got Dalton in our hands," Jack said. "It's a perfect cover. Rotate special agents inside the range acting like shooters with their guns in plain sight—not standard FBI issue. Have them dress like casual shooters, not like agents. And be damn sure none of those agents were ever posted with Dalton while he was with the bureau."

"Shall we apprehend on sight?" Rex asked.

"No. While he's shooting, have them attach a magnetized satellite tracker to the underside of his car and then let us know. They're not to apprehend unless he realizes he's spotted. It's possible Dalton is so accustomed to the route between his home and that range that he may be more careless about looking for a tail, but don't rely on it. Make sure the outside agents are very familiar with vehicle-surveillance tactics. Include both wheel and pavement artists capable of using a floating-box. . . . Hey, everybody. This guy is a crack shot."

"Why don't we just grab him?" Marsha asked.

"We're short on proof this is our guy," Jack answered. "We haven't connected him to a single one of the killings or even the red cap. His father wrote some strange letters that connect with LW's communiqués, and his FBI file shows he's violent and a crack shot. That's all we've got except that he fits a general description that would prob-

ably match up with half the guys in his jury pool. That's enough for
a search warrant, but not an arrest."

By half past two the morning of June twenty-first they were ready.
Isaac Dalton's car registration and his driver's license showed the address in the FBI file. Isaac Dalton drove a 1999 dark-green Ford Explorer. They had the license plate number.

An FBI drive-by called to report a dark house and a closed
garage. Rex had gotten a federal judge out of bed to get a search warrant for Dalton's house, his car, and any places he frequented, such
as storage units, second homes, or lockers at clubs. A sharp attorney
might argue they were a bit light for that broad a warrant, but Jack
had expected they could find a judge who would be accommodat-
ing and they had. This asshole had killed judges — Supreme Court
judges. The judge also approved the installation of electronic surveillance equipment.

Jack picked between three thirty and four in the morning for
their assault. In covert ops, two-to-three hours before sunrise was a
prime infiltration time.

# CHAPTER 47

LW has killed fourteen people and there have been no arrests. Rumors persist there aren't even any suspects.

—*Marian Little, NewsCentral 7*

Tomorrow, on the anniversary of his father's death, Dalton would assassinate Thomas Evans, the chief justice of the United States, the king on the chessboard of the unelected government.

The U.S. Supreme Court had already been forced to stand down for lack of a quorum. Assassinating Evans would jettison the rudder from America's already sinking judicial ship.

Dalton felt sexually aroused as he often did when he was about to make a kill. Since Kitt in San Francisco, he hadn't taken the time to find relief. After a few minutes with the D.C. phone book, he used one of his disposable cell phones to call America's Finest Escort Service. He hoped their name stood for more than a marketing tease.

"My name is Tim LaRue," he said to the woman who answered. "I'm at the airport. I'll be checked into the Capitol Hill Hyatt Regency on New Jersey Avenue by eleven thirty. I want your finest woman at my room at twelve thirty—that's half an hour past midnight."

"All our ladies are fine," she told him. "Perhaps you'd like to be specific about the woman you have in mind."

Dalton thought of his mother's dark hair and full figure, then said, "She must have black hair, long black hair, be busty, and she must look clean-cut."

*Momma had always been a classy woman.*

Dalton showed his black market Tim LaRue drivers license, paid cash, and carried his own luggage up to his suite in the Hyatt Regency. His larger bag contained the rifle he'd chosen. The smaller bag held his tearaway casual pants, sweatshirt, sweatbands, and several red baseball caps. He also had a roll of orange florescent tape, the kind joggers and bikers wear so cars could see them at night.

He watched the news for a while. There was nothing new. Then he found a music channel and went down the hall to get some ice. He had brought a bottle of wine and some Scotch in case the woman wanted a drink. He would take the bottles with him when he left.

Fifteen minutes later he heard a quiet knock on his hotel room door. He turned up the music, but not too loud. Frank Sinatra was singing "Luck be a Lady Tonight." Dalton knew he was about to get lucky, and also knew that whatever the woman outside his door was, she was no lady.

The woman left his room at four in the morning. Dalton had paid the agreed fee and a tip of an extra hundred. He could not imagine his next sexual collision topping this one, but he planned to try, perhaps to celebrate his ending the reign of the chief justice of the United States.

Already naked, he decided to risk taking a shower. It would make his DNA discoverable, but there were many places at which that could be true. He remained confident the authorities would have no reason to take note of a room rented under the name Tim LaRue.

After taking a long shower and rechecking his gear, he decided to go downstairs for breakfast. Before leaving the room, he slipped the do-not-disturb sign into the door's outside card-lock slot, and wedged two tiny slivers of transparent paper behind the sign in such a way that they would be dislodged if anyone moved the sign to insert a card key.

Forty minutes later, after swallowing the last bite of a Belgian waffle, Dalton left the hotel and walked south on New Jersey Avenue, crossed Louisiana Avenue, and entered the National Mall near the Taft Memorial. He stopped next to the Peace Monument and watched the rising sun create a nimbus around the Capitol Dome. He was sure the sighting was a symbol from God, or perhaps his father. There would soon be a new dawning for America.

Near the Smithsonian Institute, he cut over to pick up Ninth Street, then veered right at Constitution Avenue to start his trip back to the hotel. Along the meandering route, he selected the spots where he would leave the red baseball caps and several places where he could slip out of sight.

His first choice would be the bushes behind the café in the Sculpture Garden between Constitution Avenue and Madison Drive, across Seventh Avenue from the West Building of the National Gallery of Art. If events prevented him from getting there, he would duck into either the Sudworth arborvitae and false cypress near the southwest corner of the garden, or the bushes beside the yellow buckeye tree at the corner of Seventh Street and Madison Drive. The latter would provide the poorest cover, but be directly on his route back to the Hyatt.

He would make the final decision on the fly, as circumstances dictated.

After long practice he had reduced to twenty seconds the time needed to remove the velcro-attached leggings, pull off his sweatshirt, slip on the orange sweatbands and, if he had a few extra seconds, stick some bright-orange reflective tape onto his running shoes. After that he would emerge from hiding with his appearance changed from a man in full-length pants, a sweatshirt, and a red baseball cap, to just another jogger in shorts and a T-shirt.

Then transformed, he would cross Madison Drive and, under

cover of the trees, move east with the tourists and other pedestrians. To return to the Hyatt he could take either Third Avenue to D Street, or Constitution Avenue to New Jersey Avenue.

At seven he eased his way down the hall to his hotel room and silently pulled out the do-not-disturb sign. The paper slivers softly fluttered to the hallway carpet. He smiled. No one had entered his room.

He set the alarm clock and, for a backup, called downstairs for a noon wake-up call.

*I cannot be late. Today, is Daddy's birthday.*

# CHAPTER 48

Nominees are delaying their appearances, waiting
for Jack McCall or his rumored replacement to
put an end to the terror of Commander LW.

—*Marian Little, NewsCentral 7*

JUNE 21, 3:37 A.M.

For centuries, agents and soldiers had filled their solitary time before dangerous missions with prayers and silent messages for their
loved ones, entrusted to the telepathic winds. It had likely been that
way since the beginning of soldiering. It was in that kind of quiet
that Jack and the members of his squad traveled north on I-95, followed by an unmarked FBI SWAT van.

After parking on a tree-lined side street, they quietly moved to
the edge of Dalton's property. The moon, peeking in and out from
behind passing clouds, brightened and darkened what appeared by
all reasonable measures to be just another sedate suburban home.

In the distance, the tires of a car squealed rounding a corner. A
residential street light, nearly defeated by a canopy of tree branches,
brought an illumination similar to a jungle in the refracted light pre-
ceding sunrise.

Jack could see the west side of the garage and enough of the front
to know its straw-like yard suffered from neglect. He had limited the
number of SWAT agents to four plus their squad leader and two electronic surveillance experts. In foreign ops he had handled tougher in-

filtrations with less manpower. If they didn't catch Dalton, Jack didn't want the neighbors and, through them, the media to learn of this raid. Given the tense state of the union, anything even possibly about LW became instant news.

The FBI SWAT team used a FLIR scope to confirm Dalton had not applied the heat-generating chemical on his own home.

SWAT Team Leader Mike Edgerson dispersed his four SWAT men to the four corners of Dalton's house. These positions would allow two shooters a view of the front, back, and each side of the house.

"Set. Set. Set. Set."

The four shooters whispered in rapid sequence to indicate they had taken their positions out of sight off the corners of the house. It also meant they had set up portable lighting to illuminate the perimeter. The lamps would not be lit unless they heard the command "light it up," or heard gunshots in or around the house. Everyone involved in the assault was wearing dark SWAT jackets with reflective FBI lettering on the back.

Jack, Colin, and Rachel crept toward the front door where a vine-covered trellis provided cover from the closest neighbor, while Frank, Nora, and Rex moved toward the back door.

Jack turned his attention to picking the locks and at 4:23 a.m., with the yet unseen morning sun throwing orange across the eastern sky, he whispered into his radio.

"Ready."

"On your command," Frank replied, letting Jack know he had also picked the lock in the rear door.

"Now."

The hinges screeched as Jack nudged the door. For a moment he stood frozen to the spot listening for any noise from inside. Hearing only quiet, he pushed the door far enough for them to enter. There were no more squeaks.

The smells of old food and stale air crowded them as the narrow light tubes from their handheld flashlights bleached out hunks of darkness, beyond their lights the sense of an ancient Egyptian tomb. An arcing light in the kitchen, the size of a quarter, told Jack that Frank, Nora, and Rex had successfully entered through the back of the house. Frank held his hand in front of his flashlight and raised his thumb. Jack raised his. The ground floor appeared clear. Frank's team moved to check the two-car garage.

The SWAT team had been instructed not to use their radios once Jack's squad got inside other than to say one of three words: front, back, or garage. If it came, the one word signal would mean they were about to have company and the expected point of entry. If more than one person approached, a number would be added after the one word. Jack had instructed the SWAT team to let whoever arrived enter without interference.

Frank came close and whispered. "It looks like he's gone."

"Car?" Jack asked.

Frank shook his head. "Gone."

Jack knew there were reasons why a person might be home without their automobile. He told Frank to stay downstairs with Rachel and Nora in case an entry alert came from outside, then motioned for Colin and Rex to follow him upstairs.

The three men inched up the stairs keeping their feet to the sides where stairs were least apt to complain to a step. When the stairs creaked anyway, the three men stood motionless, sweat beading on Jack's forehead. But there was no sign their quarry had been alerted. After Colin nudged Jack, they continued on without stopping until they reached the landing at the top.

They worked the upstairs landing from left to right, communicating with only their hands. Jack focused on each doorknob. Colin kept his focus on the entire door, and Rex stayed alert for an assault originating from the remaining doors to their right.

The first door opened into a linen closet. The next, a full bath. The room beyond that was a study with a desk, computer area, and file cabinets. There were framed photographs covering the walls, many of them of a man, but the majority were copies of documents.

From the news accounts he recognized Isaac's father. As for Isaac himself, Jack had seen one picture, but that was enough. The rest were likely some of the older Dalton's writings, the stuff Marsha had found in the archives.

A muted sound came. The three men froze. The low clattering came again. The muscles in Jack's stomach tensed. He saw Colin rotate his hand in the air before pointing toward a narrowly open window where irregular breezes were pulsing the metal blinds against the sill.

The next room, a bedroom, was empty except for a tanning bed placed in the center of the floor. A woman's clothes hung in the closet, inside plastic bags the way they would come from the dry cleaners.

Then another bedroom, this one stained with the blunt smell of body odor. Clothes were strewn everywhere. Jack's flashlight found an empty Cracker Jack box, its contents scattered, the beam chased a cockroach into a pile of clothes. Pictures of women crowded the top of the dresser. No. The pictures were all the same middle-aged woman. The room had a messy closet and the attached bathroom was filthy.

Isaac Dalton's bedroom. It had to be.

When the three joined the others downstairs, Jack raised his radio and said, "Clear." That one-word instructed SWAT Leader Edgerson to send in the two electronics experts. Jack met them at the door.

"One up. One down. You know what to do. Keep it moving. We need to be out of here as quickly as possible."

The experts turned on the small lights in their headgear and spread out to plant cameras and listening devices in the living room, kitchen, the upstair's office, and Dalton's bedroom. They would also bug the phones.

Jack took his squad upstairs. "See what you can, but leave things as you find them. And be ready to go when the electronics guys are done. Estimate twenty minutes. Rachel, get on that computer. The rest of you look for files on the targets. Frank, let's look downstairs."

The next twenty minutes passed like two hours. At 4:59, Jack leaned into the office doorway and looked first at Rachel, then at Nora. They both shook their heads.

"The electronics are done," he said. "We're out of here. Leave everything just like you found it."

Rachel turned off the computer and repositioned the keyboard and mouse to the precise places she had found them.

"Nothing in Dalton's computer had been encrypted or even protected by a password," she told Jack. The two teams left the house the same way they had entered. "I copied his files and e-mail onto a CD," Rachel said. "He had no electronic address book."

In the spreading predawn light, Jack saw a FOR RENT sign in the yard of the house across the street.

"Check that out, Mike," he told the SWAT leader. "If it's empty, occupy it and man an observation post until we can get agents here to relieve you."

Edgerson nodded and alone started across the street. The others waited in the trees. A minute later, Edgerson's voice came over their shoulder-mounted radio. "Vacant." His SWAT team set up cameras to watch the back door of Dalton's house before they crossed the street to join Edgerson. On their way, one of them removed the rental sign.

"Rex, as soon as we get back to the CIA, get ahold of that property owner. Have them tell the leasing agent they are taking the property off the rental market. Tell the owner the government will be using the house in an investigation and that the use must be confidential. If the owner is not cooperative see Director Hampton. Within the hour I want a sign on that house designating it as a health hazard, with a do-not-enter sign carrying a phone number answered at FBI headquarters. Callers are to be told there's no danger as long as they don't trespass, and that an environmental contractor will abate the hazard within a week to ten days."

Five minutes later they were back on I-95 heading south. In the distance the headlights from a steady stream of early traffic pierced the withdrawing darkness as if chased by the rushing beams of light.

After minutes of tense silence, Nora broke the ice. "That upstair's office was a goddamned shrine. It felt creepy."

"He had a beautiful computer desk," Rachel said.

"So were the walls," said Colin. "The room had cherry wood wainscoting with forest green vinyl wall covering above it and a cherry wood floor with an expensive Persian area rug."

"I didn't know you were into interior decorating," Nora remarked.

"What can I say? It's a gift."

They all laughed, a bottled-up nervous kind of laugh.

"The important thing is that he's our guy," Jack proclaimed. "There's no doubt. Did you find anything in his computer?"

"No. Maybe Millet would have. I could have used more time but I got everything on a CD."

The car continued south fifteen miles an hour faster than the posted speed limit, its headlights of limited use against the early gray sky.

# CHAPTER 49

JUNE 21, 5:41 A.M.

"Did you nail his ass?" Millet asked.

Marsha leaped off the couch. "Did you get him?"

"Not home," Rex said before collapsing into one of the Bullpen's green overstuffed chairs. "We bugged the place and set up an observation post."

"Christ," Nora said. "I hope he's not off somewhere visiting one of his targets. Rachel, let's call and alert the protection squads again. Let them know Dalton may be on the hunt."

"Use LW, not Dalton," Jack cautioned. "Let's keep his identity on a need-to-know basis."

Rachel tossed the CD to Millet. "I copied his hard drive. He had no e-mail sent or received. His address book had nothing in it."

Lana Kindar, the Kurdish woman Jack had saved in Iraq, and got jobs for her and her husband, Zaro, as a coffee service worker at CIA headquarters, walked into the Bullpen and went to Jack. She reached up and cradled his cheek in her open palm. Her calloused hand somehow felt soft. When she turned to leave, he rested his hand on her shoulder. She stopped and turned. Jack hugged her. She smiled and left.

"Frank, can you get an all-points bulletin out on Dalton's Explorer without it getting to the press?" Jack asked.

"The media and ambulance-chasing attorneys listen to the police radio," Frank said after shrugging.

"It's your town. How do we find this Explorer without tipping off the media and starting rumors? He'll bolt if he hears the police are looking for his car."

"We could go to the station and talk with the watch commander," Nora said after digging a finger full of raspberry jelly out of one of the fresh pastries Lana had just left. "Ask him to spread the word face-to-face, not use the radio. That might keep the lid on for a while, maybe twenty-four hours, certainly no longer." Her eyes slightly crossed as she watched her red finger approach her mouth.

"Keeping it hushed for even twenty-four hours would take a bunch of luck," Frank said, standing to flex his tall frame. "Certain media people spend a lot of time and money maintaining contacts on the force. This is not just another big city. It's the nation's capital."

Jack gulped his coffee. "So, if we're going to get him today, it might be a good idea. If not, it stinks. Is that what you're telling me?"

They had found neither the perp nor any conclusive proof at Dalton's home, and now they were running into problems with what Jack had hoped would be a simple APB on a car. The luck he had prayed would hold was slipping away.

Frank twisted his shoulders. "You can't tell anything to that many people and expect it to remain a secret."

Millet walked over from his computer. "Rachel had it right, Jackman. That CD had nothing that helps one fucking bit."

Adrenaline raced through Jack. He got out of his chair, left the Bullpen, and walked the halls of the CIA complex. When he got back, he had made his decision.

"If Dalton wasn't home at four thirty in the morning, it's a good guess he's out of town. Rex, take charge of an FBI squad to check the parking lots at D.C.'s airports and Baltimore International. Give them the description and license number of the Explorer. They're to get inside the car without making it obvious. His parking stub will likely be in the car. Have them get the time on the stub and call you. From where he parked, the entry time on the stub, and the home cities of his likely targets we should be able to shorten the list of possible flights. Maybe make a decent guess at his next target."

"Then we can alert that target's protection squad." Rachel said eagerly.

"Something like that," Jack said. "If we're lucky."

"It sure as hell beats turning in circles," Frank volunteered. "If he's out of town, his car may be at the airport."

"Include the train and bus stations," Jack said as Rex waved back over his shoulder on his way to the door.

JUNE 21, 9:00 A.M.

Jack held a cold, sweaty bottle of spring water against the back of his neck. Three hours had passed without hearing from Rex. He called Mike Edgerson. Nothing had happened at Dalton's house either. Jack noticed Nora playing the children's hand game of here's the church and here's the steeple, open the door and see all the people. Colin, working on calming his nerves, sat hunched building a card house. Rachel reclined in her chair, her arms dangling toward the floor, staring at their paper graveyard. And Millet, having found nothing meaningful on the CD Rachel had brought back from Dalton's house, kept swigging cranberry juice between his dog-in-heat gawks at Nora.

A few minutes after nine, Rachel's phone rang. She answered to hear Special Agent Martin, the agent in charge who had relieved Mike Edgerson's SWAT team. Martin reported that no one had been seen coming or going at Dalton's house.

At nine thirty Rex called. He had fifty agents on the job but with three-quarters of the lots at the airports, bus stations, and train stations checked, they had not found Dalton's Explorer.

"We're going back!" Jack said, after rapping his knuckles twice on the table. "Millet, you've never been on a field op. How'd you like to come along?"

"Just watch my back. I'm no fucking secret agent man."

JUNE 21, 10:00 A.M.

Press Secretary Addiena Welch stood on her tiptoes to speak into the microphone that had been raised to the setting for her boss.

"Ladies and gentlemen," she said, "the President of the United States."

President Schroeder strode directly to the microphone. "Thank you all for coming. This will be short. I stood before you a few days ago and spoke of the bipartisan effort to expedite confirmations. Late last night, in special session, Duncan Carillo and William Ladd were confirmed by the Senate's Judiciary Committee and approved by the vote of the full Senate to take seats on the bench of the U.S. Supreme Court. I'm pleased to announce the U.S. Supreme Court has a quorum and is back in business. In addition, Dr. Elizabeth Hancock took a seat on the board of governors of the Federal Reserve System. To facilitate their prompt relocations to D.C., these appointees will not appear before you this morning.

"Throughout the history of our great country, patriots such as these three appointees have always stepped up to the plate in our times of need. America's greatest strength continues to be our citizens and their commitment to serve their country.

"My thanks go to Senators Marshall Leland and Ruth Ann Mitchell, the chairpersons of the Senate's Judiciary and Banking Committees, for their tireless attention to this matter. Senators Leland and Mitchell have assured me their committees will soon confirm more nominees.

"Ms. Welch has the background handouts standard to such appointments. Thank you, ladies and gentlemen."

The president tamped straight his two-page statement and turned to leave.

"Mr. President! Mr. President!"

"I refer you to the confirmations committees for any details or updates," Schroeder said, and again started to leave.

"Mr. President! Mr. President!"

The president turned back and leaned toward the microphone. "I said no questions. There will be none. However, I will take this opportunity to make a brief statement on the matter of this self-appointed Commander LW and his band of renegades."

He cleared his throat. "I and the leaders of your government's law enforcement and intelligence agencies have recently met with Jack McCall. Mr. McCall reported that his team remains positive and hard at work. Beyond that, it would not be appropriate for me to comment. I assure all Americans that their president and the intelligence community continue to support Jack McCall as the right man for this nasty job. Anything you may hear to the contrary is without merit."

# CHAPTER 50

President Schroeder continues to stand firm:
"McCall remains in charge of the LW case."

—*Mel Carsten, D.C. Talk.*

JUNE 21, 10:17 A.M.

Rachel twisted around and looked at Millet sitting behind her in the van. "There have to be files on his targets."

"Dalton killed Roberts in his mistress's apartment," Jack said, twisting to the left as Frank turned the wheel hard to the left and accelerated around a FedEx truck. "Neither the FBI nor the Supreme Court Police knew about Jenny Robinson. Dalton did. The details of that information about Roberts and the others must be in that house."

"Drive this sucker, Frank," Millet said. "It's so cool to not have to sweat getting a ticket. Hey, Jackson, when are we going to stakeout that grave?"

"Colin," Jack said, "what did you find out?"

"He's been there," Colin said.

"How could you tell?" Nora asked.

"Most of the graves have grass that has grown out over the stone markers. Grass too low for the mower blades, but the grass growing out over Dalton's father's grave marker has been trimmed by hand."

"Maybe the cemetery did it?" Millet asked.

"No," Colin said. "If they had, there would be a pattern as to which markers had been trimmed. The few that had been clipped were scattered about the cemetery. They had to have been done by people visiting those graves."

"Couldn't it have been someone other than Isaac Dalton?" Rachel asked.

"I suppose it's possible, but Harry Dalton has only one living relative, his son, Isaac."

"Okay," Jack said impatiently, "okay. What are we doing with this information?"

"I've got a detail watching the cemetery twenty-four seven," Colin said. "If Isaac Dalton enters the cemetery, I'll be called before Dalton gets to his father's grave."

Jack snatched the beeping cell phone from his belt and held it to his ear.

"Jack. Rex. No dice. No dark-green or any color Explorer with Dalton's plate number. He could've switched plates, but we have nothing that indicates he's not playing his true identity straight."

"Either that or he parked away from the airport in one of the economy lots and took their shuttle to the airport," Jack replied.

"I guess we're all dressed up with nowhere else to go," Rex said. "I'll get back to you."

"I'm calling the rental house," Jack told them while dialing. "I want Agent Martin to know we're on our way." He spoke into his cell. "We're about five minutes from you. What's the status at the house right now?"

"The same as I reported last time," Martin said. "No one has approached Dalton's house. The environmental hazard sign keeps the neighborhood curious about this house."

"We'll park on the side street and approach Dalton's home from the south through the trees," Jack explained. "When we're in position, you'll hear from me or Agent Johnstone. Can you provide a distraction?"

"No problem. The few neighbors still at home watch everything we do. A couple of my guys can make a commotion out front and then leave to the north. That'll hold the attention of any curious neighbors. I'll have the agents wear an earpiece so I can give them their timing as you give it to me. Let me know when you're in position."

JUNE 21, 10:41 A.M.

"Agent Martin. Rachel Johnstone. We're in position in the trees. Have your guys do their thing. Keep this line open and stay in communication with your agents going outside."

"Can you see the front of the rental house?"

"Yes." Rachel moved a small branch that was blurring her view. The street was bright with the morning sun, but oak trees shaded the side of Dalton's driveway, as well as the side of his house.

"My men are ready to come out, Agent Johnstone," Martin said. "Watch them and make your own judgment on when you go. Your end will move quicker if we cut out the back and forth talk."

"Roger that."

Three agents wearing overalls and dirty T-shirts came out the front door of the observation house carrying boxes, then loaded those boxes into the back of a van. Two of the men walked toward the far north front of the property, stood back, and stared at the roof of the rental house. The third agent backed the van into the street and pulled up to park at the curb, then joined the other two talking and pointing. After a minute or two, one agent got back in the truck and drove north while the other two walked slowly back inside the rental house.

While the agents had been playing their roles in the front yard of the rental house, Frank had run for the back door through the shadows in a crouch. After picking the lock, he motioned to the others.

Inside, they heard nothing other than the occasional complaint of an old house railing against the stresses of time. They quickly confirmed Dalton's house was still empty just as the observation team had reported.

"I know it's an oven in here," Jack said, "but don't touch the thermostat. Most people won't adjust their temperature when they leave for less than a full day. His is set at eighty-five, so he's likely gone. But we don't know how long he's already been away. If he comes home, a cooler temperature could alert him when he opens the door."

Stabs of light slicing through small breaks in the lowered window shades illuminated the dust particles seemingly drawn to the beams of light as metal is drawn to a magnet.

"The team across the street will let us know if anyone approaches," Jack said, "so let's get to it. Rachel, get Millet upstairs on that computer. Frank. You and Nora take the rest of the upstairs. Colin and I'll take the downstairs."

In a kitchen that looked like it had come straight out of the fifties, Jack and Colin searched the drawers and cabinets, opened containers and everything in the refrigerator.

Nothing.

Frank called softly from upstairs. "Jack. Come up here."

Jack found Frank standing in the doorway of the bedroom at the far end of the hall. The doorway to what had they figured to be Dalton's bedroom. The bed covers were balled up in the center of the mattress and the pillowcase was heavily soiled.

On the nightstand on the far side of the bed stood a framed picture of a woman. Jack recognized the woman as Mrs. Harry Dalton from her photo in the newspaper article about Harry Dalton's suicide. In the black-and-white picture she wore a skimpy two-piece bathing suit. The wall above Isaac's dresser held a collage of several more mother pictures, her poses ranging from those of a young mother cradling her cherubic son to the seductive cheesecake shots of a middle-aged lover.

"Some nutcase, eh?" Frank said as they headed down the hall to check on the progress in the office.

"Yeah." Jack nodded. "Both him and his momma."

"This thing is filled with household and family stuff," Nora said, shutting a drawer in the file cabinet. "There's nothing on the targets, not a damn thing. It's as if we have the right guy and the wrong house."

"Not possible," Rachel snapped, "this shrine to Harry Dalton proves this is the right place."

"This fucking computer is lifting its skirt," Millet bellowed. "But I can't get it to put out."

"Okay. Let's all cool it." Rachel said, motioning downward with her hands. "Just stay with it."

Nora began checking for loose or hollow sounding floorboards.

"The evidence must be here somewhere," Frank said. "I'll check behind his father's speeches."

Millet slammed his hand against the desk top. The echo vibrated through the room.

"Take it easy." Rachel massaged his shoulders. "Loud unexpected noises are not recommended in covert ops."

"If I could find where to stick my dick, I'd just fuck this computer and be done with it."

"I'd unplug it first," Rachel said with a straight face.

Millet laughed. "I'm okay. Really. Sorry for the coarse language."

"I've heard it before." She slapped his shoulder. "From you, now that I think about it. Now settle down and stay with it."

Despite Rachel's words of calm and encouragement, a moment later Millet again swore at the computer, then wiped his runny nose on his shirtsleeve.

"There's nothing behind this stuff on the walls," Frank said.

"C'mon Frank," Jack declared, "let's go give Colin a hand downstairs. Nora, search his bedroom and the rest of the upstairs."

They found Colin in the garage. "You finding anything?" Frank asked.

Colin, who had been poking around a shelf of paint cans, looked at them expressionlessly. "Just garage stuff, nothing incriminating. Is Millet having any luck with that computer?"

"Its looking like a dry hole," Frank answered. "Jack, you want me to start taking off the air grates and get in the attic crawlspace?"

"Help us finish the garage," Jack said. "Then if we still have nothing, the three of us will divide up the attic and registers."

"This looks like a standard-sized double garage," Colin said, looking around. "Twentyish-plus feet wide and about the same front to back."

"So?" asked Frank.

"When we were waiting in the bushes, while you picked the lock, I crouched across from the side of the garage. From the outside, that window," Colin motioned with his head, "was in the middle of the garage wall. Here on the inside, it's much nearer the back wall."

"I've often been amazed at your capacity for noticing the shape of every woman," Jack said. "I never knew that talent extended to garages. I—"

"Don't move." Colin said sharply, starring at the cement floor. "See that discoloration? Someone's walked back and forth here a lot."

After pointing out a pattern of steps to the back door of the house, Colin pointed out a fainter second path that Jack could not see, that he said led to the back wall of the garage.

"The discoloration ends here," he said. He shut his eyes, then reopened them. Jack watched Colin as he felt around until he found a push release that unlatched to reveal an eight-foot-deep room, the width of the garage.

Inside were file cabinets, a TV, a computer set-up, and a chessboard with a partially completed game. A red baseball cap hung on a nail. Popcorn dotted the green indoor-outdoor carpet. A stack of partially uneaten TV dinners stacked on a coffee table in front of a leather recliner functioned as a cul-de-sac for the army of ants that marched back and forth from the baseboard behind the TV.

"Colin, get Millet and Rachel," Jack said. "Tell them unless they've found something by now to shut that computer off and get down here. Fast!"

They had found the mother lode. But could they find Dalton?

# CHAPTER 51

The opposition minority leader is demanding to
know why Jack McCall has not been replaced.

—*Headline News, June 21*

JUNE 21, NOON

Dalton swung his legs over the side of the bed, poked the off button
on the alarm, hacked up and reswallowed a wad of phlegm, popped
an antacid, and slipped into the white terry cloth robe provided by
the hotel. A moment later the wake-up service rang the phone.

*Time to get to work.*

Today would be an important day. Today he would take a giant
step toward freeing Americans from those who had captured the
country.

He rechecked his Galil sniping rifle and its scope and again
made sure that he had an adequate supply of the same Winchester
cartridges he'd used in Dallas to eliminate Capone. For one final
practice, he assembled the Galil in twenty-eight seconds, then dis-
assembled it and wedged it into his backpack.

He showered and dressed, then surfed the news networks. The
channels were all regurgitating the same message: McCall had
made no progress and his job was hanging by a thread. The president
kept saying otherwise, but the standard procedure in politics and pro
sports sounded the same: McCall was the president's man.

*At least until the president sacks Jack's sorry ass tomorrow or the next day.*

Dalton entered the hotel restaurant wearing his tearaway long pants, a sweatshirt over his T-shirt, and his backpack. He slipped off the backpack, put it on the floor with his foot on the strap and ordered a salad and a glass of peach iced tea.

After eating and leaving cash on the table, he returned to his room for his carry bag, and took the hotel's elevator down to the underground level. He stowed his bag in his Explorer, and told the parking attendant that he would do some sightseeing before taking his car.

The sunlight warmed him as he emerged from the garage. Clutched in his hand, in what appeared to be a brown-bag lunch, were the six red baseball caps he would leave in the National Mall. In the cargo-styled pocket of his pants, he had orange sweatbands for his wrists and head, and the reflective tape for his shoes. He'd kept one red cap in his backpack with the rifle to wear when he ran from the killing zone. Today would be the last time he'd wear his trademark red cap, but it would go out in glory—the elimination of the chief justice of the Unites States.

JUNE 21, 12:47 P.M.

Millet's fingers moved on the keyboard like slam dancers in an underground New York club. The others spent the time searching the file cabinets and documents stacked on the floor.

"Holy shit," Millet shouted. "Remember Justice Monroe, killed with oleander-laced ginseng?" He didn't wait for an answer. "Dalton kept a doc titled, Diary to Dad. It says, 'This morning I followed Monroe, the one with the twitchy nose who insisted on driving himself. When he stopped for breakfast, he left his car door unlocked and his ginseng bottle in his seat-side console. I swapped out the capsules. I admit I was nervous, but it was easier than I imagined. Our resurrection of America has begun.' "

"I'll be damned," Nora said. "The man stopped for breakfast and died."

Millet held centerstage, the keeper of the secrets. "They're all in here. All his killings." He read more. "'Daddy, do you remember that old picture of grandma pushing momma in the carriage? Well, I found that carriage and that old dress in the attic and used it to spook Santee. When I put the dress on, I called myself Grandma Moses—you remember that's what I called Grandma. I never liked her. I named the invisible baby in the carriage, Shirley, after that silly little twit—'"

"Millet," Jack scolded, "we want to hear all of it, but right now let's find this guy. Fast-forward to the end and read what's there."

"Okay, Jackman. Don't get a knot in your shorts. The diary ends with his eliminations of Justice Roberts and Jenny Robinson, but nothing we don't already know, unless you want me to read his description of her ass. . . . Okay, Jackman. Okay. The next line just says, 'to be continued.'"

They all stopped what they were doing when Jack's cell phone rang. It was Agent Smith.

"Jack. Rex. I've got good news."

"So do we. Did you find his Explorer?"

"Not in an economy lot, so we figured he might have taken a hotel shuttle. Bottom line, his Explorer is in the underground parking at the downtown Hyatt Regency on New Jersey. The hotel says the Explorer belongs to a guest named Tim LaRue who checked out less than an hour ago. The parking lot attendant identified Dalton's picture as LaRue. The hotel manager opened the suite Dalton had rented. It's empty. We marked it as a crime scene and called in an ERT. They should be here any min—"

"Rex," Jack injected, "you got anything that tells us where he is right now?"

"Dalton told the parking attendant he had checked out, but he would leave his car for a few hours while he walked to do some sight-seeing. The attendant said he left about fifteen minutes ago with a backpack slung over his shoulder. We can guess what's in the back-pack. Dalton is within a few blocks of where I'm standing!"

"Hold on, Rex." Jack held the phone down near his waist. "Everybody! Dalton's on foot downtown. Get on your phones to the protective squads. We need to know which of the targets is or will be in D.C. today, and where." Jack brought the phone back to his ear. "Great job, Rex. Stay where you are. In a few minutes we may know the identity of his target. That may tell us where Dalton's headed. I'll call you back. In the meantime, get agents around you who know downtown D.C."

"Jack!" Rex shouted to stop him from hanging up. "What's your good news?"

"Dalton's house has a secret room with a different computer set-up in it. We found a red baseball cap in that room. The witnesses did see him."

Time always moved at the same speed. It just gave the impression that it moved much slower when you were desperate for some-thing to happen.

"All the Federal Reserve governors, including the one confirmed this morning, are in their respective districts," Rachel called out. "None in D.C."

"Justice Budson is in New York," Colin added. "Sanders is visit-ing his mother in Orlando. Huckaby's in Chicago. The two new jus-tices left town before the president announced their confirmations. None of the nominees are local."

"Agent Cawley, hold a moment." Nora said, while her face lost its color. "Chief Justice Evans is about to leave the Court for a two forty-five dental appointment a few blocks from the courthouse. He plans to walk. Here's the info on the dentist." She handed Jack her scratchpad.

Jack knew they had to move fast if they were to save the life of the chief justice of the United States. He grabbed Nora's phone.

"Agent Cawley, this is Jack McCall. I'm going to speak up so that you can hear what I'm saying to my squad: Listen up! Here's how we play it. Agent Cawley, the chief justice is not to leave his office. Lock him in his closet if necessary. Keep three agents with him at all times. Get an agent made up to look as much like the chief justice as possible in the time available. The height must be very close. In war we've used stand-ins for generals. The Secret Service body shields the president. We need an agent with that mind-set. Get him in body armor. The stand-in must volunteer. If no one does, get back to me fast."

He raised the phone to his ear. "Agent Cawley, you still with me?" After she said yes, Jack continued, "Have the stand-in walk to the dental appointment. Send agents with him on foot and a tail car trailing, the same as you had planned to do with the real chief justice. No different. This guy knows FBI procedures. Put everyone in body armor. Walk a bit slower than usual. Miss a few traffic lights. We need to pick up extra minutes. Dalton's ready. We're not. Get the stand-in to the dentist's building three to five minutes late. No later. We don't want Dalton getting suspicious. Do not report or discuss this activity outside your detail. Keep your focus on carrying out my orders."

After making sure that Agent Cawley had understood his instructions, Jack dialed Rex's number as fast as he could.

"Rex, Dalton's after the chief justice who has a dental appointment at two forty-five. The dentist is only a few blocks from the Court, within walking distance of the Hyatt. As soon as I hang up, we're on our way. Get your guys moving on foot. It looks like another sniper shot. Evans's dentist is Dr. Jonathan Eberhard. Agent Cawley will have some of her agents walk a stand-in to the dental appointment. Eberhard's office is on the third floor on S—"

"Sixth, just north of F Street. Eberhard's my dentist."

"Okay. Great. I'll call again when we're on the road. Stay as inconspicuous as possible, but get a feel for the dentist's building and the nearby area. We don't have much time for preparation. You'll need to wing it some."

"I got this end, Jack."

"Rex! Get an agent in the dentist's office. Dalton will expect the chief justice to have an FBI escort, so I doubt he'll be inside. He'll be watching though, so—"

"The building lobby has a rear exit to the alley."

"Good. That ought to work. We don't need patients running out of the building. After you confirm Dalton is not in the dentist's office, keep it under surveillance. Distribute copies of Dalton's picture to your agents and Cawley's."

"I've got copies of the pictures and the parking attendant's description for everyone," Rex said. "Get your mind off us, Jack, and get your ass down here."

Jack hung up and said, "I wish we had more time to plan."

"A good plan today," Frank said, "is better than a perfect plan tomorrow."

Rachel called across the street to the observation post. "Agent Martin, we're out of here. There's no time to explain. Count to thirty and have several of your people run out the front door. Hopefully that'll distract any neighbors looking our way. If Dalton comes back, let him get inside. Then surround the house and call us. Don't repeat this message to anyone outside your squad at that house."

"I don't know about that last part, Agent Johnstone," Martin said. "I was told to report potentials for action to my section leader."

"We don't have time for this, Agent Martin," Rachel snapped. "Do exactly what I've told you or you'll wake up in charge of a new field office in Iceland, with no heat and your balls frozen to the chair."

While Rachel had been talking with Agent Martin, Jack had made a call.

"I've got a priority call, Agent Johnstone, please hold." A moment passed before Agent Martin was back on the line. "Director Hampton has just ordered me to do exactly as you have instructed. I am also to inform you that a supervisory agent is being dispatched to replace me and that he will answer to a different section leader."

"Fuck you, Agent Martin." Rachel said after hanging up. Then she turned to Jack. "Now let's get out of here."

Jack had been standing at the chessboard in Dalton's secret room. At first glance the configuration of the pieces had looked familiar, but they were more than just familiar. This board was an exact duplicate of the chessboard in his own home. His opponent had been Isaac Dalton, playing as Harry, Isaac's father's name.

Jack moved the black bishop to f–5, his fourth move, the one not yet posted, then he tipped over the white king, grinned and said, "Checkmate, Isaac Dalton." But Jack knew the real game wasn't over and wouldn't be until they had Isaac Dalton in custody. Hopefully, before anyone else died.

# CHAPTER 52

The FBI receives numerous LW leads.
We're looking into each and every one.

—*Fred Hampton, FBI Director*

JUNE 21, 2:03 P.M.

A soft breeze stirred Dalton's hair as he casually strolled through the National Mall leaving red baseball caps on several benches. If he was right, those hats would soon be on the heads of other people. If not, no problem, for by the time he entered the Mall any pursuers would be looking for a man wearing a red cap. They would find either several or none.

2:10

"Mr. McCall. Agent Beth Cawley. The chief justice is safe in his office. Three men are with him. Special Agent Ira Bullock is standing in for Evans. He's wearing body armor, but we both know that won't help if Dalton uses a head shot like he did to kill Capone in Dallas, so let's get this bastard before he fires. We're about to leave for the dentist. As you ordered, we'll arrive a few minutes late."

2:19

Dalton walked out of a Starbucks in the three-hundred block on Seventh Street, NW carrying a venti, nonfat, no-whip mocha, busily playing the role of a rubbernecking tourist.

2:38

Dalton sat atop one of the cement pylons along the F Street side-walk adjacent to the Oriental Building Association building. He wrestled with his impatience for a full minute before taking the final gulp of his mocha. Then he casually stepped over the pylon and entered the empty lot that filled the area on the west and south sides of the OBA.

He crushed the cup in his hand and jammed it into his back pocket. After looking both ways and seeing no one, he ducked inside the air duct and scurried up the rope ladder onto the OBA's fifth-floor rooftop. A strong wind was blowing across the top of the building. He tugged the red cap tight on his head and stayed low, crossing to the northeast corner where he took off his backpack and leaned it against the equipment shed. A moment later, he looked over the edge while staying back far enough to prevent anyone from seeing him who might look up from the street.

2:45

There he was. Evans. His appointment is at two forty-five and he's not yet in the building. There's three, no four agents with him. He also expected a tail car, and spotted it when the car pulled to the curb near the Metro Transit building.

*Mr. Chief Justice, you'll never again make anyone wait.*

2:50

"McCall, Agent Cawley here. When Dr. Eberhard didn't see Chief Justice Evans we had to brief him. Eberhard will stay with Agent Bullock for the time appropriate to the scheduled treatment. Then we'll leave. Give us three minutes to get to the street. We should be exiting the building about three thirty. Special Agent Rex Smith is with me. He wants to talk to you."

"Jack, what's your ETA?"

"Frank tells me three fifteen."

"Have him drive to Seventh and Pennsylvania Avenue. I'll meet you there."

Frank floored the accelerator, throwing Jack hard against the back of his seat, and pulled onto the right shoulder to get past side-by-side cars clogging the lanes.

Rex slapped his cell phone closed and turned to face Agent Cawley. "Call me before you leave the dentist's office to be sure we're set."

He went down the elevator into the lobby and out the rear door to the alley behind the dentist's building where several more agents awaited his orders.

"The stand-in for Chief Justice Evans should be coming out at three thirty, give or take a few minutes," he told them. "Cawley's detail will take the lead if Dalton goes after Evans up close. I want two of you at the first corner in each direction from this building. That's E and Sixth to the south, and half a block to the north at G Street. Curtis, Bradley, get on top of the OBA building at Sixth and F. We didn't have time to get you up there before Evans arrived, but I want you there to cover his return. The OBA's boarded up and it's too old to have an elevator. There should be a fire escape on the back side. Break in if you have to and use the inside stairs. And you four," he ordered, pointing at the remaining agents who had not yet received their assignments, "two each at Seventh and E and F."

If they were going to stop Dalton without another murder, today had to be the day and Rex was right where he wanted to be, in the middle of it all. He wondered what he was missing. As the last of his agents neared the end of the alley, it hit him.

"Stop!" he hollered. "Don't all of you go out the same end of the alley, a few out each end, and when you get to the sidewalk turn away from Sixth and circle around. Move casually. We've got time before Cawley brings the stand-in out of the building. Agent Curtis, you and Bradley need time to set up on the OBA so go back through the lobby out onto Sixth. Draw some attention to yourselves as you go. Agents wouldn't do that, so don't act like agents. You're heading back to your office, carrying your attaché cases in plain sight. Kid around a little. Take off your tie, Agent Curtis. Bradley, hang your purse back over your shoulder. Let it dangle from your fingers. Clown around some. Giggle. Then get on top of that building. Oh, and before any of you leave, if nothing happens, Agent Cawley will escort the stand-in all the way back to the courthouse. In that event everybody moves with them, keeping your spacing.

"Now go. Go! Now!"

With his squad dispersed, Rex headed toward Pennsylvania and Seventh to meet Jack and his team. On the way he called Special Agent Crenshaw.

"Crenshaw, are your agents spread out in the Mall south of Constitution Avenue from Fourteenth to First Streets?"

"We're set."

"If the suspect gets in the Mall," Rex said, "I'm guessing he'll exit near the Taft Memorial and then work his way back to the Hyatt for his car. Keep an agent near any motorcycles in the area. Get a couple of agents on the tourist trolley the next time it stops at Constitution and Twelfth. Don't worry about Dalton's Explorer. There are agents in the Hyatt's underground parking."

"I've already got two agents on the trolley," Agent Crenshaw replied. "They have orders to stay put unless in hot pursuit."

Rex picked up his pace as he talked his way across the intersection of Seventh and D Street. "Crenshaw, your guys are dressed casually. If pursuit begins, get your FBI hats on. We don't want our squads shooting one another."

"Gee, Mom, I didn't know you cared."

Rex looked at his phone, grinned, and jammed it in his pocket.

They were set for action. As set as they could be. He would soon know if it would be enough.

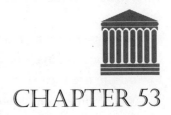

# CHAPTER 53

California State Court justice shot.
The FBI says this one's not LW.

—*Marian Little, NewsCentral 7*

JUNE 21, 3:08 P.M.

After finishing the assembly of the Israeli sniping rifle, Dalton settled into the narrow space between the back of the equipment shed and the edge of the OBA's roof. The Galil had not ranked particularly high in his shot group test. But in the end, he had chosen the Galil because with its folding stock it fit into his backpack.

He could not have used the less-precise Galil for the surgical shot he made on Capone in Dallas, but it would be adequate for this much closer elimination of Chief Justice Evans. The cement wall of the Metro building on the northeast corner of Sixth and F would be a perfect shooting backdrop.

3:14

Dalton heard a clanking sound. *The wind's blowing hard. The sound could be carrying from a distance,* he thought. He strained to hear it again. He didn't need any surprises at this juncture. Then he heard it again. Clank. No. *That's not a clank. Its a grating sound. No. Rubbing. Yes. Rubbing. Metal rubbing and a clank. Yes, a clank, too.*

He noticed the metal pipes along the side of the fire escape

where they curved up and over the edge. They were loose and rat-
tling.

*Someone's coming onto the roof.*

Then a woman came over the top. She turned and looked back
toward the fire escape.

*More? How many more?*

A man's head appeared. He handed the woman an attaché case,
then a second case. The man and woman looked in Dalton's direction, but it was clear from their lack of expression that they hadn't
seen him. That they hadn't really expected to see anyone.

Dalton leaned back for a count of ten, then inched his head forward at an angle until he could see them with one eye. The couple
appeared to be satisfied they were alone on the rooftop. From where
the two stood, the equipment shed he was behind appeared to butt
against the roof cap.

The man and woman knelt over their cases. Black cases.

*Rifles. They're starting to assemble rifles. Of course, they're FBI
snipers. They're up here to cover Evans on his way back. They should
have been here for his arrival. They ran me off and kept these incom-
petents. Sloppy. No wonder the country's falling apart.*

Dalton pulled the Glock from his waistband and screwed on the
noise suppressor. After a quick peek confirmed the agents were still
assembling their rigs, he leaned out from behind the shed and fired
twice.

They had died without knowing they had gotten closer to LW
than had any member of McCall's squad.

*We all hope to learn from our mistakes, but these two just flunked
their final exam.*

He dragged the agents' bodies over next to a tarp partially covering a jumble of whole and broken roof tiles. The man's credentials
from his pocket gave his name as Ben Curtis. Dalton kept the cre-
dential and put Curtis's radio in his pocket and the earpiece in his
own ear. After pulling the tarp over to cover the two agents, he an-
chored it against the wind with some roof debris. If the FBI sent a

chopper into the area, the two agents would be hidden from view. Dalton then took one of their FBI caps to put on in the event he needed to look over the rooftop.

*They'll expect someone to be up here, Dad. If I'm seen wearing the FBI hat—well, I'll go over it all with you later.*

An idea came in a flash. He liked its poetic justice. He would finish assembling the FBI rifle, then use it instead of the Galil. He would enjoy watching the media ask McCall how he could bungle the job so badly as to let Commander LW use an FBI rifle to eliminate the chief justice of the United States.

Agent Curtis's radio crackled: "This is Agent Cawley," the voice said. "It's three thirty. We'll be exiting the building in a minute or two."

*Damn! No time. I'll have to use the Galil.*

After the shot he would take the rope ladder to the ground. Fast. Unseen. He'd leave the scene carrying his hand gun so that bystanders would report seeing a man carrying a gun, wearing long pants, a sweatshirt, and a red baseball cap. Headed that way!

*I'm way ahead of you jerkoffs.*

The radio squawked again, "Cawley here. Agent Curtis, are you and Bradley in position?"

Dalton put on the FBI hat, turned the radio so that the wind gusting on the roof would slam against the mouthpiece, and raised up to peer over the edge of the building. "Yes," he answered. The fewer words the better. Things were moving too rapidly for Cawley to focus on his reply as Agent Curtis.

*Daddy, your birthday present should be here in a few minutes.*

# CHAPTER 54

A CD was received at a San Francisco radio station: "I'm an LW recruit. I killed the state court judge to protest the failures of the courts in California to stand up against the Federal government's repeated encroachments of state's rights." An unnamed FBI source, said, "Different case. Different nut."

—*San Francisco Chronicle*

JUNE 21, 3:20 P.M.

Jack opened the van's side door as Frank skidded the van to a stop at the corner of Pennsylvania Avenue and Seventh. Agent Rex Smith jumped in.

"Agent Bullock, the stand-in for Evans will be leaving the dentist in about ten minutes," Rex said. "There are two snipers on top of the building at the nearest intersection. I've positioned agents at each corner in all directions. Agents are at all the entrances to the metro system within five blocks. Hopefully, we have enough vehicles in the area to block off the exit from any underground parking garage. Agent Crenshaw's squad is positioned in the National Mall. Other agents are scattered along as many possible escape routes as we could identify and staff in the time available."

"The concentration of agents should be south of the dentist," Jack said. "How is it set up?"

"That way," Rex answered. "I agree. South is Dalton's more likely route, given the location of his car. Only four agents are north of the dentist. If Dalton heads north, the agents positioned south will follow turning the pursuit into a large floating box. Agents are staking out any observed motorcycles. We have two agents on the trolley and two more near the Union Station Plaza. I'll radio to get the agents moving should we learn he's heading that way. More agents are watching the entrances to the Metro Rail System inside Union Station. A chopper's holding at the bureau on Pennsylvania and Tenth. It can be over this area in a few minutes. We should be able to corral Dalton once he shows himself. In the event of foot pursuit, agents will put on FBI hats."

Rex handed Jack and his squad FBI hats. "If that happens, get these on your heads."

Jack grabbed the front of Millet's shirt. "Stay in this van. Keep the doors locked. Like you said, 'You're no secret agent man.' You are not to participate in any pursuit or get out of the van for any reason."

Jack thought briefly about ordering Rachel to stay in the van as well, but she had a job to do and he knew she was good at her job.

"Where do you think Dalton will head?" he asked Rex.

"The Mall. It's got trees and shrubs and pedestrians at all hours."

"Frank. Nora. You agree?"

"It's the one place where he could anticipate agents might lose sight of him while he stays on the move," Nora said as she turned to step out of the van.

"That's where I'd head," Frank said. "I wouldn't be surprised if he tries some kind of misdirection in an attempt to blend in with the citizens."

Jack nodded. "All right. Lock and load. Rex, join your agents. Frank, position the five of us near the entrances to the Mall."

"You heard the man," Frank said, "except for Millet, everyone out of the van. Colin, I want you to take a position near the Mellon Fountain. It's in the small triangle where Sixth Street, Pennsylvania, and Constitution come together. If we fail to get him before he gets to you, he's yours. If he surprises us and heads north, Rex will radio a position two command. That'll mean you're to move toward the Hyatt as will the agents from the Mall. The agents at the Supreme

Court will move west. The agents from the west will move east. Those positioned near Union Station will swing around and drop down to finish the moving box."

Jack watched Colin's smooth gait as he picked up speed moving east on Pennsylvania Avenue.

"I'll take Nora with me to Ninth and Constitution," Frank told Jack. "You and Rachel cover Seventh Street between Pennsylvania and Constitution Avenues."

"If he crosses Constitution," Jack said, "he'll be in the Mall. Dalton will have a plan for once he gets into the Mall. So, if the opportunity presents itself, let's take him on the streets." Jack turned back toward Millet. "As soon as we're gone, roll up this window and lock the door. I meant what I said. Keep your ass in this van."

"Wilco, Jackman, the hero shit's your job."

Frank and Nora walked away quickly in the direction of Ninth Street.

"I'll set up next to the Federal Trade Commission on the northeast side of Seventh and Pennsylvania," Jack said to Rachel. "You cross to the west side and take a position near the National Archives Building."

Jack held Rachel's arm for a moment and softened his voice. "Be careful."

She smiled and touched him on the heart.

JUNE 21, 3:29 P.M.

Dalton tucked the heavy gloves he had worn to climb the rope to the rooftop inside his pants at the waist. He would need those gloves again when he went down the air duct. He still wore the latex gloves he had put on before assembling the Galil.

Earlier he had considered coming up from one of the underground parking garages to take the chief justice from up close. But then he had realized that the FBI could have a contingent plan that would quickly block the exits from those nearby garages. And even if he got out to the road, once they had identified his car it would be difficult to avoid capture. After days of plotting out all possible alternatives, he had decided his best escape would be on foot. It would be slower, but it would not be what they expected. Besides, it would allow him more flexibility to get into the National Mall and back to his car.

His stomach felt as if an alien was gnawing at the walls of its captivity. After popping an antacid, he wiped the sweat from his brow, rubbed his latex glove on his pants, and tightened his grip on the rifle. After steadying his stance with one knee down, he put his red cap beside him, and put the FBI hat on his head.

He drew in a breath and let it out long and slow, then another, and another. He would use a chest shot this time. In a later communiqué he would tell America that not everyone in his militia had the shooting skills of the volunteer recruit who put down Capone in Dallas. Mommy always said, "When you get lemons make lemonade."

*There he is! There's Evans! He's such a creature of habit. He'll turn left at F and walk back to the Court the same way he came. The FBI agents are moving in a standard protective pattern.*

Slow slight movements of his hand allowed the scope to keep its crosshairs on Chief Justice Evans or the agent immediately shielding Evans. The choreographed group moved closer to the corner, just a few more steps. The grand moment was near.

The corner would be the weak spot in their protection scheme. The spacing between the agents nearest the curb had already begun to spread due to their wider arc compared to the agents turning the inside of the corner. The tail car, lagging back some, could effect his escape, but would not effect the killing of the chief justice.

*Now.*

Whap! Whap!

Dalton's two shots, divided by an instant, struck dead center on the chest of the gray-haired man he believed to be Chief Justice Thomas Evans. Through the scope, he watched the man collapse against the wall of the building, watched his eyes go big, his tongue lolling from the corner of his mouth. Then his legs buckled and he went down.

The minute the shot rang out, everyone looked up.

Dalton squeezed a few indiscriminate rounds into the crowd bunched at the corner. Through the scope he saw a slug chip fragments from the building's masonry wall. Then a woman clutching her chest fell to the sidewalk. Another shot struck a man standing sideways. His nose exploded. He grabbed his face, blood oozing between his fingers.

Dalton swung the Galil to the FBI tail car. It looked empty. The passenger-side door flew open, then the driver, who had leaned over to push open that door, came back into view.

*The Fool! Evans is dead.*

He took careful aim and again brought his finger tight against the trigger. The driver slumped forward, his body falling against the horn. It blared. People were screaming and scattering like cattle spooked by night lighting. He could feel their confusion. Taste their panic.

Dalton knew that FBI agents would soon identify the OBA building as the source of the shot and they would swarm the boarded-up building. They would not find him. He would be gone.

After moving back from the edge of the roof, he rose, dropped the Galil, and jammed the FBI hat into his armpit under his sweatshirt. Next, he yanked off the latex gloves and stuffed them in his back pocket, and put on his red cap. The Glock he had used to put down the two agents, went inside his waistband at his back. He tugged the coarse gloves free from his pants, pulling them on while dashing for the opposite corner of the rooftop.

An announcement came over Agent Curtis's radio: "Evans is down. I repeat. Evans is down. Shots fired from the top of the OBA building at Sixth and F Streets. All agents in the immediate area are to converge on the OBA."

Dalton ducked under the curved top of the air duct and grabbed the rope, wrapped his legs around it and using the knots, half slid and half rappelled to the bottom. It took only seconds to cross the weeded lot and reach the wall. He stuffed his red cap inside his sweatshirt, opened the door and stepped through, closing it behind himself. Then walked south on the Sixth Street sidewalk, using the L-shaped turn in the wall to conceal his presence.

When a man wearing an FBI hat came running wide around the corner onto Sixth Street, Dalton hollered, "What happened? Did I hear gunshots?"

The agent ignored him and ran faster on the straightaway.

*It's done. I'm home free. Happy Birthday, Daddy.*

At D Street Dalton turned west. Without pursuit he would not take out the Glock or his red cap. He wanted onlookers to report the gun and the hat. But without pursuers there was no reason to call attention to himself. The FBI agents would assume he could not get down off the building quickly without an elevator. Right now they were likely surrounding the OBA while he was already outside their hastily constructed web. He grinned.

Dalton continued toward the Sculpture Garden, confident he would have time to complete his metamorphosis in the Mall and emerge to laugh at the collectors unable to catch him in their net.

*Daddy, it's going better than I expected.*

"What do you mean, you lost him?" Jack yelled into his cell phone.

"Everyone's holding their positions," Rex replied. "He thinks he's shot the chief justice. He doesn't know we know his identity. He'll come to us, Jack. He has to. He'll go for his car. He left the Hyatt wearing full-length tan pants, a white sweatshirt, and white sneakers."

"Anything else?" Jack asked.

"Yeah. Dalton killed Agents Curtis and Bradley after I sent them up to the roof of the OBA building to provide cover. Dalton must have already been up there. Agent Curtis's FBI hat is missing and his radio. Dalton may try posing as an agent."

"Okay, Rex. We'll hold our positions."

"I just used the radio to tell the agents not to use their radios," Rex said, "you probably heard that order, so Dalton did too. But it only told him we knew he had a radio. He would have anticipated our knowing that once we found Agent Curtis's body on top the OBA."

Jack hit his end button and cursed under his breath before punching in the numbers to call Rachel whom he could see standing across the street in front of the National Archives Building.

"Our boy's on the run," he told her. "He could be anywhere. Keep your eyes open."

After filling in Rachel on the description, including the missing FBI hat and radio, he again used his cell phone to relay the news to Frank and then Colin.

Jack was certain now of only one thing. Right now had to be it. He couldn't let Dalton kill again.

Dalton turned south toward the Sculpture Garden. South toward his new appearance. South toward safety.

Near the corner of Eighth and D Streets, he stepped into a drugstore to get out of sight while watching for pursuit, but there was none. He knew what he needed to know. They had discovered Agent Curtis's body and learned of his missing radio. He dropped the radio into a trash bin, but kept the FBI hat under his arm, under his sweatshirt.

When the sidewalk grew busy, he stepped out of the store, merging into a sea of chattering clothes carried forward on wingtips, tennis shoes, and flip-flops. He continued south with the crowd. Eighth Street, below D, near Pennsylvania Avenue had been permanently closed to vehicles and developed into a U.S. Naval Memorial. There he paused and loitered like a tourist, while studying the far side of Pennsylvania Avenue.

When he felt it safe, he starting to move again as part of a formless group of walkers. A few minutes later, he stopped near the corner of Pennsylvania Avenue and Seventh Street, loitering behind some bushes in a raised planter that included another of D.C.'s numerous statues.

The agents near Evans would be tied down for a while. They had a dead chief justice of the United States and three dead agents, not to mention a crowd of frightened and injured citizens. He knew that agents dispatched from the FBI building on Pennsylvania Avenue would be swarming the area like locusts, but even that coverage would dilute as they spread out trying to cover all of the downtown area.

Dalton crossed Seventh to the opposite corner and slowed near the Monument to the Grand Army of the Republic. He had to get past Pennsylvania and Constitution Avenues before he would get into the Sculpture Garden, change his appearance, and become a jogger to cover his retreat back to the Hyatt.

With the next green light he stepped from behind the monument and started across Pennsylvania Avenue. Halfway into the crosswalk, he saw Jack McCall fifty yards ahead, moving out from under a tree near the Federal Trade Commission. He had a cell phone in his hand. He turned his back to Dalton.

*Dad. You orchestrated this, didn't you? Its time isn't it? Time to kill Jack McCall.*

Thirty-five yards.

Killing McCall would derail the government's godless investigation. While the government reorganized, he would eliminate the newly confirmed aristocrats and the senators who chaired the confirmation committees.

*I see your thinking, Dad.*

Thirty yards. McCall's back made a broad target. An easy shot.

Twenty-five yards.

He tugged the Glock free of his waistband and slipped it out from under his shirt.

Twenty yards.

A few pedestrians saw his gun and shrank back, terror on their faces, their mouths open. To Dalton their screams sounded as though they were coming from underwater.

Ten yards.

He raised the Glock.

The pedestrians scurried to avoid Dalton's line of fire.

Out of the corner of his eye, he saw a woman crossing from the National Archives building on the west side of Seventh.

Her arm came up.

*It's that bitch, Rachel Johnstone!*

*She's aiming at me.*

Jack watched as Rachel turned slightly to her left. *She's drawing her Sig,* he said to himself. With his eyes still on Rachel, he heard nervous commotion behind himself. Reflex put his Baretta in his hand as it had countless times before. He spun in a direction matching Rachel's turn, but lagging behind her as a shadow lags behind its master.

Dalton pivoted on Rachel. He would take her first. McCall would pause when he saw Rachel killed. That would give him the split second he would need to turn back and kill McCall.

Jack saw the reason Rachel had drawn her Sig. Dalton. Things were moving at jet speed, yet, as to detail, in slow motion. Jack could see the tendons stiffen in the killer's forearm as the man they hunted tightened his grip on the trigger. Dalton's gun aimed at the woman Jack loved.

Dalton saw the spit-flash at the muzzle of Rachel's gun at almost the same instant he felt her bullet burst through his ribs, ripping a path to his heart. Saw his own shot thrown high by the impact from her bullet. And felt his resolve draining from his body. His purpose diminishing.

As he went down, he saw McCall fire. A dull thump rocked the side of his chest, but he never truly felt McCall's bullet, only the thud against his body, the shudder of a fastball hitting a bat.

Jack and Rachel reached Dalton at the same moment. Jack kicking the dropped Glock away from the blood-soaked red baseball cap that had fallen from under Dalton's sweatshirt.

The madman's eyes closed and then, in the moment of death, snapped open. His stare cold and straight. Gravity took his head to the side, his right arm flopping limply across his chest as if he were about to recite the pledge of allegiance.

# EPILOGUE

On July first, Rachel resigned from the FBI. Jack left the CIA on the same date.

They were married three months later in the Rose Garden at the White Hose. President Samuel Schroeder and the First Lady sat in the front row.

Colin Stewart stood up as Jack's best man, Nora Burke acting as Rachel's bridesmaid. The entire squad had come to the wedding. The heads of the intelligence agencies were also there. And, Ms. Gruber.

After a long honeymoon, Jack and Rachel planned to open McCall Investigations in Washington, D.C. Nora Burke had agreed to join them. But Frank Wade, having reconciled with his ex-wife Sharon, had decided to stay with the Metropolitan Police Department.

The newlyweds moved into Jack's home on Potomac Avenue NW. They would adopt two or three children, after taking the first year or two to get acquainted as husband and wife.

# AUTHOR'S NOTE

As I often do, I got by with a lot of help from my friends. The comments of discerning readers including Jody Madden, Mary Lee, Ellie Brooks, Toni Jaskowitz, and Jeanne Bishop, as well as John Logan, who has a wonderful ear for dialogue, Frank Evans, Dick Houser, Beth Eggers, and the invaluable observations and keen eye for detail of Kim Mellen provided direction and insight into the shaping of the story. Thanks are also due the fine folks at the U.S. Chess Federation, who provided insight into the fascinations and functions of multiyear e-mail chess tournaments.

The contributions offered by law enforcement officers from the FBI, CIA, and the D.C. Police Department, as well as the U.S. Supreme Court Police, and the White House Secret Service during my research visit to Washington, D.C., provided critical points of confirmation and enhancement.

The professional staff of Oceanview Publishing including, but not limited to, Pat Gussin, Frank Troncale, and Susan Hayes provided the invaluable guidance that can only come from experience in and knowledge of the publishing of fiction. And I cannot forget George Foster, who somehow wed his wondrous talents to the scattered thoughts of this author to create the book jacket.

The generous contributions of these people as well as others I may have inadvertently failed to mention were indispensable. The characters, who roam the pages of *The Third Coincidence*, were made smarter, tougher, sexier, or more villainous through your unselfish assistance. Those characters join the author to say thank you one and all.